5/20/21

WITHDRAWN

THE SKY BLUES

THE SKY BLUES

ROBBIE COUCH

SIMON & SCHUSTER BFYR

NEW YORK   LONDON   TORONTO   SYDNEY   NEW DELHI

SIMON & SCHUSTER BFYR

An imprint of Simon & Schuster Children's Publishing Division
1230 Avenue of the Americas, New York, New York 10020

Text © 2021 by Robbie Couch
Jacket illustration © 2021 by Jeff Östberg
Jacket design by Krista Vossen © 2021 by Simon & Schuster, Inc.

SIMON & SCHUSTER BOOKS FOR YOUNG READERS
and related marks are trademarks of Simon & Schuster, Inc.
For information about special discounts for bulk purchases, please contact Simon & Schuster
Special Sales at 1-866-506-1949 or business@simonandschuster.com.
The Simon & Schuster Speakers Bureau can bring authors to your live event.
For more information or to book an event, contact the Simon & Schuster Speakers Bureau at
1-866-248-3049 or visit our website at www.simonspeakers.com.
Interior design by Hilary Zarycky
The text for this book was set in Minion Pro.
Manufactured in the United States of America
First Edition
2 4 6 8 10 9 7 5 3 1
Library of Congress Cataloging-in-Publication Data
Names: Couch, Robbie, author.
Title: The Sky blues / Robbie Couch.
Description: First edition. | New York : Simon & Schuster Books for Young Readers, [2021] |
Audience: Ages 12 up. | Audience: Grades 7-9. | Summary: Seventeen-year-old Sky, openly gay but
under the radar, decides to make a splashy promposal but his plans are leaked by an anonymous,
homophobic hacker, moving his classmates to help him expose the perpetrator.
Identifiers: LCCN 2020030133 | ISBN 9781534477858 (hardcover) |
ISBN 9781534477865 (paperback) | ISBN 9781534477872 (ebook)
Subjects: CYAC: Gays—Fiction. | Friendship—Fiction. | Prejudices—Fiction. | Cyberbullying—
Fiction. | High schools—Fiction. | Schools—Fiction.
Classification: LCC PZ7.1.C6757 Skky 2021 | DDC [Fic]—dc23
LC record available at https://lccn.loc.gov/2020030133
ISBN 978-1-5344-7785-8
ISBN 978-1-5344-7787-2 (ebook)

For the tough ones

THE SKY BLUES

THIRTY DAYS

I'm standing in the shower next to Ali Rashid. *The* Ali Rashid. Sure, we're both completely naked and there are plenty of other body parts my eyes could wander toward. But I can't look away from his eyebrows, of all things. His big, bushy, glorious effing eyebrows. I've never even noticed another person's before Ali's, I don't think. But his are different, I guess. I've stared at them so many times—mostly across crowded classrooms or dreamily through Instagram filters—I bet I could sketch them from memory, follicle by follicle. That's a super weird, gay thing to admit, I know.

But hi, I'm a gay weirdo, apparently.

"Can I kiss you, Sky?" he asks.

The hazel of his eyes disappears behind long, curly eyelashes. They're as beautiful as the brows; so jet black and thick, they could, like, sign a modeling contract all on their own, I swear. I can't wait to tell our gaybies (gay + babies) about this moment someday—their dads' first kiss. They'll probably be grossed out, but that's okay.

"Sky, let's go!" Bree's mom yells right outside the bathroom door. My whole body jolts awake from my daydream. Er, my . . .

shower-dream? Yeah. That's more like it. Let's call it that. My Ali shower-dream. I have them from time to time.

Rattled, I reach out to grab the shower curtain to regain my balance—and the whole thing rips beneath my weight. My flailing body goes spilling out onto the bath mat like some white, scaly-ass fish caught in Lake Michigan. It seriously sounds like a bomb went off—a wet, soapy, incredibly embarrassing bomb. I yelp, more out of shock than pain.

"Oh my God!" Bree's mom gasps on the other side of the bathroom door, as the dangling nozzle sprays water literally everywhere. Bree's pit bulls, Thelma and Louise, start barking a few drywalls away.

"Are you okay, Sky?"

"No," I groan. "I mean, yeah—"

But it's too late.

The door cracks open and I see the bright red rims of Mrs. Brandstone's glasses for a microsecond before I screech in protest, lying there totally exposed on the slippery floor. She squeals too, and slams the door shut.

I'm mortified. I am completely, totally, full-stop mortified.

This has to be a top-five most embarrassing moment, really. Way worse than when my best friend, Marshall, let out a massive fart in seventh-grade gym and ran away, leaving everyone thinking it was me.

"Don't worry, I didn't see anything," Bree's mom lies through the door. "And even if I did, I've seen it all anyway, honey. But hustle, please! Bree is waiting outside. You two are going to be late."

And just like clockwork, Bree—my other best friend—starts

honking her horn out in the driveway, as if the apocalypse will ensue if we're thirty seconds late to first hour. She's going to kill me.

"Tell her I'm coming!" I stand and turn the shower off before fixing the rod and curtain. Half the bathroom floor is covered in a puddle.

What an absolute mess. This bathroom *and* my life.

My guess is, Ali's probably shower-dreaming about someone else this exact moment over at his house on Ashtyn Drive. It's the third house from the corner; the one with the seafoam-green shutters, and the cat, Franklin, moseying around in the front window.

Yes, okay. I'm in love with Ali Rashid.

I'm not proud of it. I'm anything *but* proud of it. I'm annoyed of it. I'm sick of it. I wish I could snap my fingers and forget Ali Rashid even exists. But he does, and I'm hopelessly, helplessly, eternally infatuated with him, his seductive eyebrows, XXX-rated eyelashes, and the way his skin crinkles a bit when he laughs at one of my jokes. Especially when he snorts a little, too, because then I know it's genuine.

Crushing this hard is confusing, though.

In my seventeen years on this planet, Ali's the only boy that's ever made me feel this way. Actually, the only *person*, period. Falling this hard isn't all euphoric and heavenly, like in the four hundred million rom-coms I've watched way too many times to count.

Like when Lara Jean finally confesses her love to Peter on the lacrosse field in *To All the Boys I've Loved Before*, and everyone gets their happiest possible ending. Or like in *Booksmart*, when Hope shows up on the doorstep to give Amy her phone number *right before* Amy bounces to Botswana for the summer. (What convenient timing.)

Okay, sure, some days it does feel like that. Some days I feel like Simon Spier on the Ferris wheel. I have my moments when I swear cupid flies in and slaughters me with his big gay arrow, and my eyes turn into heart emojis and I can't catch my breath for a solid five seconds.

But the problem is, Ali is straight. Well, he's *probably* straight. . . . Maybe straight? I don't know! We're friends-ish, but not in That Way. At least not yet. I don't think?

Anyway.

Bree—who is now literally holding down the car horn outside so the noise is nonstop and off-the-rails annoying—believes I have a shot with him. She and the rest of the Brandstone family are the only ones who know of my Ali Rashid obsession, and I'm going to keep it that way. Well, for another thirty days, at least.

Thirty effing days.

I turn to face the cloudy bathroom mirror and swipe my hand across its slippery surface. My sopping wet sandy hair, plastered across my forehead, probably needs to be trimmed soon, and I'm pretty sure I'm getting a pimple on my nose. At least I still like my eyes—probably my favorite thing about my face (although they pale in comparison to Ali's). Mine are the color of toffee, my mom once told me as a kid. For some reason, I never forgot that.

The mist on the mirror fades away, revealing more of my chest, and I immediately remember why I implemented my number one rule since moving in with the Brandstones: Never, ever, *ever* look at my reflection right after I get out of a shower. Because the hot water always makes Mars—my burn scar—look infinitely worse than he typically does.

Mars has been lurking on the left side of my chest, right over my heart, ever since the accident. He looks pretty damn bad as is, honestly, but ten minutes under some hot water? He's a million times more fire-engine red than usual. Which makes me look like one of those characters you see about halfway through an apocalyptic zombie movie—you know, the guy who just got bitten and is on his way to becoming a cannibalistic beast? That's me!

My mom doesn't have big mirrors in her tiny, suffocating house, so it was easier to avoid seeing Mars when I lived there. That was one perverse advantage me and my older brother, Gus, had growing up with hardly any money, clothes, or space: fewer opportunities to accidentally catch a glimpse of Mars in a reflection. That's not the case here at the Brandstones', though, standing in front of a mirror the size of a classroom chalkboard.

God damn Mars.

Bree is still blowing up the car horn out in the driveway, which has now turned from being obnoxious to hilarious. She is bonkers about school stuff, in general, but especially so between seven and nine a.m., when the sugar rush from her daily hot cocoa is in full swing. I think she's trying to honk to the rhythm of the new Ariana Grande song she's obsessed with? I don't know. It sounds completely absurd.

"Sky!" her mom bellows from the kitchen, now sufficiently annoyed with both me and her daughter. Thelma and Louise are going extra nuts too, barking up a storm. "Come *on!*"

I stifle a laugh and assure her I'm coming.

Three minutes later, I'm jumping into the passenger seat with my backpack, hair still dripping wet. "Sorry—"

Bree slams her foot onto the gas pedal. "I'm going to murder you," she says, half serious. The car roars in reverse down the mile-long driveway. (It's not really a mile long, but their front yard is huge.) "I wanted to get Yearbook stuff done before first hour."

"Is it possible for you push pause on your editor-in-chief duties for one day?" I say as the car lurches into forward drive and squeals down the Brandstones' mansion-stacked street. "I've had senioritis since sophomore year."

"Believe me"—she sips her cocoa from her Thermos, peeling out of the cul-de-sac—"I know."

If you only saw the Brandstones' subdivision, you'd probably think Rock Ledge was a top 1 percent kind of town—but you'd be dead wrong. Because Bree lives along the coast—the only area in this zip code with money. And even then, many of the houses are just vacation homes from downstaters—not locals. Their street is nestled into its own quiet peninsula, with its own quiet private beach, with its own definitely-not-quiet stay-at-home moms. The road's even been paved within the last decade.

The real Rock Ledge, though? Imagine the decrepit towns you see in depressing political TV ads focused on how awful the economy's gotten, where there's empty sidewalks in front of closed storefronts, and sad old people gathered on porches reminiscing about the good ol' days. That's the real Rock Ledge.

We race through a stretch of woods into the non-touristy side of town—farther inland and away from the bed-and-breakfasts selling framed maps of Lake Michigan for $800—and the sight is pretty depressing. Because in March, the snow has mostly melted around here, but the trees are still completely bare, and pee-colored grass and poop-colored mud cover just about everything.

"So." I clear my throat. "Just so you know . . ."

Bree's blues eyes burst with intrigue. "What?"

"Your mom walked in on me. . . ."

"Walked in on you where?"

"The bathroom."

"What?"

"When I was in the shower."

Bree inhales, pure shock and delight draped across her rosy, lightly freckled face. She immediately forgets about me making her late.

"I was naked," I add.

"Well, I *assume* so." Bree thrives off a good plot twist. She says she hates drama, but I've noticed all the people who say that are the most dramatic people I know. "Did she see anything?" Her eyes dart back and forth between me and the road, the car weaving between the peeling yellow and white lines.

"No. Well, I don't know. She said she didn't."

"Please, for the love of God, don't tell me you were masturbating."

"Stop!"

"You totally were, weren't you?"

"I can barely tie my shoes before eight a.m. I don't have the motivation to do that before school, Bree."

She ignores me, pulling her long, brown hair into a tight bun atop her head. "You were jacking off to Ali. No need to lie." She's steering with her knees while fixing her hair in the rearview mirror. I'm holding on for dear life.

"I was *shower-dreaming* about him, sure. But that's it."

"Shower-dreaming?" She tilts her head, confused, as we fly through an intersection. "Is that gay for 'masturbating'?"

We come screeching into the senior parking lot right as the tardy bell for first hour is echoing across the soggy front lawn. "Meet for lunch outside Winter's?" She jumps out of the car and sprints toward our prison of a school before I give her an answer.

"Yep," I sigh to myself. "See you then."

I follow in her path, much more slowly, weaving through cars toward the main entrance along with a handful of other tardy seniors with terminal senioritis. Our last semester is dying a slow, inconsequential death, so there's been a growing number of us out here each morning avoiding our first hours with gas station coffees and increasingly loud playlists blasting across the football field. Today it's in the dozens, and the song of choice is some country song I've been sick of since October.

I pass by some jock douchebags and feel their eyes judging my every move. A few of them smirk at me, and the group's most deplorable, Cliff Norquest—naturally, their ringleader—imitates my walk to laughs.

My heart sinks.

My hips are swinging too much, I realize is what they've spotted. So I try to walk straighter. Like, literally *and* in the heterosexual sense. When you're an openly gay kid at Rock Ledge High who reads about as straight as a curly fry, you think about these things. Constantly. Almost as much as you think about Ali Rashid's eyebrows.

Oh, and my books. I need to carry them hanging loosely against my upper thigh with one arm—not with the bottoms of the books pressed against my hip, like Bree always carries hers. It's a gay giveaway.

Also, my shirt! Damn it. I would have grabbed something else out of my closet had I had time to think, between Bree's honking and Mrs. Brandstone's yelling for me to hurry up. It's okay to wear this shirt to, like, the movies, or to the mall, or anywhere else. But not to school. Not to *this* school, at least. It's a pale pink button-up, which, if a guy like me has it on, screams *gaaaaaaay*. If I wear it like I'm "supposed" to wear it, I'd have it buttoned all the way up. But this isn't Paris, France. This is Rock Ledge, Michigan.

So I undo the top button.

I know—if everyone in Rock Ledge already knows I'm gay, why does it matter? I should be allowed to wear the gay shirt. Carry the books like I want to. Walk the way I walk. But people in this town have a low threshold for different, and I don't want to press my luck.

"Hey, idiot." Marshall comes crashing into my right side, clasping his hand around my shoulder. He's like a big puppy, always bouncing out of nowhere, with a smile on his face. "What's up?"

"You'll never guess—" I almost dive into the Mrs. Brandstone drama, but see Marshall's track friend, Teddy, is by his side. I bite my tongue.

Nothing against Teddy—he's nice enough—but he's built like a bodyguard, has a voice a hundred octaves lower than mine, and gives off this intense Straight Guy Energy that makes me a bit more closed off when he's around. If my personality were to be

9

compared to Teddy's using a Venn diagram, there would be *no* overlapping section.

Marshall gives me a look after I pause. "What won't I guess?"

I think fast, rolling my eyes. "Just that Bree's mad at me for making us late to first hour."

Teddy pulls the straps of his backpack forward and looks at me curiously. "Did Brandstone already run out of tardies for the semester?"

"It's not that," I say.

"It's more, she hasn't gotten senioritis like the rest of us yet." Marshall sighs.

They start talking about track stuff as we trek through the school's soggy front lawn, so my eyes begin to wander across campus in search of Ali. I bet he's nearby. Seriously, sometimes it's like I have a sixth sense—not seeing dead people, but knowing when Ali is within one hundred feet. M. Night Shyamalan would be so proud.

"Yo," Marshall says, nudging my shoulder.

"Huh?"

He nods at Teddy, who's apparently talking to me.

"Oh." My neck swivels in Teddy's direction. "Sorry."

If it's not my Ali shower-dreaming getting me in trouble, it's my Ali daydreaming.

Teddy laughs. "No worries. I just asked where you got your shoes. They're sweet."

I look down at the ancient pair of sneakers on my feet, yellowed and speckled with mud. They're a pair of Gus's that he left at my mom's forever ago. I can't remember the last time I had the money to buy a new pair of shoes, let alone where Gus bought these ones probably, like, five years ago—but Teddy doesn't need to hear the whole story.

"I'm not sure where these are from, actually," I say. "But thanks."

"Gotcha." Teddy starts to break away from us for a different school entrance. "I have Butterton first hour. See you guys later."

"Later," Marshall says.

"Bye," I add.

Once Teddy's out of earshot, I divulge the *real* news.

"Oh, by the way," I say to Marshall. "Mrs. Brandstone walked in on me naked in the bathroom this morning."

Marshall gawks, offering me a piece of cinnamon gum. He's the cinnamon gum guy. "Why would she do that? Was she being creepy?"

I take the gum and explain exactly what happened. Well, almost exactly. I tell him Mrs. Brandstone startled me, that the shower curtain betrayed me, and that she probably saw . . . everything. But I leave out the Ali shower-dreaming part for Marshall's straight guy ears; I haven't told him about my massive, all-consuming crush on Ali.

Marshall closes his eyes and pops them back open again to express just how wild it is to imagine that horror scene unfold. For two straight people, my best friends really are the biggest drama queens ever, I swear.

He starts cracking up and prodding me for details. "What all did she see?"

"I don't know."

"Do you think she came in on purpose, knowing you were naked?"

"God, I hope not."

"Did she see your ding-a-ling?"

"I'm not answering that."

"Is that a yes?"

"No. And why are you calling it ding-a-ling? Ew."

"Fair point, but—"

"Anyway!" I cut him off. "How did your track meet go?"

"Got murdered." We avoid a puddle of mud that's been steadily expanding, in its conquest to turn the entire front lawn of the school into a swamp. "Like, knife through the chest, sledgehammer to the face, poison to the lips *murdered*."

"Poison to the lips? Is that a thing people say?"

"I won my races, Teddy killed it, and Ainsley ended up being able to come, though. I'm happy."

And there she is: Ainsley. He almost made it through an entire conversation without bringing up his new (and first-ever) girl-friend. Almost.

I don't mean to sound like a jealous crank—I'm rooting for them like a good best friend, of course—but his obsessing over her has gotten to be a bit much. It's nothing like my obsessing over Ali. Duh. But still. It's a bit much.

Speaking of Ali. There he is.

Hazel eyes, eyebrows, and eyelashes, my nine o'clock. I'm defi-nitely not shower-dreaming this time. He's leaning against the school like some *GQ* model, talking with his best friends, who are the luckiest people on the planet, I swear.

How is he so flawless? Like, how did X and Y chromosomes from two relatively normal humans unite to create such a perfect specimen? Science may never know, honestly. We'll have colonized the moon before we've cracked the code of the Hotness of Ali Rashid, is what I'm saying. He looks so cool, too, in black denim jeans and a backward, bright-yellow hat. Wait. Does he know yellow's my favorite color? Is he sending me some kind of sign?

Of course not. It's just a yellow effing hat. But this is my mind on Ali Rashid.

He catches me staring and grins back. My heart melts a little. Actually, a lot. It melts a whole lot. I really like this boy. I really, really like him.

Here's the thing. The crazy, sort of embarrassing thing.

In thirty days, I'm going to prompose to Ali Rashid. Like, I'm actually, literally, honest to God going to ask him to prom. Why? Because I'm nuts. But Bree's helped convince me I have a real shot. A small shot? Probably. I'm not *that* naive. But it's a shot.

Plus, I want to make a point.

What better way to stand up to Cliff and his cronies than to show up at prom hand in hand with one of the hottest popular guys in school? That'll be the biggest clapback to their buffoonery in the history of clapbacks at Rock Ledge High.

I know asking Ali is a risk. A big one.

He could very well be as straight as an arrow, and I could very well end up looking like a total idiot. But what's the quote on that poster with the basketball hoop you always see on teachers' walls? *You miss 100 percent of the shots you don't take*, or something like that? That's what's been going through my head lately. Which is so beyond cheesy and ridiculous, I know—but it's sort of true. I have to shoot my damn shot, even though there's a very big chance it'll be a horrendous air ball.

I'm scared. Downright terrified. Barely able to function, the dread is so intense. But I'm a gay senior with terminal senioritis, ready to put it all on the line for the boy I think I might love.

I have thirty effing days.

THIRTY DAYS

I t doesn't help that I have three classes with Ali this semester: Trig, Anatomy, and Yearbook. His big, beautiful face and bushy eyebrows are always hovering nearby, begging me to stare. It's the absolute worst.

Like, right now, during a pop quiz in Mr. Kam's first hour, he keeps scratching his ear—just scratching his ear, that's it—but I'm mesmerized. Like he's Nick Jonas strutting down Hollywood Boulevard naked.

I'm already not so great at math and science, so throw in a heaping handful of Ali Distraction to Anatomy and Trig, and I'm barely making it to graduation.

In the middle of our quiz, Marshall discreetly passes back a folded, bright-orange piece of paper. It makes me nervous, because four-hundred-year-old curmudgeon Mr. Kam will lose it if he catches us. But it's safer than getting a text; Mr. Kam can sniff out a buzzing phone like one of those TSA dogs at the airport.

I unfold it quietly. It's an event flyer for the Senior Beach-Bum Party. Marshall's terrible handwriting reads *IT'S FINALLY*

HERE! scrawled across the top. My skin crawls with excitement and dread. Is that a thing? Excited dread? It should be, if it's not. Actually, maybe excited dread is just nerves.

The Senior Beach-Bum Party has basically been my nightmare fuel since Gus told me about it when I was in middle school. Every April, the seniors throw a beach party on Lake Michigan, which is nuts, because it can still be cold in April, and the water is undoubtedly freezing. But the risky weather and pneumonia-inducing swim are all part of the excitement. Or something. I don't know. I don't get straight teenagers in small towns. It sounds like a great time if you're a guy like Marshall, who's ripped, and loves to swim, and is friendly with almost everyone. But not for guys like me. Because when I'm standing there shirtless on the beach, Mars—ugly, attention-grabbing Mars—will steal the show. And not in a good way.

If it wasn't obvious, Mars got his name because he looks like the planet. Pinkish red, a little bit potholed, and completely irreparable. I got him in a car accident when I was five. A crash in an ice storm, which is almost too on-the-nose for a family in northern Michigan. My dad lost his life and I gained Mars. Yay!

Gus named him Mars shortly after the crash, and it just . . . stuck? The overwhelmed skin-doctor-dude at the clinic for broke families used to say Mars will keep healing. "You won't even see it in a few months," I remember my mom assuring me after one appointment, not very sure of herself.

So, yeah. I'm stuck with Mars, and Mars is stuck with me.

That's exactly why I've chosen the Senior Beach-Bum Party in thirty days to prompose to Ali. I'll be shirtless and terrified, no doubt, but it's the end of my senior year, damn it, and I refuse to go out a shrinking gay violet.

I write *!!!!!* and draw a smiley face on the event flyer before quickly handing it back to Marshall—and proceed to get two of the last three questions on the quiz laughably wrong. Seriously, I hate Trig so much. Like, when will cosines or tangents ever be relevant outside this class? Get real, Mr. Kam.

Ali nudges me with his shoulder on the way out of Trig. Every time he acknowledges my existence, butterflies fill my gut. And my chest, and my head, and . . . basically everything else.

I mean, not *everything* else.

At least not right now.

Anyway.

"Sky High," he says. That's his nickname for me. "What's up?"

"Nothing!" I reply, awkwardly loud and trying way too hard to play it cool. I can feel my heart beating in my throat. I think I'm walking pretty gay again too, so I straighten up.

"What's happening in Anatomy today, do you know?" Ali asks. "I might skip, but not if Zemp is going over something new."

"Hm." I try to think of something—anything!—the least bit witty to say. "Zemp's probably going to go on and on about his cat's liver problems some more. I'm sure you won't miss a thing."

It's clever enough to get a laugh out of him. A little one, but it does the trick. "You're probably right," he says, grinning. I can never tell if I should interpret this very specific Ali Grin as flirting or just Ali being a nice guy. He nudges me with his shoulder again before peeling away with his friends, leaving a subtle sniff of his earthy cologne behind. "See you later, Sky High."

. . .

It's tacos for dinner at the Brandstones'.

Clare, Bree's older sister and the unofficial chef of the family, laid out a massive spread that could feed the whole neighborhood. There are three different kinds of marinated meats, a variety of cheeses, and an entire garden of veggies, all adding up to about a week's worth of soon-to-be leftovers.

"Sky, have another scoop," Mrs. Brandstone basically threatens, eyeing my plate after I go light on the guacamole. "We have a lot, and it won't keep anyway, hon. Eat up."

She's not lying. At least ten avocados lost their lives to supply this bucketful of guacamole.

Tonight—like every weeknight at the Brandstones'—is total chaos. Bree's twelve-year-old twin brothers, Petey and Ray, are fighting over the salsa spoon for some unknown but apparently critical reason. Clare is blasting Drake on her huge-ass headphones, wearing a bright-pink pullover that comes with a unicorn horn attached to its hood. Thelma and Louise are begging for scraps, hoping someone will drop something edible onto the floor.

Plus, everything feels ten times louder and echoey because Bree's house is one of those "open floor plan" homes, as her mom always reminds guests; the kitchen, dining room, and living room meld into one cavernous space with high-rise ceilings that confirms to everyone, "Yes, the Brandstones *are* upper-upper middle class."

I weirdly like all this mayhem, though.

The Brandstones are so loud and always invading your privacy and yelling at one another. But it feels like an actual family lives here. I didn't get that at my mom's, so it's nice. Sometimes I just sit back and watch them like they're a sitcom or something. It's like *The Brandstone Bunch*—except with way more F-bombs.

Annoyed with both his human and four-legged children, Mr. Brandstone turns up *SportsCenter* to the maximum volume so he can hear the commentators over Drake, and the barking, and the salsa spoon fight. "Chill out!" he yells at no one in particular. He catches my eye in the process. "Listen to Mrs. Brandstone, Sky, and help yourself to some more avocado dip." He smirks. "But don't drop any on the floor. We wouldn't want anyone, you know . . . slipping and falling."

He gives me a wink.

Petey starts cracking up; Ray follows suit. Bree tries not to laugh, but can't help but grin too. The only person who doesn't seem to notice is Clare, who probably wouldn't hear a nuclear bomb go off next door, through those headphones.

My cheeks begin to burn.

"Mark." Mrs. Brandstone sighs, refilling a bowl of shredded cheese. "Don't listen to him, Sky. Like I said, I didn't see a thing."

"Mom," Bree interjects. "That's the second time you've said you didn't see anything, and the more times you say you didn't see anything, the more we're convinced you definitely saw something."

I smile to let them know I'm okay with his dad jokes, but really, I'm mortified. Forget my *ding-a-ling*, as Marshall's apparently calling dicks now; Bree's mom has never seen Mars. I wonder if she did this morning, and I wonder if she was grossed out.

Probably yes to both.

"Can we talk about anything else, please?" I joke to make sure they know I'm laughing *with* them. "Politics? Religion? The meaning of life?"

The Brandstones are like family to me—I've been best friends with Bree since sixth grade and have been living under their roof since Christmas—but Mr. Brandstone can still melt me into a puddle of embarrassment in two seconds, flat.

"Your birthday!" Mrs. Brandstone gasps. "Let's talk about that! It'll be here before you know it."

Ugh, okay—anything else *except that*. I actually rather would talk about the meaning of life with Mr. Brandstone than my birthday. All the extra attention and pressure? No thanks.

"I don't want a party," I say, smiling at her to be polite. "Honestly."

"Eighteen!" Ray lights up. He has autism and really gets into birthdays.

"That's right." Mrs. Brandstone points at him, giving him thanks for backing her up. "Eighteen is a big one, Sky."

"Everyone leave him alone," Bree cuts in, chomping through the remainder of her taco and rolling her eyes at me. "He's never been a big birthday person. We'll do something low-key."

"*Oooh*, what about that new indoor skydiving place in Cadillac?" Mr. Brandstone pipes in. "That'd be fun."

"Indoor skydiving's not low-key, Dad."

"We could throw a scavenger hunt in the neighborhood!" Mrs. Brandstone squeals. "How fun would that be!"

"He's also not turning ten," Clare chimes in. Apparently she can hear a lot more through those headphones than I thought.

"Those are great ideas, thanks," I say to Mr. and Mrs. Brandstone. "Let me get back to you."

"Okay, okay." Mrs. Brandstone surrenders. "Don't wait forever, though."

I get why Bree gets annoyed with their constant caring; she doesn't know what it's like to have parents who don't care at all.

Bree stands and signals for me to follow her out of the kitchen.

"Where are you two going?" Mrs. Brandstone asks before her lips melt into a smirk. "To scroll through Ali's Instagram, I bet."

Mr. Brandstone lets out a howl. Clare grins.

And just like that, my face starts burning again.

"Mom!" Bree jabs. "You two are insufferable today."

"Ohhh, don't get all huffy and puffy." Mr. Brandstone chuckles, looking away from *SportsCenter* and wiping his mustache. "Yeah, what's been happening in that department, Sky? Have you made any moves yet?"

"Dad!"

"What?" He raises his arms, napkin and fork in hand. "Are Ali and Sky a thing or what? What would your couple name be? *Sah-lee? Ah-kai?* Nothing rolls off the tongue."

My face? Definitely burning. *On. Fire.*

"Please shut up." Bree recoils.

"Don't tell your dad to shut up." Mrs. Brandstone takes a big bite of her taco, sour cream smearing across her upper lip. "But really, Sky," she says, lowering her voice. "*Is* Sah-lee happening?"

"We're getting ice cream," Bree announces, frustrated with her intrusive family. She snags her car keys off the counter. Ray perks up, but before he can put in an ice cream order, Bree cuts him off. "Be back in a half hour."

"No speeding!" Mrs. Brandstone warns.

"Or texting behind the wheel!" Mr. Brandstone adds.

"Thanks for the tacos, Clare," I say, nudging her shoulder on our way out. "They were delicious."

Bree's sister nods, collecting carnitas on her fork. "Anytime, love."

Embarrassingly enough, Mrs. Brandstone was onto my unending pursuit of Ali Rashid. Except it's not his Instagram feed we're watching tonight—it's his actual house.

Bree parks in the street a stone's throw away from the Rashids' driveway. This has been one of our favorite things to do since we got our driver's licenses in Boring as Hell Rock Ledge: eating junk food, listening to Bree's melancholy playlists, and stalking my crush at his home. Yes, like complete and total losers.

It's pathetic, sure. (And illegal? Is stalking illegal?) But whatever. Today we decided on Blizzards from Dairy Queen as our junk food of choice. Hers: Butterfinger, large. Mine: Reese's, also large. The sun's dropped low enough that we feel somewhat hidden, lurking outside like the thirsty teens this terrible town has forced us to become.

The Rashids live in your standard Rock Ledge neighborhood, which is a tad bit nicer than my mom's—and *nothing* like the Brandstones' near the lake. Most of the houses in this town are droopy and sad, with cracked concrete driveways busted up by weeds. Those driveways are my pet peeve. Like, can't you people spray some weed killer every decade or so?

But it's peaceful out right now, and nature's beauty is trumping Rock Ledge's ugliness. I roll down my window and glance around at the flat lawns and leafless trees beneath a purple sky. The air has that sweet spring smell that confirms the worst of winter has passed. Even though I can't see it, I know Lake Michigan disappears into nothing just beyond the tree line—one of the few comforting constants that's kept me sane the past seventeen years. It makes sense that tourists downstate flock here to escape their own lives, even though most of us are trying to get out.

"Whatya thinghe's doing-er-now?" Bree asks something through a mouthful of Butterfinger.

I turn my attention back to inside the car. "Um, what?"

She swallows, staring at Ali's house in deep thought, knees pressed against the steering wheel. "What do you think Ali's doing right now?"

"Hopefully shower-dreaming about me."

"You're creepy."

"You're creepier."

We smirk at each other.

"Oh! Is that—" Bree gasps, spotting movement in the front window.

"What?" I say, cranking my neck.

"*Uck*, nothing."

It's just Ali's cat chilling on the windowsill.

"Freaking Franklin," she says. "False alarm."

It's weird, because I know Bree doesn't love Ali like I do. She claims he's only "a little bit cute," and not, like, an eleven out of ten, which he clearly is by any objective measure. But my Ali obsession has worn off on her the past couple months, even though she won't admit it. It makes all this (possibly illegal) stalking a lot more fun, honestly. Unlike a newly hitched Marshall, Bree and I have both been single our entire lives, so keeping tabs on Ali is the closest we've come to having boyfriends.

Holy crap, that's super pathetic.

But whatever. That's us.

Another shadowy figure pops up in front of Ali's big bay window, but this one is definitely too big to be Franklin. We freeze like deer in headlights. Whoever is there, they're possibly looking right at us—it's too difficult to tell for sure.

"Wait, can . . . can they see us?" Bree whispers, like they might be able to hear us too. She ducks below the steering wheel.

"I don't know," I say, also low-key panicking. I pull my hood over my head and slip on sunglasses—like in that one *Mean Girls* meme—desperate to be invisible too.

The shadowy figure brushes a curtain to the side and leans closer to the glass. It's bespectacled, bearded Mr. Rashid.

And yep, he's looking outside. Right at us.

"Go!" I scream.

"Crap, *crap*," Bree yelps, fumbling to place her ice cream in a cup holder and accidentally bumping the gearshift. The engine roars to life and the car blasts backward, nearly taking out a neighbor's trash can and mailbox. The wheels screech against the asphalt like daggers, killing the neighborhood's silence, as Bree flips the car into forward drive, cranks the wheel, and peels away like a bat out of hell.

Once we're safely out of view, we both start laughing—and we can't stop. Tears are running down my face. Bree is holding on to the steering wheel with her left hand, white-knuckled, while her right is clamped firmly against my thigh. She's hunched over the wheel, hardly able to catch her breath, the crisp air from outside whipping her force field of hair into my face.

"That was so *close*," she screams over a Lizzo song. We're rocketing down the road at an absurd speed, fueled by adrenaline, as if we're in a high-speed race to the Canadian border. I glance backward, checking for red and blue sirens. Luckily, there are none.

A part of me knows that someday soon I'll miss moments like these.

We drive home toward the nearly set sun. Once the lake is in view, the final maroon hues reflecting off its glittery surface before all goes dark, the homes transform from dilapidated huts to McMansions like *that*. I see families huddled behind big bay windows eating dinner, bundled-up dads shooting hoops with their kids on paved driveways with no cracks or weeds. It makes me wonder how different life would have been if me and Gus had grown up in the Rock Ledge 1 percent—in a neighborhood like the Brandstones'—and the car accident had never happened.

Dad would be here. Mars wouldn't be. Mom would still be normal. Gus would come around a lot more. Our family could have been like one of these ones (minus the disposable income).

Bree stops at an intersection and I read a decorative rock sitting next to a mailbox, with the engraved text, THE CLOSER THE COAST, THE FEWER THE WORRIES.

They think they're being cute and clever. But they have no idea.

Ray is excited to see us when we get home, hoping Bree would secretly bring him back a treat too, despite Mr. Brandstone's rule banning sugar after seven p.m. for the twins. Ray is not disappointed. Bree slips him a half-melted chocolate sundae with a threatening stare that says, *Don't you dare tell Dad*, and I give a tiny lick of my leftovers to Louise.

Mr. Brandstone asks us to help him clean the kitchen. He's extra nice to me while I put all the silverware into the dishwasher; I think he feels guilty about the falling in the shower and Ali teasing digs earlier. Which, in all honesty, he shouldn't. I can take harmless dad jokes. It's kind of nice to be on the receiving end of them from time to time when you grew up without any.

Then me and Bree head to the basement to veg out—and, more importantly, plot my Senior Beach-Bum Party Promposal.

For the past year, the Brandstones have been putting in a rec room—or a mini movie theater, or something else bougie, I can't remember—down here in the basement. It's basically been this massive, sawdust-covered empty space ever since I moved in. Every time I hear Mr. and Mrs. Brandstone fight, which is not that often, it has to do with paint swatches or blueprints or some other dumb stuff. You know, Rich People Problems.

The basement is also where I've been living since my mom wanted me out. Actually, I still don't know if I should say "living." Staying? Hanging out? Whatever. The Brandstones' basement is where I've been sleeping at night since the holidays.

"We should throw a party down here," Bree says as we cross the huge, barren room, our footsteps echoing off the concrete.

"We have to have way more friends to throw a party."

"True."

"But you, me, and Marshall could set up the projector one weekend and binge *Lord of the Rings*?"

Her face lights up. "Order Mario's?"

"Why haven't we done this yet?"

My bedroom is nestled away in the farthest corner from the stairs, which gives me the type of privacy the other Brandstone kids can only dream of. Hardly anyone comes down here but for the occasional construction worker, Thelma and Louise, and me and Bree when we feel like forgetting about the rest of the world, which has been most of senior year. The downfall is, my room is also part of the renovation. Let's just say it's not uncommon to feel sawdust between my bedsheets.

Like every other wall in the basement, the ones in my bedroom have been primed boring-ass white. My deal with Mr. and Mrs. Brandstone is that, for letting me stay at their house indefinitely, I have to paint the room a color of my choosing at some point. Which, c'mon, has to be *the* most reasonable rent agreement ever.

Knowing I'll be painting over the primer eventually, me and Bree decided to utilize one of my bedroom walls like a blank canvas while we still could, and covered a patch with dry-erase paint Mr. Brandstone had in the garage. At first we used it to keep track of all the movies we wanted to see together.

But it quickly became one of the most egregious manifestations of my love for Ali Rashid yet.

"It's coming along nicely," Bree says, plopping down on my flattened futon bed and scanning the wall left to right.

I sit next to her, scooping the remaining Reese's from my cup. "We have a *lot* to choose from."

High up on the wall, DAYS LEFT: 30 has been written in thick erasable marker. Right below that it reads SKY IS GAY FOR ALI:

PROMPOSAL IDEAS. And yes, the wall has become exactly what it sounds like: a daily countdown to the Senior Beach-Bum Party, along with all the ways we've brainstormed about how I can ask Ali to prom.

Did I mention we're extra?

Here's the catch. I can't just *ask* Ali to prom. At Rock Ledge, promposals are A Whole Big Thing for seniors, and there's an annoyingly high bar. So beneath DAYS LEFT: 30 and, SKY IS GAY FOR ALI: PROMPOSAL IDEAS, there are three columns where we've been writing down all our ideas to pull it off. REAL POSSIBILITIES, MAYBE, and LOL HELL NO (just to document our most absurd proposals).

Like, one time, Bree truly thought it'd be a good idea for me to prompose to Ali dressed in drag as Megan Fox—the hottest actress alive, as Ali once told a friend while I was eavesdropping in Anatomy. I think Bree was extra slaphappy after we'd played Mario Kart with Petey for three hours that Friday when she suggested it. Petey laughed so hard, he had to spit out his Coke, which gave us our answer. MEGAN FOX DRAG went on the LOL HELL NO list.

"Oh!" Bree says, leaping up from the futon, still holding her ice-cream cup. "I noticed a Detroit Pistons bumper sticker on his car tonight. Is he a fan?"

"A huge one."

She bites her bottom lip in excitement. "Okay, so . . ." She begins to pace. "What if you write, 'Prom or Pistons?' on a basketball, then ask him to play a game of one-on-one at the courts next to the lake during the Beach-Bum Party. . . ."

"I'm listening."

"Then, when you guys are playing, he'll see what you wrote on the ball, and that way, in case he's a little hesitant to say yes to *prom*, he has the option to go with you to a *Pistons game* instead. Get it? Prom or Pistons?"

I stare at her.

"You're providing a second option to him that may be an even better option for you!" she clarifies, annoyed I'm not immediately overjoyed.

"Okay, but how is a Pistons game a better option for me than prom? I hate basketball. The only sport I like is men's Olympic bobsledding."

"Oh, right. Because of the skintight uniforms."

"Exactly."

"At a Pistons game, you'll be alone with Ali. Well, except for the million other people in the stadium. But they'll be strangers. At prom, you'd be stuck with every other annoying person in *our class*. The basketball game would be a legitimate date. And who knows, maybe he'd say yes to both?" She winks.

I roll my eyes, grinning. "Could I borrow your car to drive to Detroit?"

"Duh."

I think for a second. "I like including the game as an option, but I hate the idea of playing basketball at the beach and looking like a complete idiot." I think some more. "Let's say MAYBE."

"Yes!"

There's no way I'm doing it, but Bree looks especially excited over the idea. I don't want to let her down.

She grabs the marker, hops over to the wall, and scribbles *Prom or Pistons?* in the MAYBE column, right under SPONGEBOB

SQUAREPANTS SPONGE CAKE—an idea from Clare that has since devolved into a definite LOL HELL NO.

Then, with the sleeve of her sweater, Bree rubs away 30 in the daily countdown and replaces it with 29.

Twenty effing nine.

Things are getting real.

Bree crashes down onto the futon and opens her laptop. "*Kimmy Schmidt*? She spreads out across my blankets. "Or *Schitt's Creek*?"

I cozy up to her, pulling a blanket over my torso, because the basement's chronically cold, and angle my head so I can see the screen too. "Your choice."

Thinking about promposing to Ali is fun and all. But truthfully, I mostly like spending time with Bree down here, not thinking about my mom, or Mars, or where I'm going to live after I graduate, or if I'll end up being able to afford community college in the fall, or all the awful people in this terrible town.

Down here, we're basically twelve-year-olds again. I don't know how the outside world so easily fades away beyond these primed white walls, but it does. I think that's the real reason we've been going over promposal ideas for weeks and still haven't decided on an idea to run with. It's not entirely about Ali after all.

TWENTY-EIGHT DAYS

Don't look now, but Dan, to your right," Marshall reports through his teeth without shifting his eyes around the food court. "Should we say hi?"

Dan and Bree have gotten close this year, so we probably should at least nod his way. But seeing people who aren't your friends outside school can be fatally awkward.

I glance over quickly; Dan's sitting with his younger sister near Sbarro hiding under a thick winter hat and hoodie. "Do you *want* to say hi?"

"No."

"Then nah."

"Dan's gay, right?"

I roll my eyes.

The truth is, Dan probably *is* gay. At least that's been my impression from our brief interactions throughout the past few months, after Dan transferred to Rock Ledge from a school in the Upper Peninsula and started hanging around Bree more often. But what's it to Marshall?

Straight people needlessly speculating over sexuality is a nails-on-chalkboard-level irritant to me. If you don't care either way, why make A Whole Big Thing? Comments like that one are why I've been hesitant to tell him about my crush on Ali. "I don't know," I answer, clearly annoyed. "Why do you care?"

He shrugs. "I don't. Dan just seems gay. Isn't your gay-dar supposed to be better than mine?"

I give him a look.

Then I decide the guilt of ignoring maybe the only other gay kid in school trumps the potential awkwardness of acknowledging each other's existence. I crank my head Dan's way and stare, waiting for him to notice. I wave when it looks like he might see us—but he doesn't react.

"Damn," Marshall says. "He's straight up ignoring our asses."

As nice as it'd be to have a gay friend in Rock Ledge, Dan's never shown an interest in building that bridge, and Bree's never attempted to build it for us. So I guess we're stuck painfully avoiding eye contact in food courts for the foreseeable future.

Whatever. It's not a big deal.

We return to our LMEP burgers and cheese fries. That's pronounced "el-mep," by the way—as in, Lake Michigan Entertainment Plaza. We could just say "the mall" like normal people. But me, Bree, and Marshall kind of have our own language at this point.

LMEP is the best, because—unless you're into chilling at Taco Bell until it closes, or getting stoned in a friend's basement—there's nothing to do in Rock Ledge on weekends during the winter. It's about an hour's drive away, in Traverse City, and it keeps me, Bree, and Marshall sane. Seriously. All three of us are big movie people, and LMEP has the closest theater with actual good film options and new releases—even though it's still behind the times on reserved seating and IMAX. It's become our Saturday night go-to ever since we got our licenses.

LMEP can also be the worst, though, because it feels like every Rock Ledger has the same plan in mind. You're bound to spot approximately one million people you don't want to interact with.

Case in point: awkward Dan Christiansen.

Marshall, whose stomach must be larger than mine and Bree's combined, starts going in on my fries because he's already done with his. I push his hand away. "It's your turn to get the goods, by the way," I say through a mouthful of burger. I nod across the food court toward Moe's.

We take turns sneaking snacks into the movies each week, and Moe's is this convenience store type of place that sells candy a third of the price of the theater's. We just smuggle it inside.

"I thought I got the candy last week?"

"Last week was *Revenge of the Whales*, and I got Sour Patch Kids and Sno-Caps. Remember?"

He remembers, and angrily steals more of my fries. "We can still take turns paying, but I think you should always sneak in the snacks."

"How would that be fair?"

"Because it doesn't look good if the only Black kid in the mall gets caught sneaking candy into the theater."

"Don't be an idiot," I say, pushing his hand away from my fries yet again, more aggressively this time. "You're the only Black kid in northern Michigan—not just in this mall."

He grins. "Touché."

I'm one of the very few people close enough to Marshall to joke around like that. Even Bree would probably get yelled at (or at least a mean look).

I don't blame him, though; he has to put up with a lot of crap being literally one of four not-white kids at a school with a nauseatingly high number of MAKE AMERICA GREAT AGAIN bumper stickers in the parking lot.

Marshall somehow manages to always stay bubbly and keep a cool head despite it all. I don't know how. The only time I've seen him show any kind of emotion over race stuff was when he got into it with Cliff in junior year History debating if Confederate monuments should be taken down.

Seriously. Cliff is the worst.

And his awfulness doesn't stop with Marshall, either.

Cliff's had a thing for Bree since freshman year, but she keeps rejecting him for obvious reasons. He's gotten the hint more recently, though, and is now just a straight-up dick to her, too—like how seven-year-olds make fun of the kids they have a crush on. And of course, I'm her gay best friend, so he mouths "homo" at me in the hallway and mocks how I walk in the parking lot, as if he's playing the role of "bully" in a nineties comedy.

So now, me, Bree, and Marshall are all on his shit list for challenging his asshole-ness in our own unique ways—which means we must be doing something right.

But it really does bear repeating: Cliff's a complete garbage human.

"Okay, you're right," I say, my skin crawling, remembering how soul-crushing that Confederate monument debate was. "I'll sneak in the snacks from now on."

Marshall points at me with a grin to say thanks.

"I'm already giving it a nine-point-five out of ten," he says of the new Ava DuVernay film we're about to watch, before sucking up the last of his Faygo. "I'm setting my expectations low."

"You shouldn't do that," I warn. "Your pro-Ava-DuVernay bias will mess with your ability to see the movie for what it is."

"I don't have a *pro-Ava-DuVernay bias*." He shakes his head. "I have a *good movie* bias. It just so happens all DuVernay movies are flawless in every single way."

Our phones go off at the same time.

Marshall sighs. "Again?"

"Yup," I say, glancing at the screen. "Again."

It's a text from Bree, who's in meltdown mode because she's stuck at Petey's swim meet instead of with us. We really do feel sorry she couldn't come tonight, but her excessive FOMO means she's been blowing up our three-way chat and sending us TikToks nonstop in an attempt to feel included from afar.

"She does realize I'm seeing the movie with her again next weekend, right?" Marshall says, shaking his head and reading her latest text, which asks what food court option we decided on. "I told Teddy I'd see it with him on Saturday. You're coming too, right?"

"Next weekend?"

"Yeah."

"Hrm."

This is the first time Marshall's proposed that Teddy hang out with the three of us, and it catches me off guard. Don't get me wrong—Teddy's always been nice to me, but a fourth would definitely throw our friend-group equilibrium off.

"If the movie's not complete garbage, potentially," I say to mess with him, already knowing I'll be there. "But that's a big if."

We trash our napkins and empty cups and walk toward the candy store, passing Dan on our way. I try to make eye contact again to break the glacial ice that took over the entire food court while we ate, but fail.

Yep, he's definitely avoiding us.

"I vote Whoppers and M&M's," I say. "Is that cool?"

Marshall thinks through his options as we walk to Moe's. "How about Whoppers and Raisinets?"

I fake vomit everywhere. "Raisinets?"

"What's your beef with Raisinets?"

"You know how I feel about Raisinets."

"Junior Mints?" he asks.

"Deal."

We pass mall workers who are just now removing Christmas ornaments from the ceiling. Around here, people take Jesus pretty seriously. It's not just my mom.

"Question," Marshall says. "Do you think Ainsley would appreciate yellow roses or normal roses more when I ask her to prom?"

Ugh. We're back to Ainsley again.

Marshall went on and on about her basically the whole drive here. I know I should be happy for him, but he never used to talk to me about the girls he liked until she came along—and I am *terrible* talking girls with straight guys. Even—especially?—with Marshall.

"By 'normal' roses, do you mean red roses?" I ask.

"Yes," he says. "Yellow is her favorite color, but I also read that yellow is the color of friendship. I don't want to subconsciously suggest I'm more friend-zone material."

"The concept of the friend zone is inherently sexist, FYI, but I'd go with yellow anyway, because I think she'd care less about society's meaning and more about that you remembered yellow's her favorite color, *buuut* . . . " I pause to breathe. "I'm biased because, as you know, yellow is also my favorite color. So take it with a grain of salt."

Marshall nods slowly, trying to keep up.

We snag the Whoppers and Junior Mints and head to the theater, where I breeze by the usher with the candy tucked under my jacket. We're twenty minutes early, which is typical because Marshall's super particular about his seat. Once, we had to watch a movie in the first row because Bree's car ran out of gas and made us late, and Marshall never recovered from staring straight up into Robert Downey Jr.'s humungous nostrils. I really wish LMEP theater would enter the twenty-first century and get reserved seating already; it'd probably cut the number of our friend fights in half.

After we take off our layers of late-winter garb and stuff the surrounding cup holders with our snacks, Marshall is back to Ainsley. Seriously, I can barely get a word in about anything else.

He goes on and on about how she has the "quirkiest, best laugh," walks me through the day he knew she was "the one" (spoiler: Marshall learned she, too, wants to get a husky puppy one day), relishes in their shared love of everything Ava DuVernay, and blah, blah, *blah*. Kill me now. It's not that I don't like Ainsley. She's one of the nicest people at our school, always smiling at others in the hallway and giving rides home to the freshmen who live in her neighborhood. She *does* have a great laugh, too, for what it's worth. But I get really uncomfortable trying to give Marshall any sort of Straight Guy Advice, and I now associate Ainsley with all that awkwardness.

It's definitely not her fault, but Ainsley's part of a bigger . . . *thing*, that's happening between me and Marshall. The straighter he's gotten, the more uncomfortable I am showing my gay around him. It's weird.

He hasn't actually gotten *more heterosexual*, obviously, just like I haven't gotten any *gayer*. But now he has his straight track friends, like Teddy, and a girlfriend he can't get enough of. Last week, he mentioned the possibility of joining one of the bro-y frats at MSU; I had to suppress the urge to projectile vomit directly into his face.

My point is, the more he's leaned into his new life of Teddy, track, and Ainsley, the less I want to do things like tell him about my crush on Ali. No wonder my blood runs cold at the thought of Marshall discovering the promposal wall. He's never been down into my basement bedroom at the Brandstones', and I'm going to keep it that way until the room gets painted.

There's a lull in his monologue praising Ainsley's preference for Cool Ranch Doritos over nacho cheese, so I seize the opportunity to change topics.

"What are you doing next Friday?" I whisper at him as the lights go dark and everyone gets quiet. I'm hoping he'll want to see the new outer-space action-drama starring Mark Ruffalo and Amy Adams, but two trips to LMEP in one weekend might be kind of excessive—even for us.

"Ali invited me to his big house party that night," he answers nonchalantly, splitting open the bag of Junior Mints. "Aren't you going?"

My stomach drops a million feet all at once.

"Uh . . ." I swallow hard as the intro warning us to turn off our phones starts to play. "Like, this coming Friday? As in, six days away?"

"Yeah."

"A house party?"

"Yep."

"Ali Rashid?"

He looks at me suspiciously. "Is there another guy named Ali at our school?"

I sink deeper into my seat, thankful the dark theater is helping hide the devastation draped across my face.

"Wait, hold up," Marshall whispers, oblivious. "Why is the friend zone inherently sexist again?"

"I'll explain later."

Damn. The love of my life is throwing a house party. A *big* one, apparently. And I'm not even important enough to make it onto the guest list. Which means I'm definitely not important enough to be his prom date.

This blows.

TWENTY-EIGHT DAYS

I have this terrible, throbbing knot in my stomach.

It feels like when I was in third grade and I fell off the monkey bars and landed on my chest and got the wind knocked out of me. Or when I was a kid and the pastor at my mom's church implied there were "wicked spirits" dancing inside Ellen DeGeneres's soul because she doesn't like D. (Okay, that's actually hilarious to think about now, but it definitely wasn't at the time.) Or the moment when the skin doctor at the poor people's clinic finally surrendered to reality and admitted Mars would probably be around well into adulthood.

Ali doesn't want me at his party. And that really, *really* sucks.

"Did you get an invite?" Bree asks, storming into my bedroom out of breath.

I pause Netflix and give her a look.

"Damn it. How'd you know what I'm talking about, then?"

"Marshall. Ali invited him."

She slumps into the room and dumps the backpack she took to Petey's swimming competition onto the floor. The fact that her first question wasn't about the DuVernay movie shows how invested Bree is in my promposal plans too.

"Just come with us!" she says cheerily, trying to be glass half-full. "Who cares?"

I grunt disapprovingly.

"It's going to be a big party anyways. It's not like you'd be crashing a small get-together."

"Did Ali ask you? Like, directly?"

"Carolyn texted me and said Ali wanted me to come"—she must read the expression on my face—"which is, you know, *weird* because you're closer to Ali than I am. Obviously."

I grunt again, knowing full well I'm being a whiny drama queen, and return to watching *Bird Box* for the fourth time. I'd rather be stuck in its fictional apocalypse than in the nonfiction one I'm experiencing right now. Especially if it meant being shacked up with Trevante Rhodes.

I learn on Monday that at least, like, sixty people were invited. The fact that I didn't make the cut proves that not only is Ali certainly *not* going to say yes to any prompsosal coming from me, but I barely even register as a friend on his radar. Or, as Marshall might say: I'm not even in Ali's friend zone.

"Are you going to the party on Friday?" Carolyn whispers at me in Mrs. Diamond's Health class, apparently reading my mind while passing back a study sheet on STDs.

"No."

"Why not?"

"I wasn't invited."

"Oh." She cringes, giving me this look over her shoulder like she just learned about a terrible medical diagnosis. "So sorry, Sky."

Is it that obvious to everyone in this godawful school how desperate I am for Ali Rashid to like me?

"What do you think, Sky?" Mrs. Diamond asks from the front of the room, spotting my being distracted.

Damn it. Now Carolyn's big mouth is getting me in trouble.

I clear my throat. "I didn't hear your question, sorry."

"What disease am I describing?"

My face burns red as more heads crank toward me. "Ah . . . chlamydia?"

"Nice shot in the dark, but no. Gonorrhea."

"Question," Cliff interjects, raising his hand near the front of the class. Because of course he's going to use this opportunity to humiliate me.

Yeah, Cliff and a bunch of his cronies are in Health with me too, which somehow makes learning about sexually transmitted diseases even worse, if you can believe it.

"Go ahead," Mrs. Diamond says, nodding at him, her massive golden earrings dangling on either side of her exhausted, fed-up face. Mrs. Diamond is one of those teachers who probably should have retired a decade ago.

"What about gay people?" Cliff asks.

My stomach drops.

Mrs. Diamond's eyes narrow on him. "What about them?"

Cliff licks his lips and thinks for a second, as all his friends start smirking at one another. "This class doesn't really talk about gay people or gay sex or anything."

My face is now burning hot, and my stomach is *still* dropping—

under my chair, through the floor, into the ground. It's halfway to China by now.

I hate this.

"What are you getting at?" Mrs. Diamond asks, as if she doesn't know.

"I'm just saying, it's the twenty-first century. Doesn't this school care about the sexual health of our gay students?" Cliff's mocking tone makes me want to curl up into a ball and disappear. Why won't Mrs. Diamond cut him off? Why won't *anyone* jump in and say something? Anything?

Cliff glances around the room looking for support, but keeps his laser-blue eyes glued on me a second longer than on anyone else, accompanied by a nasty grin. "Shouldn't gay students be able to learn about gay sex? I personally think it's gross when it's dudes—"

"*Cliff.*"

"—but it should still be part of the curriculum. Right?"

Mrs. Diamond rests her hand on her hip. "Are you finished?"

A few girls sigh and mutter, "Oh my God," annoyed by his antics. Cliff's friends are trying and failing to hide their laughter. Carolyn glances back at me in pity—cementing the fact that everyone knows this is an attack on me—which makes everything a million times worse.

"Just my two cents," Cliff says, shrugging in victory. "I'll speak up for the gays because no one else will."

There's so much to hate about Cliff. He's Rock Ledge's most egregious example of an arrogant bigot, which says a lot. But the worst thing about him is that, whenever he's an asshole to me, I'm immediately, without fail, reminded of my mom.

Because, sure, she might *love* me, technically. But she's still a huge homophobe.

She got swept up into an old-school church and gargled the conservative Christian Kool-Aid right after my dad died, when I was five. Not all churches are nuts—the Brandstones go to a chill, inclusive one up the coast on Christmas Eve—but the congregation my mom joined? Completely bonkers.

Gus told me one time that he can remember what she was like before her literal come-to-Jesus moment, but I can't. Apparently she smoked pot sometimes and cursed a lot in the pre-accident era. I wish we still had that version of her. It sucks, but I know the hate hiding behind Cliff's nasty grin and my mom's moral policing are the same exact thing.

They just take different forms.

I should be taking notes on how not to get gonorrhea, but now my mind is spiraling, rewinding back to holiday break—the night when everything hit the fan with my mom.

We were both sitting on the living room sofa and *It's a Wonderful Life* was on, but playing softly enough that we couldn't really keep up with the story. Our house had this distinct-but-nice double-whammy smell of cheesy potatoes—my mom had baked a pan to take to church the next day—and this gargantuan vanilla candle she only lights in December. Gus was at a friend's, or his girlfriend's parents' house on the lake, or at the bar, or something. He was always looking for a reason to not be home, even when he was just visiting for a few days around Christmas.

Out of nowhere, my mom—without even looking at me—asked, "Do you have something to tell me?"

I knew she knew.

I'd already come out at school, so I understood I was living at constant risk of her finding out. Rock Ledge is tiny. People talk. And people at her church *really* talk. Still, it was naive of me to think I'd muster up the courage to tell her myself before the grapevine filled her in. I never did ask how she found out I was gay, because it didn't really matter anyway (although I'm fairly certain the pastor's son, who's in my Trig class, was the culprit).

So I owned up to it. I told her I'm gay.

She wasn't angry. Just devastated in the disappointed parental way that's much, much worse. I would have preferred her screaming, breaking plates, promising me I'd be grounded forever. She looked completely depleted—this soul-crushing, irreparable level of sad I'd never seen on the face of another human before.

"Have you acted on your urges?" she finally asked in this restrained tone that made it feel like we were speaking in one of those church confessional booths, not on the same family room couch where we used to play Clue.

"No," I remember answering, unsure if the porn I'd watched counted to her.

My mom doesn't wear her heart on her sleeve all that much. Not since Dad died, Gus says. But I glimpsed over just long enough to see the light from the Christmas tree shimmering off her cheeks, so I think there were tears.

Then she went in for the kill.

"What would your father think?" she asked, intending for it to sting.

And it did. It definitely stung.

It still does.

I hate to admit it, but sometimes I think about that question when I'm walking through the parking lot and my hips are swinging a bit too much. Or when I'm giggling with Bree watching *Kimmy Schmidt* instead of hanging out with Marshall and Teddy and the guys on the track team. Or when I hear my voice played back in an Instagram story, and I think I sound—I mean, I *know* I sound—totally, 100 percent, bright-pink gay.

I don't know what my dad would think. And I don't want to think about it.

My mom waited a few minutes longer before asking if I wanted to sleep at a friend's that night. I said no because it was Christmas Eve, and Bree and Marshall both had family stuff going on. I didn't want to intrude.

She thought it'd be best, though. So I packed a big bag, walked the three miles to the Brandstones', and never looked back.

The school bell rings, jolting me awake from my anxiety-dream—not to be confused with my much more preferable shower-dreams and daydreams. I brush past Carolyn, who I can tell is about to get all maternally sympathetic about Cliff's comments, and I bolt out of the classroom and into the hallway as Mrs. Diamond finishes a final thought about condoms.

"What?" I hear Cliff quip to his giggling asshole friends on the way out, a few of them glancing my way. "It was a valid question! Sex-ed needs to be gayer!"

I don't know why, but sometimes everything just hits me at once, you know? Cliff. My mom. Mars. (Freaking Mars.) They circle through my brain on a loop like a snowball rolling down a hill, gaining size and speed, before it becomes this unstoppable boulder of gay gloom. I have to let it smash into whatever's lying at the bottom of the hill before I can feel better. I just hate that it's about to smash right here, right now, in the middle of a crowded hallway.

I'm fiddling with my locker combination and keeping my head down—I'm not sure how watery my eyes are, so better to not look up at all—when a hand grabs my shoulder.

"Sky High! What's up?"

Oh no.

I quickly wipe away my tears and turn around, forcing a smile at Ali. "Good. Er, nothing. Nothing is up."

His face drops. "Everything all right?"

"Yeah, of course," I say, blinking away the wetness. "Sorry, allergies. How's it going?"

He's not buying it. "You sure?"

"Yeah."

"Okay, well," he says, moving on, probably sensing my embarrassment. "I wanted to make sure you're coming with Bree and Marshall to my party."

"Oh."

"My house. Friday. Think you can make it?"

"Yeah, definitely."

He flashes an Ali Grin. I try to flash one back. Then he floats away.

I shouldn't let one person have this much sway over my emotions, but I immediately feel much better.

TWENTY-TWO DAYS

S crew our promposal ideas." Bree burps, interrupting my thoughts, and licks the aluminum lid of her chocolate pudding. "You should just prompose to him tonight at his party!"

I jump, nearly spilling my orange juice. "Shh!"

"What?" She glances around the hallway. "No one is listening to us, Sky. No one cares about our boring existence here. We might as well be invisible."

"You're practically screaming, though."

We weren't even talking about Ali, but Bree must have noticed the chronic smile spread across my face—the one I haven't been able to shake since Monday after Health class. On Tuesday, I found out Ali only invited forty people to his party. Forty! To be in Ali's top forty—and not floating in ice-cold space outside his friend zone—might be my biggest high school accomplishment yet.

Maybe I do have a shot at going to prom with Ali Rashid.

"I say go for it tonight," she continues, this time quieter. "Who knows? Your chances of getting a yes might be better if he's buzzed, which will *definitely* be the case tonight—"

"Who will be buzzed?" Marshall says out of nowhere, plopping down onto the floor next to us outside Ms. Winter's classroom.

Ugh, Teddy is right behind him too, lumbering along like Marshall's much larger shadow.

Just the sight of Teddy makes it feel like my body is a balloon being pumped with vaporized dread instead of helium. There's this pressure to be extra careful not to say or do something too gay around Teddy, because then it could embarrass Marshall.

"Hello?" Marshall repeats, after me and Bree stay silent, handing us two pieces of cinnamon gum. "Who will be buzzed?"

"Ali. Sky wants to ask him for his Anatomy notes," Bree lies for me nonchalantly, sticking the gum into her mouth.

Yes, I know, I know. I need to get it over with and tell Marshall about my promposal plans for Ali. But with Teddy around?

Definitely not right now.

"LMEP is happening tomorrow, yes?" Bree points between all of us. "Ava DuVernay?"

Marshall lights up. "Yes! I will see that movie at least three more times in theaters."

"Dude, that's so much money," Teddy says, jaw dropped, crouching down to join our group. He's like, six foot three, so it reminds me of a circus clown on stilts bending in half to talk to kids. "How do you justify spending that much money on one movie?"

"*DuVernay*, bro," Marshall says before turning to me. "You're in, right?"

How are they even thinking ahead to Saturday? Ali's party is *tonight*, and it is literally impossible for my mind to focus on anything beyond that. My calendar currently includes Ali's party, a bunch of years after, then death.

"Just say yes," Bree says, rolling her eyes. "What else do you have going on? A night filled with Ali shower-dreaming?"

It's like she dumped a bucket of ice water on my head.

"A night of what now?" Teddy perks up, confused.

"Fine, yes, I'll be there," I say emphatically, feeling my cheeks getting toasty.

Bree winks at me.

Thankfully, the lunch bell rings, helping to end the discussion. Teddy departs for whatever his next class is, as me, Bree, and Marshall walk into Yearbook.

"Tardy," Winter jokes without looking away from her computer screen, a half-eaten sub sandwich in her hand dripping with Italian dressing. "Suspensions for all of you." She knows it's us because we're almost always the first to arrive for her class.

"Ha, *ha*," Bree mocks as we cross the classroom. "As if you could survive a single day in here without me steering the ship."

Winter shrugs, conceding Bree's point.

Even though she's only been teaching at RLHS for a few years, Winter has the kind of worn, stuffy classroom that suggests she's been working here since the 1970s. The walls are plastered in historic magazine covers from decades past, large posters showing off her love of all things typography, class photos from previous yearbooks, and layered bulletin boards that she's only added to since she began teaching here—like a tree's rings that show its age. If I have a comfort zone in this school, it's in here.

"DuVernay," Marshall says flatly, sliding one of his butt cheeks onto the corner of her crowded desk. "Thoughts?"

"First of all, nope," Winter warns, staring disapprovingly at his leg infringing on her paperwork. He slides back off the desk as quickly as he slid on. "Secondly, you know I can't weigh in on that, Jones."

"Why not?" Bree says as we take the three computers closest to her desk, like usual.

"Because," Winter answers, tucking her endless black hair behind her ear, revealing small and sparkly hoop rings. "I can already tell by the way you said 'DuVernay' that this is a fight waiting to unravel between the three of you. Don't think I forgot about the Lady Gaga debacle."

The three of us grin, admitting she's right.

Last fall, Incurably Straight Marshall had the audacity to claim that Katy Perry's Super Bowl performance—yeah, the one featuring Left Shark—was better than Gaga's *and* the J.Lo/Shakira extravaganza. It became A Whole Big Thing for obvious reasons and set off a bitter Yearbook fandom civil war that hasn't technically been settled yet. Ali took my side, though, which put me on cloud nine for a week.

Yearbook is the only hour I look forward to during the day. For one, it's the only class in four long-ass years at RLHS that me, Bree, and Marshall have had together. But also, Yearbook has exactly zero Cliff Cronies in it and an eclectic group of fun, creative weirdos instead. Even the few popular kids in here, like Ali, are chill. Winter being the coolest teacher at this school is the cherry on top.

Once the tardy bell rings, Winter closes the door and scolds everyone to shut up. She yells a lot, but it's always half-hearted and a little bit playful—like an older sibling calling you out for something stupid. "Settle your oversugared selves," she says, waiting for the final voices to die down. She's wearing a flowing, oversize gray sweater that dwarfs her slender frame, and her freshly painted nails are a green color that remind me of the guacamole from Clare's taco night. "Everyone knows their assignment for the day, right?"

The class gives mixed responses of yesses, hesitant shrugs, and nos. Winter squints around at individual faces to get a more detailed picture of who's staying on top of their work and who's clearly not. After a few minutes of back-and-forth so everyone's on the right page—like, literally—we get to work.

Bree goes into Bree Beast Mode, as me and Marshall have been calling it. As editor-in-chief, she's in charge of designing and drafting the weekly e-blast on Fridays, which gets distributed early on Mondays. It's basically a newsletter for seniors and parents of seniors about what's going on with the yearbook—deadlines for photo submissions, info about ad sales, that sort of thing. It's one of the most important responsibilities for the EIC, so Bree's type A perfectionism truly shines when she's on e-blast deadline.

Marshall is the techy one in the class—and, like, in life—so his latest task is figuring out a new font issue some students are having in Memories, the program we work in to build out pages and do All Things Yearbook. Well, I think that's what he's been doing. I'm not even sure, really. Marshall plays the part of IT Guy in Yearbook, and I don't ask too many questions.

Then there's me.

I'm not the driven editor-in-chief type, nor am I technologically literate enough to be a computer nerd. But I do love movies. Winter assigned me a Films of the Year spread last week. It's definitely one of our "filler" spreads, as Bree accidentally referred to it once in front of me (aka no one would even notice if we end up having to cut it—unlike the varsity football page). But I don't care; it's probably the most fun assignment I've ever had.

I've interviewed students on their favorite movies (and I've learned that their opinions about Hollywood are usually complete trash) and I'm doing box-office research today so I can create this cool infographic thing listing the year's biggest blockbusters. Not to brag, but this will definitely be the best spread in the book. Well, besides the full-page ad Ali's parents bought for him. It's filled with pics of Ali; I can't compete with that.

"Are you including the new DuVernay movie on your Films of the Year spread?" Winter whispers into my ear, bending close. "Is that why you and the other two Stooges were arguing about her earlier?"

I look over my shoulder at her with a smile. "No. Marshall's just annoyingly obsessed with all her movies, is all."

"Ah." She nods, straightening back up.

"We saw the new one Saturday, though."

"The verdict?"

"I'd say three out of five stars. Marshall loved it, of course, but—"

"*Blah, blah, blah,*" Bree begins yelling next to us, typing furiously.

"What's her problem?" Winter asks me.

"She didn't see it yet."

"*Blah, blah, blah,* sorry, I'm seeing it tomorrow and can't hear spoilers, *blah, blah, blah.*"

Winter pats Bree's shoulders before moving down the row of students. "Okay, no spoilers, Brandstone, I promise."

I would never in a million years become a teacher in Rock Ledge—why would anyone voluntarily sign up for that kind of torture?—but if I did, I'd want to be a teacher like Winter. She's from here originally, but you'd never guess it. She's cultured and forward-thinking and doesn't belong in this deteriorating town, with its endless rows of cracked concrete driveways.

After high school, Winter jetted off to South America to backpack for a year. Like, I've seen that cliché played out in the movies a hundred trillion times, but who actually does that? Then it was off to Seattle—then San Francisco, then New Orleans—scraping by working waitress jobs and living in big houses with dusty curtains and artists with infinite stories.

She worked reception at a Miami Beach hotel, spending lazy afternoons in white sand and late nights on dance floors. She lived in Brooklyn nannying for the kids of a single Wall Street banker "who was on a strict diet of whiskey, corned beef, and women who were too good for him," as she put it. There was her stint managing a camp for kids with disabilities in Utah; her move to Austin, Texas, for a man who stole her heart—before stomping all over it.

Seriously. She's been everywhere and seen it all. Her life sounds like a story filled with twists, turns, and cherished memories even the best writer couldn't piece together.

Winter did what so many people from Rock Ledge never do after high school: she escaped. But many years later, she decided to come back. Or, as she phrased it to me, Bree, and Marshall one evening eating cold pizza in her classroom as we finished up page deadlines: "I finally grew up. I missed the blues." She nodded at a photograph on the classroom wall taken from space of the northern Michigan coastline—the spectrum of turquoise, indigo, and navy meeting the rigid, crooked green of land. I remember she popped a pepperoni into her mouth and had this sparkle in her eyes. "The blues are bluer up here."

That's the part of Winter's story I will never understand.

Why come back to this hellhole of a town after seeing what else is out there? Whatever *blues* Rock Ledge has to offer, they can't possibly compete with the flavors of New Orleans or the energy of San Francisco. Right? I'm grateful she returned, though. Otherwise, I never would have known her.

The bell rings, which is nuts, because I barely made a dent in researching box office results for my spread. Okay, I admittedly spent way more time than planned glancing over at Ali, distracted by the way he was grooving in his chair to Frank Ocean with his headphones on. And yes, I know it was Frank Ocean because I made several unnecessary trips to the printer to peek at his Spotify. The point is, it's hard to concentrate on anything when those eyebrows are so close.

"Hey, you," Winter calls across the room as everyone's collecting their things to leave.

She's talking to the party boy.

"Yeah?" Ali answers, stopping in the doorway on his way out. He's wearing a gray T-shirt that fits him very nicely and a brand-new pink watch. If I wore that watch, it'd look way too gay. Ali can pull it off, though.

"A little birdie told me you're having a party tonight," Winter says, shuffling papers around her desk before giving him a look.

Ali swings his bag around his shoulder, a grin creeping into his cheeks. "What little birdie told you that?"

"Word spreads fast around here."

My and Bree's eyes are darting back and forth between the two of them like it's a Wimbledon match.

"Please make good decisions," Winter says.

"Always." He nods.

"I mean it, Rashid. Your parents better be home too."

"They will be."

"Remember, the drinking age is twenty-one, and I assume no twenty-one-year-olds will be there."

"Got it."

Ali disappears out the door, unscathed. But a minute later, the three of us get caught in the line of fire too.

"I assume you're all going tonight?" Winter asks us.

Damn it.

We all turn around slowly, just inches away from the exit.

"Going where?" Marshall plays dumb.

Winter drops her chin at him knowingly. "Ali's party."

"Oh, is that tonight?" Bree says in the high-pitched tone she makes when she's feeling guilty. "I didn't realize that was tonight."

"Save it, Brandstone. Just be smart, you three."

"We will be," I say, unsure if I'm telling the truth.

TWENTY-TWO DAYS

I t all comes down to this.

Well, not really.

I need to stop hyping up Ali's party like it's my life's make-or-break moment. It's not! I'm not even sure what I want this party to accomplish, anyway. Is my goal to further cement my friendship with Ali? Get better, more personal promposal ideas from seeing inside his house? Just stare at him creepily across the room, fantasizing about what our lives could look like together ten years from now? Lose my virginity to him?

A girl can dream.

Bree and I have eaten about ten thousand calories in a dozen stalking operations outside the Rashid household, and now we're entering Ali's lair—by *invitation*. This may not be my make-or-break, but it's still big.

I'm wearing that pale-pinkish collared shirt I wore to school the Thursday before last. Yeah, it screams "gay" and I'm a little insecure about that. But I scream "gay" too, right? Plus, it makes my arms and chest look more muscle-y, I think.

I hope.

I don't know.

Marshall floats over to Bree's car from his front porch wearing his favorite puffy, red vest coat and light denim jeans, clearly trying to look good for Ainsley. He's almost to the car when his dad comes flying out the front door behind him in a flash.

We should have known.

"Here we go," Bree sighs through gritted teeth behind the wheel, turning the music down. "Don't say anything stupid."

Mr. Jones is one of those annoying overprotective *guy's guy* type of dads. He rarely laughs, he makes fun of vegetarians, and he has never been seen not wearing an earth-toned polo shirt.

Marshall hops into the back seat. "Heads up," he warns as his dad beelines to the car.

"Oh, we know," Bree says, unrolling her window and clearing her throat. "Hey, Mr. Jones."

"Hi, Bree." Mr. Jones places one hand on the roof of her car and bends down to scan the interior. "How's everyone doing?"

"Good," Bree and I say in unison.

"Headed to a get-together, I hear?"

"Yep," Bree answers.

"Will there be drinking?"

"Nah," I say, smiling.

Mr. Jones doesn't smile back. He gives each one of us an individual mini stare-down. This is beyond awkward, even for Mr. Jones's standards. I already know Marshall is mortified. "If any of you digest even the tiniest sip of booze, don't you dare get behind this wheel. All right?"

"Dad, c'mon," Marshall mumbles.

Mr. Jones ignores him.

"Of course not," Bree answers in her high-pitched voice.

"Got it," I reiterate, nodding and pointing out that my seat belt is buckled—as if a buckled seat belt is somehow related to not driving drunk.

Mr. Jones zeroes in on Marshall in the back. "You be safe, OK?" His tone softens—like suddenly me and Bree aren't even there— like it's even more critical Marshall hears his every word.

"I will, Dad."

"Don't put yourself in a situation."

"I won't."

"All right. Well." Mr. Jones nods at me and Bree. "Have fun, kids. Be back by curfew."

Bree rolls the window up and backs out of the driveway.

"Sorry," Marshall sighs.

"Marshall, *please*," Bree says, sitting up straight so she can see his face in the rearview mirror. "The world is a better place because of your dad's terrifying threats to avoid trouble."

"But now we *really* can't get caught drinking tonight," I say, turning the music back up loudly and raising my voice. "Because I don't want to live in a world where both Winter and your dad catch us."

Marshall leans forward from the back and turns down the music. "Can we not?"

"Seventy-year-old Marshall and his aversion to loud music," Bree mutters, grinning.

"I'd appreciate it if I could actually *hear* the conversation up there," he says defensively, handing us two pieces of cinnamon gum. "Oh! Promposal question. I'm giving Ainsley a gift when I ask her to go with me."

"In addition to the yellow roses?" I ask.

"Correct. So, what's better: A framed picture of us together, or an inanimate object that sort of symbolizes the start of our relationship?"

"What's the inanimate object that symbolizes the start of your relationship?"

"The movie ticket stubs from our first movie together."

"Movie ticket stubs," Bree and I say promptly and in unison.

"Hands *down*," I emphasize.

"I have to admit," Bree says, "that's going to be pretty damn cute, Marshall Jones."

"Yeah?"

"Yeah." She shakes her head in disgust. "It makes me sick."

We park on the street near Ali's house and walk toward his yard. This is the first legitimate popular person party I've been to, now that I think about it.

A wave of nerves ripples down my body, accompanied by irrational, panicked thoughts. What if Ali ignores me all night? What if I get too drunk and prompose to him *here*? What if Cliff randomly crashes the party and ruins everything? What if a playful Franklin's claws accidentally get stuck in my gay shirt and rip it off, exposing Mars to everyone?

The boulder of gay gloom starts rolling down the mountainside in my head—

"You okay?" Bree whispers, saving me from myself and wrapping her arm around my middle.

"Yeah, of course," I answer, trying to act chill. I'm very aware Marshall is right next to us, completely unaware of my Ali obsession. "Why wouldn't I be?"

She smiles.

We're almost to the front door. The air has that sweet spring smell again, just like when we were parked nearby last week, but the pulsating bass coming from inside the house means the neighborhood is way less quiet than it was then.

Jeff Blummer, a stoner if I've ever met one, lets us inside. "Hey," he mutters, probably not registering who any of us are.

The house is filled with bodies. The living room couches that are supposed to fit four butts are actually fitting seven. People are meandering between the living room and kitchen, nodding at friends and singing along to the music. Every single surface—the coffee table, kitchen countertops, the mantel above the fireplace— is covered in bottles and beer cans. I spot Franklin dashing around pairs of feet, wide-eyed and overwhelmed.

I want to start drinking ASAP to take the edge off. Not to get *drunk* drunk, of course—I've only been wasted one time, after the homecoming football game last year, and it was not an experience I want to relive at the moment. Not when I need to be at least somewhat cognizant around Ali.

But still. I want to feel loose.

Marshall already arranged for our group to split a thirty-six-pack with his track buddies, so I grab two Coronas for me and him—Bree agreed to DD, and doesn't really like drinking anyway—and crack them open.

Then comes the awkward standing. *So* much awkward, *so* much standing. If I've learned one thing about the, like, three parties I've been to in high school, it's that there's always a lot of hesitant stares and waiting around for the alcohol to kick in.

We situate ourselves in a corner of the Rashids' dining room.

"So . . . what now?" Bree says, glancing around coolly and holding a red cup filled with Sprite. Behind her, a row of Rashid family photos lines the wall; his younger sister's soccer pics, his smiley mom kayaking, a group shot of Ali's dad, using a selfie stick, alongside people who I'd guess are extended relatives from Iraq. The Rashid family's cuteness level could easily qualify them for a spot on *Family Feud*, I swear.

We mostly keep to ourselves for a while. Bree chats about the difficulties of parallel parking with this girl she took driver's ed with last summer. Marshall is our trio's true social butterfly, so he strikes up the most convos with passing randos.

Then Dan arrives wearing his typical baggy-sweater-big-hat combo, joining us in our corner of the dining room. He hugs Bree shyly before waving at me and Marshall. He's sporting a pierced ear and bright red corduroy pants. It's a cool look.

"How was the pizza?" Marshall asks him, making things awkward.

"What?"

"Sbarro. We saw you at the LMEP food court last weekend."

"Oh." Dan nods. "Right. It was good."

"Wait, you were at the mall last weekend too?" Bree says, mouth hanging open.

"I told you," Dan says softly. "My family thing? In Traverse? We stopped at the mall on the way back."

Bree closes her eyes, remembering. "Right. Still. The FOMO is real."

A few minutes later, Teddy—more animated than usual with his hair gelled back—shows up and joins our group too. Which feels more okay than when he crashed our trio outside Winter's class at lunch, because it's not just the three of us hanging out now.

Still. I wish me, Bree, and Marshall could stay in our own little world.

Teddy turns and asks me something, but I wasn't paying attention.

"Sorry, what?"

"I just asked how Yearbook is going," he repeats, sipping a beer. "Marshall told me you're in charge of a movies page, or something like that?"

"Oh yeah," I say, glancing around for Ali. "It's going well." I don't want to be rude to Teddy, but the party host's whereabouts is taking up about 95 percent of my brain capacity, and I have yet to see him in his own damn house. I'm getting antsy.

Teddy asks me something else. This time, it's more that the party is crazy loud and less me being too preoccupied to care. But I still didn't hear him.

"Huh?" I ask, leaning toward him. "Sorry. It's loud in here!"

"I just said"—Teddy cranks up his voice, bending down so we're closer in height—"I'm excited for the movies tomorrow night!"

"Yeah, me too!"

"Marshall said the movie is awesome."

I roll my eyes, grinning. "He's somewhat blinded by his DuVernay bias. But, yeah, it was very well done."

A few minutes later, Ainsley appears in the dining room in a brown faux-leather coat, small purse strapped across her chest. She makes her way toward us.

"Hiii," she says, beaming, her pink face extra rosy in the uncomfortably warm house. She gives each one of us a hug. Her curly red hair brushes across my face, and it smells like coconut shampoo. "I love that shirt, Sky."

"Thank you. I like your bracelet."

"Thanks! How's the party so far?"

Marshall shrugs. "Meh."

She laughs and pulls a Bud Light out of her purse, as our group fills her in on who's shown up to the party thus far. In the minute or so since Ainsley's arrived, two more big groups of seniors have squeezed in through the front door, ensuring we've broken a maximum occupancy law.

But still, no sign of Ali.

"Where are you going to school in the fall?" Bree asks Ainsley. "I don't think we've talked about it yet."

"Just the community college," Ainsley says.

"Same!" I blast, way too excitedly. Dan jumps back. Marshall's eyes pop open. "Sorry, it's just—everyone's abandoning me next year for schools far away."

"Don't worry," Dan says. "I have another year left, so I'll be around."

We exchange smiles.

"Good," I reply. "We can be here in this terrible town together. And hopefully I can scrounge up enough cash to get through my first semester."

Last fall, Winter told me about this scholarship available for Rock Ledge "students in need" with GPAs of at least 3.0. Mr. Brandstone helped me fill out all the paperwork and gave me good feedback on my essay. But I'm not getting too excited. With a 3.1 GPA, I barely made the minimum requirement to apply. If it's the least bit competitive, I'm screwed.

And if this scholarship falls through, not even community college will be doable for me.

"Either way, we'll be here for you." Ainsley winks, locking arms with Dan. "A four year university is basically a dated concept today anyways, unless your parents have money to burn."

"Or you want to be in debt until you're sixty," Teddy chimes in. "I'm going to community college too," he says with a supportive shrug.

"One word, three syllables," Marshall says, bending toward Ainsley's ear. "Schol-ar-ships."

She pushes him away playfully. "Easy for you to say, Mr. Track Star with a three-point-nine GPA."

"Three-point-nine-*eight*. And I worked hard for it too."

Marshall gets all macho and arrogant around Ainsley sometimes. I think it's because they haven't been together all that long, and he's still trying to impress her—hence him freaking out over his own promposal ideas, with the yellow roses and the movie theater stubs. I'm more forgiving than I would be otherwise.

"I'm trying to convince her to come to Michigan State with me," Marshall notes to Teddy.

"Win me the lottery, and I'm there," Ainsley says. She sips her beer, turning to Bree. "What about you? Where are you going in the fall?"

"West Island."

"West Island?" Teddy repeats, unsure. "Where's that?"

"It's a small school in California."

College talk has been my least favorite—and totally unavoidable—conversation topic all senior year. I slip aside to pet Franklin, who's finally found a safe spot away from the drunks on a dining room chair. Besides, Marshall and Ainsley are in their own little love bubble, anyway, and I got the sense Teddy was trying to flirt with Bree, so I don't mind taking my gayness somewhere else for a few minutes.

But really, it's mostly the college small talk.

I can't stand it.

Mr. and Mrs. Brandstone are paying for Bree to study graphic design at some fancy private art college in Los Angeles. And Marshall—basking in a wave of scholarships—is moving to East Lansing for track and computer engineering.

I can't be mad at either of them. Bree's been passionate about design stuff since, like, fifth grade, and she's killed it as editor-in-chief this year. And Marshall is basically on course to run Silicon Valley by the time we're thirty, or win an Olympic gold medal—or both. They really do deserve to get as far away as humanly possible from this rotten, stagnant town.

It's just that, most Rock Ledgers don't have the test scores or money to go to a four-year university downstate, let alone a private school in California. I'm a little bitter that I happen to be best friends with two of the very few who are actually escaping and leaving me in the dust. I'll just miss them.

I pop back into the group. "Anyone want another drink?"

They all turn to me, shake their heads, and go back to being straight people. (Well, except for maybe Dan.) So I head to the kitchen alone.

I chug the last few sips of my beer over the sink and throw the can into a bag of recyclables before diving into the fridge to grab another one. I think I'm starting to feel a little less anxious, which is a welcome relief.

"Sky!" someone yells behind me. "Sky will play!"

I turn to find Carolyn from Health class standing in the entranceway between the kitchen and hallway.

And Ali is standing at her side.

My stomach, now sufficiently filled with beer, does a nervous backflip.

"Sky High!" Ali says, even more happily than usual.

Bushy eyebrows. Long lashes. Perfect smile. He's wearing this adorable orange button-up too, which I've noticed he saves for special occasions. "You made it."

"Yeah." I smile, shifting my weight nervously. "I made it."

"Sooo are you down or whaaat?" Carolyn slurs, blinking slowly.

Okay, I'm thinking she's drunk. "Down for what?"

She comes racing across the kitchen in her high heels, nearly toppling over every step of the way, and crashes into me for a hug.

Yeah—she's definitely drunk.

"Beer pong!" she yells into my ear. "We're going downstairs to play and need two more people."

Ali follows behind her. "Yeah!" he *also* yells into my ear, mocking her playfully. "Beer pong, Sky!"

He may be poking fun at Carolyn, but it feels dangerously close to him flirting with me.

I gulp.

It's okay. I'm feeling good. I'm feeling fine. I got this.

I got this.

"I'm sorry about what went down on Monday, by the way," Carolyn interjects out of nowhere, suddenly serious and clear-headed. "What a freaking idiot."

Oh God. Oh no.

The most obvious thing that could ruin this moment is bringing up He Who Must Not Be Named, as Bree always calls him. Literally, the only thing.

"What do you mean?" I laugh, playing dumb.

"Health class? Monday?" Carolyn says, focused intently on my face. "He's such a little rodent, Sky. Don't listen to him."

"Who's a rodent?" Ali asks, grabbing another beer from his fridge.

"Cliff," she answers.

Ali grimaces, cracking open another can. "Norquest?"

She nods at him.

"I loathe that guy." Ali shakes his head, taking his first sip. "He *is* a little rat. A racist one, too. He called me a terrorist for accidentally stepping on his shoelace once." He rolls his eyes. "Typical."

"What'd he do to you in Health class?" Ali presses.

I hesitate.

"It's not eeeeven important, Ali," Carolyn says loudly—maybe to save me from having to explain, or because she's trashed and doesn't realize it's kind of rude to abruptly change subjects on a topic you brought up in the first place. She hiccups. "So, aaaare you in, Sky, or what?"

"In for . . . ?"

"Beer pong!"

"Oh, right. Um . . . sure?"

"Have you ever played before?" Ali asks.

I think about lying to sound cool, but decide against it. "No. Is that a problem?"

Ali shifts his kissable lips to one side. "That's unfortunate," he says, shaking his head. "Because it's really complicated. We're only taking people who know the rules already."

"Oh," I say, deflating. "Well . . . okay. Sorry."

"Sky." Carolyn punches my shoulder. It hurts more than she probably realizes. "He's just messing with you."

Ali grins at me with his Ali Grin. "It's very easy to learn," he says.

"Then yes," I say, grinning back. "I will happily play beer pong."

They lead me away from the kitchen. I turn and lock eyes with Bree in the dining room—hers widen when she sees who I'm with—before me, Ali, and Carolyn disappear from view.

"So, can I adopt your cat?" I ask Ali, feeling a bit more confident with about one-point-five beers slowly seeping into my bloodstream.

"Why?" he asks.

"Well, first of all, he's the cutest," I say, reminding myself not to say "Franklin" out loud and give away that I'm a total creeper who weirdly knows his pet's name without having been told. "And secondly, you clearly don't know how to father a cat."

"Why do you say that?"

"He's freaking out with all these people around!" I shout. "Don't you have a quiet room he can chill in for a bit?"

Ali laughs. "Franklin will be fine, Sky High." He pats my arm. "That's nice of you to think about him, though."

We walk downstairs to the basement—I didn't even realize there was another floor—and it's packed like a jar of pickles. A few dozen people may have been invited to this party, but there's at least fifty people down here, alone. The music is blaring extra loud, it's darker and stuffier than upstairs, and—from the smell of it—there's a lot of weed being smoked too.

In a flash, we both lose sight of Carolyn.

"Where'd she go?" Ali asks.

I crane my neck, but only see anonymous silhouettes dancing and moving around. "I don't know."

"Whatever." He glances around a little more before surrendering. "Honestly, I didn't want to play beer pong anyway! Here, c'mon."

Here, c'mon.

I inhale slowly, trying to stay cool. I'm more sober than he is, which is reassuring. But I'm still nervous. I wish Bree were here. She'd be freaking out with me. Or . . . maybe I'm glad she's upstairs? Does Ali actually want to spend time with me, one-on-one?

He leads me farther back into the basement, where there's a bit more room to breathe. There are a couple of patched-up sofas and a rickety wooden chair with a few people taking a break from the rowdier area. Ali falls onto a couch as two people get up and leave. For a minute, I'm just standing there awkwardly, holding my beer. But then he motions for me to join him.

I do it.

Obviously.

How is this real life? *Is* this real life? Because it feels like a movie. I must have accidentally wandered into an alternate universe where *Booksmart* or *To All the Boys I've Loved Before* is my new reality. Because if I'd told Bree on the way here what I thought the best outcome from tonight could possibly be, not even then would I have envisioned sitting on a sofa with a buzzed and possibly flirtatious Ali Rashid.

He doesn't say anything for a bit, so I decide to break the ice. "Are you ready to be done with school?"

"What?" he asks over the music.

"School! Are you ready to be done?"

"Oh. Yeah. *More* than ready. What about you?"

"Definitely."

"Anatomy is the worst," he says.

"Right?"

"And I'm barely passing Trig."

"Same!"

"Yearbook is the only class I like, honestly."

I laugh. It's like he's reading from notes to impress me or something. "I couldn't agree more."

"Winter is next-level strict, but she's chill at the same time, you know?"

"Yeah."

"Well, obviously you know. You, Bree, and Marshall are her favorites, for sure."

"I don't know about that."

He Ali Grins at me. "Yeah, okay." His eyes travel up and down my torso for a second. "I like that shirt."

My pink shirt.

My pink, collared, gay-ass shirt.

"Thanks," I say, unsure how else to field the Compliment of My Life. Maybe this *is* my make-or-break night, after all.

"It's weird that we're graduating, huh?" he says, eyes now having wandered off, trying to take in his party—like he knows nights like these are limited. "It's bizarre."

"Yeah."

"We experienced a lot of school together, you and me." His knee taps mine. "Like basketball in sixth-grade gym!"

"Huh?"

"Sixth-grade gym. That's where I gave you your nickname, because you were taller than everyone else and could rebound like hell."

Oh my God. He remembers.

"Oh, right." I sigh, pretending I forgot about the nickname's origins—as if it's not something I think about at least three times a day. "Yeah, it's been a wild ride."

"I didn't even like high school," he says, taking a swig of his beer. "I hated it."

"You?"

"Yeah."

"Really?"

"Why do you say it like that?"

I pause to think over my answer carefully. "Well . . . I guess I just mean, it's weird to hear that a popular guy like you hated high school."

"Ha . . . yeah."

I can tell he's not saying what he really wants to say—and I'm just buzzed enough to pry. "What, you don't think you're popular?"

Of *course* Ali's popular. If Ali's not popular, I'm as straight as an arrow.

He stares ahead, unblinking, eyes glazed over in thought. It could be the beer or a contact high, but he suddenly looks uncharacteristically subdued.

"Popular," he mutters, more to himself than me. "What does that even mean, though?"

"I don't know." I think for a second. "You're funny? Guys respect you? Girls like you? All of the above?"

I want to add "and you're hot" to the list, but bite my tongue.

I'm not *that* drunk.

He finally breaks his gaze from the bodies dancing in front of us and stares into my eyes. "It's wild, because everything you said right now about me—that I'm respected, that I can get girls, that I'm popular? It sounds like you're describing someone else."

Yeah, right. "How so?" I play along.

"You're describing the person I try to be—not the real me." Oh. He's being serious.

Crap.

I didn't mean anything by it! I thought I was giving him a compliment.

I open my mouth to apologize—

"No, it's not your fault," he laughs, probably seeing the look on my face. "I've tried *really hard* to be that guy. I think everyone tries to be cool in high school. But when you're a nerdy little brown kid in Rock Ledge, you have to work a bit harder."

He takes another swig—this time, a bigger one.

I don't say anything. Mostly because I'm not exactly sure what to say. "Yeah," is eventually all that comes out.

"I should be happy I pulled off being *Mr. Popular* to some people," he says, and grins at me. "But I'm not that guy."

It's rare to hear Ali talking about anything seriously, and it throws me a bit. He's usually bouncing through the hallways handing out fist bumps to everyone, not a care in the world. I'm not sure how to respond to him. Or if I even should.

"You know what I *would* be happy doing?" He lights up.

"What?"

"Improv."

"Improv?"

"Yes!" He turns toward me, bending his knee so that his leg can curl up between us. His leg is touching my thigh. *Keep it cool, Sky. Keep it cool.* "I've wanted to join Improv Club since sophomore year."

"We have an Improv Club?"

"See?" He throws his hands in the air. A few specks of beer hit my cheek. "No one even knows about it! There's, like, four members. But it sounds so fun."

"You want to be a comedian?" I ask. "Like, after high school?"

"I don't know. I brought up joining Improv Club with my friends last year, but they all made fun of me. Now I'm scared to join."

He laughs—but it's forced. I can tell it hurt to have his goals dismissed by his friends.

"Screw them," I say, shoving his shoulder playfully. (Oh my God, I just shoved Ali Rashid's shoulder *playfully*.) "You should join Improv Club! Like I just said, you're funny. *Everyone* thinks you're funny, Ali. You should do it."

He grins, rolling his eyes. "School's almost over."

"Who cares?"

"They probably already had a cutoff date to join this semester."

"Yes, I'm sure the Improv Club no one knows about with *four people* in it has a very strict membership policy."

He cracks up—and this time, it's genuine. The skin around his eyes crinkles and he lets out a snort. My body melts into the floor.

"Touché, Sky High," he says. "Touché."

He chugs his drink, then bends closer to me, like he's about to tell a secret. I can smell the beer on his breath, but I don't mind. "By the way, can I ask you something?"

If my heart wasn't pounding through my chest before, it is now. "Of course," I say, a lump growing in my throat.

I don't know where to look. At him? Straight into his eyes? Or the wall behind his head? Do I look at my drink?

Oh my God, I don't know, *I don't know.*

I decide to make eye contact. Full on, pupil-to-pupil eye contact. Our faces are almost touching. Like, this is exactly what happens in my shower-dreams. Except we have clothes on now. And we're not soaking wet. But you get it.

He opens his mouth, pauses for a moment.

And right then, Carolyn—drunk, awful, life-ruiner Carolyn—comes crashing down onto his lap out of nowhere. "Are you two gonna make out?" she interjects, giggling. "Because that would be hot."

She nearly spills her drink, bouncing around on Ali's lap like a Labrador puppy. An obnoxious, drunk Labrador puppy. "Carolyn, can you, ah, hold up—" He tries to worm his way out from under her awkwardly, but she's not getting the hint. Her butt finally finds the sofa cushion—*right* between me and him.

Eff.

I move over to give her more room. I hate the word "cockblock" because it's as douchey as the $3 body spray scent the whole wrestling team uses, but Carolyn is being the cockiest block of all the cockblocks right now.

"So," she says, cranking her head from side to side to take in the both of us. She puts her arms around our shoulders, crossing her legs. "What's up, fellas?"

"Actually." Ali stands. "I'm going to go check on people upstairs. And *you* should probably switch to water, Carolyn."

Carolyn rises too, sighing. "You know what? You're probably right."

They both start walking toward the staircase.

"Hey," I call after him. "Were you going to ask me something?"

He pauses. And there it is again. That Ali Grin.

"Right," he says. "Some other time."

He disappears into the basement haze, Carolyn stumbling after him.

TWENTY-ONE DAYS

'm taste-testing jalapeño poppers Clare made for her cooking YouTube channel, but my eyes keep wandering over to the front door. Bree should be home any second, and she's been gone basically all day—taking Ray to the animal sanctuary (he loves, loves, *loves* goats), then Petey to swimming, then dress shopping with her mom for a wedding they have in June. I haven't been able to discuss Ali's party with her. Like, at all.

And I *need* to discuss Ali's party.

I probably shouldn't be this excited over what happened last night. Because, technically, nothing *did* happen. Ali didn't come out to me. He didn't profess his undying love. We only talked for, like, ten minutes, tops, before Carolyn ruined everything. But it felt like something. *Something* happened in that basement. I couldn't be imagining it.

I hear Bree, Mrs. Brandstone, Petey, and Ray in the foyer.

"I think that last batch had the perfect amount of cheese," I tell Clare before slipping away to the front door.

Mrs. Brandstone swings a sparkly purple dress over her shoulder to show it off. "Do you like it, Sky?"

"It's beautiful."

"It sure is. And worth every penny." She lowers her voice. "We just won't tell Mr. Brandstone how many pennies. Hey! *Hey! Shoes* off!" She scolds the twins before they trample mud through the house. "Any updates, Sky?"

I stare at her.

She stares back.

Is . . . is she talking about updates with Ali? "Huh?"

"Your *birthday*, silly," she says. "What's the game plan?"

"Oh." I close my eyes and shake my head with a grin. I should have known that's what she meant; Mrs. Brandstone will *not* stop bringing it up. It's nice that she cares so much—but she's really underestimating my disdain for being the birthday boy.

"Still deciding what I want to do," I answer. "I promise I'll let you know."

Mrs. Brandstone and the twins finish kicking off their boots and hanging up their coats. I wait until I have Bree to myself.

"So," I say, letting myself be outwardly giddy.

She's concentrating on untying the slick laces of her boots and doesn't respond.

I clear my throat. "So . . . about last night . . ."

She finally looks up at me. "Huh?"

"Last night!" I yell, glancing around to make sure no one is paying attention to us. "Last night? The party? Ali. Me. The basement. *Alone*. Well, not *alone* alone."

"Oh." She forces a smile before going back to her laces. "Yeah, what happened down there?"

Her excitement level is at, like, a two. I expected it to be a ten.

I couldn't really dish about my conversation with Ali at the party because we were with Marshall, Teddy, and their straight guy ears. And then Bree seemed exhausted and went straight to bed after we got home. I assumed she'd wake up dying to know what happened in the basement, just like I'm dying to tell her now.

That is definitely not the case.

I sit down next to her on the bench by the door as she struggles to rip the last shoe off. "He seemed flirty, Bree. Like, *flirty*. He brought up the origins of how I got my nickname. We're talking a memory from sixth-grade *gym class*. Why would he remember something that happened in *sixth-grade gym* if I didn't mean anything to him? You know?" I'm talking very fast, I realize.

"Nickname?"

"Yeah." I stare at her. "His nickname for me? Sky High?"

"Oh. Right."

"He complimented my shirt. We sort of shared this . . . *moment* together. I know it sounds disgustingly cliché, but I think there was a spark."

She doesn't respond.

"Plus, right before drunk Carolyn interrupted us, he said he wanted to ask me something . . ."

Still, no response. Only grunts as she fails to push the boot off her foot.

"Are you hearing this? He wants to ask me something!"

"What do you think he wants to ask you?"

"I don't know! To hang out after school? To go on a date?" I get quieter. "To be the one asking *me* to prom?"

She finally succeeds; the boot goes flying across the foyer, splattering ice chunks and mud everywhere. Mrs. Brandstone is going to be pissed.

"That'd be wild," she says. Except her tone implies she could not care less about anything I'm saying, let alone think it's wild.

"Are you okay?" I ask. "Did something happen with your mom dress shopping?"

"I'm fine," she says, avoiding eye contact. She stands up and heads toward the kitchen. "Just tired. I'm going to lie down."

"We have to leave for LMEP in, like, fifteen minutes."

She turns and stares at the floor, thinking. "The movies?"

"Uh, yeah? The new DuVernay movie?"

Her faces collapses in dread. "That's right."

Something is definitely up. Something definitely happened.

Because there is no way Bree would *not* be ecstatic about the Ali developments, and even less of a chance she'd totally blank on the movie. Seriously. No way.

"Are you sure you're okay?" I ask again. "We can talk—"

"Yes. I'm going to take a quick shower, and then we can go."

To match her foul mood, Bree blares a melancholy Billie Eilish song on repeat the whole way to pick up Marshall, Ainsley, and Teddy at the Jones's house. Her hair is smashed up in a wet, post-shower bun, and I notice her eyes seem a bit bloodshot, like she'd been crying.

I let Ainsley ride in the front with Bree because she gets carsick during long drives.

"Wow, this music is depressing," Ainsley jokes after hopping into the passenger side, nudging down the music. Bree doesn't respond.

Marshall and Teddy, both wearing matching Rock Ledge Rams track hoodies, slide in on my left and right, smooshing me into the back-middle seat.

"You ready for this, Brandstone?!" Marshall yells, grasping the sides of the driver's seat from behind and shaking it excitedly.

Bree murmurs something. Marshall can immediately sense she isn't her normal self and gives me a look.

I try to switch gears before this drive gets irreparably awkward for the next hour. "So . . ." I try to think fast as Bree pulls out of the Jones's driveway. "Has anyone seen any good movies lately?"

Yes, it's probably the least-original question to ask *on our way to the movies* and sounds like a very intentional icebreaker. But I'm surrounded by movie people. And at least it diverts attention away from Bree.

"Oh!" Ainsley cranks her neck backward. "Earlier this week I finally watched the *To All the Boys* sequel! Anyone else see it?"

I almost scream *yes* at the top of my lungs, but bite my tongue before it can squeak through my lips.

I adored the book it's based on and—despite convincing myself Hollywood would somehow find a way to ruin the film adaptation—was pleasantly surprised when it left me in tears (the good kind). The sequel? Just as great.

But I'm very aware of where I am right now: squeezed into the back seat between two straight guys. A straight guy sandwich, basically.

I'm sure Marshall wouldn't care all that much if I started fangirling over Jordan Fischer with Ainsley. He's not a *homophobe*, obviously, and I've gushed over rom-coms around him here and there. He's still a straight dude, though—a straight dude sharing a back seat with his straight dude friend who's quickly becoming a bestie. Maybe even my replacement. I should . . . tone down the gay. Just a little.

"I saw the first one, but not the sequel," I half lie, burying my excitement.

"Wasn't it cute?" Ainsley says, hugging her seat belt strap. "Noah Centineo . . . wow."

"Yeah, I liked it."

"Wow?" Marshall smiles at Ainsley. "What's 'wow' supposed to mean?"

"It means he's hot, Marshall," Ainsley says.

The car goes quiet—except for melancholy Billie still serving us soft vocals in the background.

"This is when you're supposed to say, 'Don't worry, babe, Noah's got nothing on you,'" Marshall jabs playfully.

He and Ainsley get swept up in a faux-fight over if and when they're allowed to say celebrities are sexy. Bree is still dead silent from the front, hands at ten and two, staring straight into the abyss, as we breeze through the rusty side of Rock Ledge.

So it's just me and Teddy.

I try to subtly move my leg so it's not pressed up against his, but the back seat is too small; there's no scooching away.

He clears his throat. "How was your Saturday?"

"Good, good." I nod, suddenly realizing my shoulder is also touching his arm. I lean away a tad. "How about yours?"

"It was nice."

Awkward silence.

"Do anything fun?" he follows up.

"Not really. Bree had a ton of errands to run with her brothers and mom, so I mostly watched TV, cooked with her sister, and caught up on laundry." The most honest version of my answer was that I lay in bed thinking about Ali, and then followed that up by shower-dreaming about our conversation at the party for nearly a half hour under the hot, running water.

But again, straight boy. He probably doesn't need to know all that.

"What about you?" I say.

"I threw around some balls."

He doesn't provide any more context. "Um . . . what?"

He laughs. "Shot put. I do shot put on the track team."

"Aha." I nod. "I knew that."

That's when I realize it's not *me* who should feel awkward about the lack of space between us. That's on Teddy and his Hulk-like shot put frame expanding across half the back seat, leaving me and Marshall to share the other 50 percent.

"We have a big meet against Frankfort coming up this week," Teddy notes. "I need to get in some extra practice."

"Gotcha."

After Marshall and Ainsley finish up their faux-fight (both agree that it's okay to say aloud that any celebrity is "sexy" or "hot," so long as the celebrity is A-list enough to be truly unattainable), Bree puts us out of our misery by blasting Dua Lipa the rest of the way there.

I'm hoping Bree's mood improves, now that we're at LMEP.

But that hope fades. Fast.

We decide to each pick out a candy at Moe's and share everything once we're in the theater. I chose Whoppers; Ainsley, mini Snickers; Marshall, Sour Patch Kids; Teddy, Twizzlers. But Bree?

"I already told you." She sighs at me, annoyed, texting someone. "I don't want anything."

"You're sure?"

"Yes."

Bree has never *not* gotten treats at LMEP. Turning down Moe's is unprecedented territory.

"Dude, what the hell is up with her?" Marshall hisses into my ear as we head to the theater. Bree is walking way ahead of us, so she's out of earshot.

"Did something happen between you two before you picked us up?" Ainsley whispers.

"No!" I say, looking between them. "I don't have a clue why she's acting this way."

"Okay, I'm glad it wasn't just me picking up on it," Teddy says, opening his Twizzlers early and sticking one into his mouth.

"I'm so confused," Marshall says, genuinely bummed. "She was stoked to see this movie with us . . ."

I shrug.

By the time we get to the ticket booth, candy stuffed away in our pockets, Bree is already inside. We're running late—well, late for Marshall's movie standards—so Teddy insists he pay for all our tickets to save time, and we agree to Venmo him later.

"Whoa, LMEP is so old-school," Ainsley says, watching the theater employee hand Teddy four tickets. "They use the vintage stubs with the marquee-looking letters. It's kind of romantic."

I glance at Marshall, remembering his promposal idea to gift her with the tickets from their first movie date. He grins back, but has to quickly hide his expression as Ainsley turns to ask him something.

Okay, I admit it. They're a freaking cute couple.

Once we get inside our theater and look up at a sea of rows, we spot Bree toward the very back in a seat that's up against the right wall of the room.

"No way," Marshall breathes, clearly agitated. "Why . . .why would she do that?"

"Do what?" Ainsley asks, sneakily pulling out his Sour Patch Kids from her purse.

"Pick one of the worst seats in the theater!" Marshall's on the brink of a meltdown. Bree, of all people, should know better than to mess with Marshall's moviegoing experience.

"All right, listen up." Ainsley stands in front us, creating a mini huddle, and lowers her voice. "We don't know what she's going through. But clearly, she's going through it."

"None of us did anything to her, though," Marshall says through gritted teeth. "She shouldn't be taking it out on us."

"Let's not make a big deal out of it." Ainsley looks between the three of us. "Let's have a good time and hopefully she'll explain what's ticked her off at some point. Deal?"

"Deal," I say.

Teddy nods.

Marshall, the most annoyed of all of us, finally sighs. "Okay."

Teddy leads the way up the stairs, and we file into Bree's row after him. Ainsley ends up sitting on the outer end of our group, so I'm stuck in another straight guy sandwich.

But honestly? I don't mind this time around. It's way better than sitting next to Bree.

As expected, Marshall and Ainsley immediately nose-dive into their flirtatious chatter and ignore the rest of us. Bree's angrily punching away at her phone and ignoring us too, for God only knows what reason.

That leaves me and Teddy awkwardly sitting in silence. Again.

What could I possibly talk to him about? We have *nothing* in common. He's a shot-putter who counts his daily protein intake. I make yearbook spreads on movies and post *Drag Race* memes to my Insta Stories.

"Do—"

"I—"

Oh my God. We both cut each other off. This could not be any more uncomfortable. This entire *night* could not be any more uncomfortable.

He laughs. "Sorry."

I do too. "No, I interrupted you. Go ahead."

"I was just going to say," he continues, "do you know what you'll major in next year? If we're both at the community college, we may end up in some of the same classes."

Ugh. College talk again. The worst. A pit in my stomach instantly forms as I think about the scholarship I likely won't be getting.

"I don't know my major yet," I admit. "I'll probably just stick with the basic required classes for now. You?"

"Same boat," he says, taking another bite of his Twizzlers. "I'm overwhelmed, to be honest."

"Why?"

He sighs, eyes widening. "I don't know, man. Choosing a major? The career field you'll be stuck in the rest of your life? I have no idea what I want to be doing when I'm twenty, let alone forty. It's scary."

I pull out my Whoppers. "I get that. I feel the same way."

"Don't you worry about what school would be like if you didn't have Yearbook?" he asks.

I'm not sure what he's getting at. "Um . . ."

"I don't mean it in a bad way, but"—he pauses to think through his words—"for me, it's track. Track takes up *all* my time. And I love it. But it's going to be gone in a matter of weeks."

"You can't play on the college team?"

He lets out a howl. "No way, man. I'm not that good." He hands me a Twizzler. "If I don't have track to keep me busy and sane, what do I have? You know?" He laughs again. "I'm going to feel so lost—and so stuck."

"Stuck in Rock Ledge."

"Stuck in Rock Ledge forever."

We quickly exchange sad grins.

I never thought about Yearbook the same way Teddy thinks about track. But he's right.

I hate Rock Ledge. I hate our school. Yearbook is the only thing I wish I could hold on to after graduation. Winter and the other Yearbookers mean more to me than I can probably even understand right now, I'm realizing. How can I find its replacement once I'm gone? *Can* I find a Yearbook replacement after high school?

My mind starts spinning, when—

"Hey." Teddy lightly shakes my shoulder, smiling. "I didn't mean to bum you out. Just venting my stress at you, sorry."

Weirdly, I immediately feel better.

"Don't apologize," I say. "It's nice to know someone is in the same boat."

I'm about to explain why I'll miss Winter so much next year, but the theater lights fade and the passive-aggressive "turn off your phones" warning pops up on-screen. Even though I already saw the upcoming trailers last weekend—and rewatched most of them on YouTube—they deserve my full attention again.

"I'll finish that thought later," I whisper.

It's wild how much I was dreading welcoming Teddy into our friend trio, when, really, he might've actually been the best part about tonight.

NINETEEN DAYS

"Y ou've got a spring in your step, huh?" Mr. Brandstone says
to me across the kitchen island, his eyes looking past the
iPad in his hands.

"Do I?" I say, suddenly aware of the involuntary smile draped
across my face.

He places the tablet down next to his plate of blueberry-walnut
pancakes. "Should I be worried?"

I help myself to syrup. "Why should you be?"

"I'm suspicious of giddy teenagers."

We're the first ones in the kitchen, which is lit up in yellows,
pinks, and oranges from the morning sun. The TV isn't on, nor
is there any playlist blaring from someone's room, and Thelma
and Louise are nowhere to be found. It's the quietest meal I've
ever eaten here. I see why Mr. and Mrs. Brandstone are morning
people.

"You two didn't do anything illegal this weekend, right?" he
continues.

"No."

"Didn't set the school on fire?"

"Nope."

"Nobody's dead?"

"Not to my knowledge."

"Hmph."

He picks his tablet back up and continues mumbling about the news.

I'm still feeling pretty great about my weekend. Ali's party went way better than even my wildest dreams could have imagined, and breaking down the Wall of Awkward between me and Teddy on Saturday night took a burden off my shoulders I hadn't even realized was weighing me down. Although Bree spent yesterday sequestered in her room, being crotchety and avoiding me and her family, I pulled off a killer peanut butter cookie recipe with Clare and the twins.

Now I'm actually excited for school. On a *Monday*.

Crazy.

"G'morning," Mrs. Brandstone says, walking in wearing pajama shorts and an old T-shirt. Her eyes grow wide when she spots me. "Sky?"

"That was my reaction," Mr. Brandstone agrees.

"You're up early." She rubs her eyes like I'm a mirage. "Everything okay?"

"I asked that too," Mr. Brandstone says, amused.

I nod.

"Pancakes?" she notes, looking at our plates. "What a pleasantly abnormal Monday thus far."

"Blueberry-*walnut* pancakes," Mr. Brandstone corrects her.

"You've outdone yourself." She rubs his shoulders for a second before beelining to the coffeepot. "What trouble did you and Bree get into this weekend?"

"Apparently none," Mr. Brandstone answers for me, eyes still glued to his iPad. "I'm not buying it, though. Sky's in too good of a mood . . . Oh!" He lights up. "I bet it had something to with what's-his-face." He looks to Mrs. Brandstone.

She looks confused. "Who?"

"Alan?"

"Ali?"

His eyes dart toward mine. "Ali!"

I laugh, feeling my cheeks getting red. "What?"

"That explains it," Mr. Brandstone declares triumphantly. "Something Ali-related turned this weekend on its head."

"Oh, knock it off," Mrs. Brandstone scolds, sipping her coffee. "Leave the boy alone."

She glances at me out of the corner of her eye, spotting my grin. I can tell she wants to ask a million questions about Ali—she is the *queen* of annoying mom questions—but instead distracts her husband with a comment on the news that she knows will get a fiery response. I appreciate her tact.

I return to my pancakes and, for probably the hundredth time this weekend, retrace the exact conversation I had with Ali. His inviting me to sit next to him. His loving my gay as hell shirt. His endearing knee tap. The Ali Grin he flashed before darting away. . . .

"Some other time," he'd said of whatever question he needs to ask me.

But, like, *when is some other time*?

My stomach flips, realizing that "some other time" could be today.

Bree appears in the kitchen, clearly still upset, and drops her backpack, jacket, and a handful of textbooks onto the counter. "G'morning," she mumbles, heading to the cupboard to snag her packet of hot chocolate.

Mrs. Brandstone silently waves to get my attention while Bree's back is turned. "What's up with her?" she mouths at me, pointing at Bree.

I frown, shrug, and mouth back, "I don't know."

"You're up early, too," Mrs. Brandstone says, watching Bree pour the cocoa mix. "Want any pancakes? You should have something other than sugar every morning, Br—"

"What do you think blueberry pancakes with syrup is?" Bree snaps.

"Hey now," Mr. Brandstone warns. "Attitude."

"Is it cool if we leave early this morning?" Bree asks me, still avoiding eye contact and stirring her cocoa. "I want to do final edits on the e-blast before it gets sent out."

Bree does edits on the e-blast from home all the time. I don't know why she'd need to leave extra early to do them on her Yearbook computer—other than just to annoy me.

I almost push back, but don't want to pick a fight in front of her parents. "Yeah, sure."

Mr. and Mrs. Brandstone eye her suspiciously as we gather our things to leave.

Bree continues giving me the silent treatment the same way she did on our drive to LMEP Saturday night, so I blast some

Lady Gaga and try not to let it ruin my morning. Once we're at school, she mutters, "See ya," and jets off across the parking lot without me.

In Trig, I ask Marshall his theories on Bree's stormy mood.

He ponders, chewing his pencil in thought while we're working in small groups on an assignment that is 100 percent over my head. "I have no idea. But Saturday night was the worst I've ever seen her."

"Right?"

"She was *pissed*."

Christina Alpine, who's in charge of mostly sports pages in Yearbook, slides her chair over from another small group and bumps into our desks, smacking her gum. "Hey, Marsh."

"Yo."

"You're a nerd."

"Hey now."

"I mean it in a good way. Why is this happening?" She puts her bedazzled, sparkly silver phone in front of his face.

I glance over; it looks like she's having log-in issues with the mobile version of Memories.

"Can this wait until Yearbook? Sky and I are having an important discussion."

"Oooh." Her eyes widen, sensing drama. She scoots closer. "What about?"

"It's nothing." I shake my head.

Her face drops. "Okay, I'll leave you alone. But heads up, Memories is being weird AF."

"How so?"

"It's making me change my password and all this nonsense. I've never had to do this before."

"I'll look at it in Yearbook."

"Thaaanks." She slides away again.

Sometimes Marshall has it rough in Yearbook. Everyone goes to him for all our technical woes. And there are a *lot* of technical woes. Fixing problems in Memories is basically his part-time job.

I glance over at Ali's empty desk. He didn't come to first hour, which has definitely sucked a little cheer out of my morning. He has a big Yearbook deadline this week, though, so I don't think he'd skip.

I *really* want to know what he was going to ask me. . . .

There needs to be better defined, more specified time frame restraints placed on the term "some other time." Because if Ali doesn't talk to me about whatever he was going to talk to me about by the end of the day, my head very well might explode.

"Last Ainsley prom question, I swear," Marshall says, still chewing on his pencil, which is now lined with disgusting teeth marks.

I look away from Ali's empty desk. "Go for it."

"Should I be dressed up when I ask her, or nah?"

"Define 'dressed up.'"

"A suit and tie?"

I nearly choke on the cinnamon gum he gave me before class. "Are you kidding?"

He frowns.

"Overkill," I say, in case it wasn't obvious.

"Really?"

"Absolutely," I emphasize. "Big, *big* overkill."

"What should I wear, then?"

"Your orange track shirt," I say—way too quickly. The answer just spewed out without me even thinking.

Marshall's jaw drops. Then he breaks into a smile. "Uh-oh. . . ."

"What?"

"You think our orange track shirts are sexy, don't you?"

"No." My face immediately starts glowing.

"That was *quite* the fast response to my question, Sky."

"Shut up."

"Do our orange track shirts bring all the boys to the yard?"

"I'm done talking about this."

Walking out of Trig, I feel a hand on my shoulder. My stomach tingles with excitement, thinking it could be Ali—

But I turn to see Winter, which is kind of disappointing.

And also very weird.

"Oh—hi?" I say, surprised. "What's up?"

She looks anxious, and that makes me anxious. Because Winter is never, ever anxious. Plus, her classroom's on the other side of the school; did she come all the way over here just to tell me something?

"Can I snag you for a second?" she asks.

"Sure . . ."

She guides me to a less busy area of the hallway, and lowers her voice. "We had an incident this morning with the weekly e-blast, Sky."

"Okay . . . ?"

"Images that were, ah . . . *unrelated* to the yearbook were sent out instead of the actual e-blast." Her tone is whatever the opposite of comforting is. Discomforting, I guess—but way, way worse than discomforting. "Have you seen it yet?"

My appendages are slowly going numb. "No. What images?"

"Can you come to my classroom?"

"Right now?"

"Yeah."

I glance around. I'm not sure why. "Uh . . . sure, but I'll be late to Zemp's class."

"I'll write you a note for Mr. Zemp."

This must be really bad. Because not only is Winter never anxious, but she also never, ever writes excuses for her students to be tardy for other classes on her behalf.

Seriously. Never.

We walk in complete silence. Well, almost. I ask her a few questions—if everyone is okay, am I in trouble—but she avoids any concrete answers, tries to be assuring, and repeatedly tells me, "Don't worry, everything's going to be fine." Which makes me think everything is definitely, absolutely, 100 percent not going to be fine.

Then I notice people are staring at me as we walk by. At least I think they are. Or am I being paranoid? It seems like eyeballs and whispers are following me. . . .

We walk into Winter's room, and Bree is standing there, pacing frantically.

And Ali is sitting in my seat.

The blueberry-walnut pancakes flip over in my stomach.

Winter motions for me to sit next to Ali. I do.

"Hey," I say hesitantly to no one in particular. "What's, ah . . . what's going on?"

Ali nods and smiles weakly—it's definitely *not* his Ali Grin—but doesn't make eye contact. He looks pissed, or sad, or distracted, or something. Maybe all three? I can't really tell. I look over at Bree, who mouths, "I'm so sorry," at me.

It looks like she's been crying.

"I hate that you have to see this, Sky, but"—Winter turns her big computer monitor so that it's facing me and Ali—"this is the e-blast that got sent out a little bit ago."

I bend forward to look, holding back the urge to spew out Mr. Brandstone's homemade breakfast. It's not an e-blast at all.

All that's there are two photos, side by side.

One of the photos shows my promposal wall in the Brandstones' basement. You can easily read it too: "SKY IS GAY FOR ALI: PROMPOSAL IDEAS," with all the embarrassing items in the three columns below.

The other photo was taken of me and Ali from Friday night, sitting close to each other on his basement sofa, grinning. Above our heads, someone photoshopped the words: "It turns out the terrorist is a fag, too."

It turns out the terrorist is a fag, too.

It turns out the terrorist is a fag, too. . . .

Tears immediately begin collecting in my eyes. This doesn't feel real.

"I'm so sorry," Bree says, her voice cracking.

I don't know what to say. I don't know where to begin.

The boulder of gay gloom starts rolling down the mountainside in my head.

"I told Principal Burger about this," Winter continues. Her

voice sounds distant, like I'm hearing it through water or some-thing. Like we're meeting at the bottom of a giant aquarium. "He's looking into how this could have happened."

Is this a dream?

Am I in a nightmare?

Bree's pacing even more frantically now. "I know I came to school early today to make sure the e-blast got out okay, Sky," she says. "But I got held up. I didn't give it a final peek. I'm so, so, *so* sorry."

"Breathe, Brandstone, breathe," Winter says. "It's going to be okay. Everything's going to be okay."

Ali clears his throat. "Can I ask who—who all gets the e-blast again?"

"Seniors and parents of seniors," Bree cuts in. "So we're talking hundreds of people. But something like this . . . I just . . . I don't know. People are going to forward it. It's going to spread. *Thou-sands* have probably opened it by n—"

"Brandstone, why don't you take a seat?" Winter says, sensing her editor-in-chief is on the brink of a total meltdown. But Bree doesn't even seem to hear her. Winter looks between me and Ali. "I'm very sorry this happened. We'll find out who did this."

"It was just a joke, though," I say suddenly, loudly, surprised to hear my own voice. I laugh a little, and can feel my heart beating in my throat. "It was all, you know, just a joke."

"What was a joke?" Ali asks, finally looking my way. "You plan-ning to ask me to prom?"

I gulp and lose my voice for a second. It was such a big gulp that it actually hurts my throat. "I—I am—I *was* going to ask you to prom, yeah."

All three of them are staring at me.

Bree's eyes are starting to leak again. Shockingly, Winter's appear on the brink of tears too.

Ali looks confused.

"I—actually, let me start from the beginning," I say, forcing a devastating chuckle that only adds to the tension in the room. "Bree and I were having this fun, stupid game coming up with ways that I could ask you to prom."

"Oh."

"But we weren't that serious about it. We were never that serious about it. I'm not sure if you're, you know . . . into guys, into girls, into both, into me, or whatever."

I'm getting more nauseous. Like, I'm actually going to be sick. Kill me now. Somebody, please just shoot me. Put me out of my misery.

The boulder of gay gloom isn't tumbling down the mountainside anymore. It's racing. Full steam. Barreling down pine trees, blasting through *other* boulders on its way. There's no stopping it. It's going to crash any second.

Bree is still pacing, but now her hands are completely covering her face. My stomach is spinning around like a laundry machine.

"Like I said." I fill the silence, just so someone's saying something. *Anything.* "It was just a stupid game. Bree and I wrote down all these wild ideas in my bedroom at her parents' as a joke. It was all just a big joke."

"You have a bedroom at Bree's house?" Winter asks.

"He's been living with me," Bree mutters. "His mom kicked him out when she found out he's gay."

I ignore the two of them and focus on Ali. "That photo makes it look like I'm *obsessed* with you or something." I laugh again—and it feels like nails on a chalkboard. "And obviously, I'm not *obsessed* with you. It's just, I thought I'd take a shot in the dark and ask you to prom—"

"But I was going to ask Bree, though," Ali says, glancing over at her. "Just as friends, obviously. I thought it'd be fun."

The room goes silent again.

"Not to make things more awkward." He starts fidgeting in his seat. "But, yeah . . . that's what I was going to ask you about at my party, Sky High. I was going to ask if Bree had plans to go to prom with anyone else."

It feels like someone punched me in the throat.

And then pushed me off a cliff.

And then ran over my body with a semitruck.

"It's okay. I, ah . . ." I stand up to leave. "I have to get to second hour."

But before my legs can follow suit, the boulder crashes. Hard.

My breakfast erupts and bright purple, half-digested pancakes come spewing out of my mouth to cover Winter's desk.

NINETEEN DAYS

Somewhere between the high school and the Brandstones', I basically blackout. I make it home somehow, though. Not *home* home. I don't have a home.

I make it back to Bree's.

The next thing I know, Mrs. Brandstone is standing there in the foyer, still wearing her pajamas, shocked to see me.

"What's wrong, Sky?"

I'm trying to find the right words, but she keeps cutting me off before I can spit out a full sentence. "Did something happen at school?" She touches my arm; her hand feels like a heated blanket against my nearly numb skin. "Did you walk here?"

"Yeah."

She dashes toward the front door and cranks her neck to see out the window, probably to check if Bree's car is there. "Is Bree okay?"

"Yeah, she's fine. I'll be downstairs."

She doesn't know how to handle me. If I were Bree or Clare or one of the twins, she'd be grilling me with questions, calling the school, or filing a police report. But I'm not her kid.

I'm not anyone's kid.

My mom deserted me. And my dad, well . . . he probably would have too. Rock Ledge dads aren't *proud* of their gay sons. More often than not, they're mortified of their gay sons. Mr. Brandstone may like me—but he's the exception, not the rule.

Even if my hadn't died in a crash and left me stuck with Mars for the rest of my life, I'd probably be exactly where I am right now: with nowhere to call home.

Mrs. Brandstone's still talking to me, but I slip away down the basement steps. Fall onto the futon. Stare straight up. Still in shock, I think.

It's like I'm dreaming. And by "dreaming," I mean drowning in the most lucid nightmare of all time. My deepest, darkest anxieties couldn't have concocted whatever just happened back there.

Ali Rashid saw the promposal wall.

Everyone saw the promposal wall.

And someone called him a terrorist, which all Rock Ledge will shortly learn, since gossip spreads like NRA pamphlets around these parts. Actually, the e-blast was sent over an hour ago by this point; the whole town certainly knows by now.

My phone buzzes, buried deep in my pocket. I have several missed notifications, and didn't hear a single one of them during my walk home.

There are three texts and a missed call from Bree: this is legit nuts call me?? and seriously where did you go? and I'm so so so sorry I'm in the bathroom sobbing. I'm so confused please respond concluded with a broken-heart emoji.

I text, I'm at your house, I'm okay.

Coming home now, she writes immediately.

Another missed call is from Marshall—damn, he's seen the

promposal wall now too—and another from the school. Either Winter or the office must be trying to get ahold of me. And to think: I thought the most embarrassing thing to happen to me this month would be Mrs. Brandstone seeing Mars.

I roll over on the futon and press my body deep into the crack between the mattress and the drywall, the smell of white primer still wafting off its surface.

I want to disappear. I wish the earth would just swallow me up whole and forget I was ever a living, breathing, miserable collection of cells on its surface. I wish that could happen. I hate to say it, but I wish I had never been born. Everything would be easier for everyone else.

That way, my mom never would have had a gay son. And Ali wouldn't be embarrassed by the creepy gay kid who was scheming to ask him to prom. And I wouldn't be another mouth to feed at the Brandstones'. If I never existed, I never would have to deal with Mars either.

Who knows? I could be the real reason my dad got into that accident. I could have distracted him, or bumped the steering wheel. If I hadn't been in that car, would he still be here?

The boulder of gay gloom is rolling for the second time this morning. And I still can't stop it.

Breathe. Just breathe.

I hear the front door burst open upstairs and Bree's muffled voice going back and forth with her mom's. Then she's rushing down the steps, toward the bedroom door.

I don't want to talk to her right now. I don't want to talk to *anyone*—but especially not to her.

Because . . . could *she* have been behind the e-blast hack?

No. Of course not. There's no way. She would never, in a million years, say something like that about Ali. Or me. Never.

And yet . . .

Bree's been insufferable since Saturday. I don't think it could be because of anything I did. But I could be wrong? Did I obliviously do something so earth-shatteringly awful, she decided revenge of this magnitude was in order?

"Can I come in?" she asks on the other side of the door.

"I don't feel like talking."

"Sky."

"I don't want to talk right now," I say.

"Why not?"

There's a really long pause.

"Did you have something to do with it, Bree?" I blurt.

Silence.

"What?" she says. "Are you serious?"

"Who would have taken the photo of the promposal wall? Your dad? Petey? Thelma?"

"I don't know."

"Was it you? Did you take that photo?"

"I honestly can't believe you're accusing *me* of the e-blast hack."

"Who's in charge of the e-blast, though?"

"Will you open the door?"

"We went to school *extra early* just so you could make sure that it was ready. How did you not see what was in there? How did you not see those photos?"

I can't hear anything from the other side of the door. I don't know if she's still there.

But I keep talking.

"You've been pissed off at me all weekend, Bree. Obviously, I could tell. We could *all* tell. We're not stupid. I have no idea what I did to you, but apparently it was enough to ask for all this."

I regret saying it, even as the words are leaving my mouth.

I regret even *thinking* it.

I run to the door and swing it open, intending to chase her down and apologize, but she's still standing there. Red-eyed, pale, and silently sobbing.

"Bree—"

"You really think I would have done this to you?" she asks softly. "You really think I would have done this to Ali?"

"I—"

"You think *I'm* capable of saying those things about you two?"

"No, I—"

"Screw you, Sky."

"Hold on."

But she's gone.

I close my door, fall back onto the futon, and start to cry too. Because now I don't just feel awful, but awful with a side of guilt.

I never treat Bree that way.

But today's a day for firsts.

Mrs. Brandstone checks on me first thing in the morning, but doesn't make me go to school. She hands me a banana, smiles, then leaves. I stay in my bedroom all day.

Well, I leave to use the sawdust-covered bathroom in the basement, and I go upstairs after everyone leaves for school, work, or errands. It's the Brandstones, so of course there's, like, a whole untouched pan of Clare's baked ziti waiting for me in the fridge. She probably made extra, knowing I'd wander up at some point.

But I don't talk to another human.

I break my number one rule, though. Intentionally.

Mars is staring back at me in the foggy reflection after a long, hot shower. And I'm staring back. He's so ugly. And so permanent. A disgusting reminder of the day my family was permanently broken.

What would your father think? My mom's question echoes throughout my brain.

What would my dad think of me now?

I'm skipping the rest of the school year, I've decided. So what if I don't graduate? Screw it. I'm probably not going to get the scholarship anyway. What's the point?

In the afternoon, I finish the rest of *Kimmy Schmidt* without Bree. I start watching *Glee* again for, like, the sixth time (but promise myself to stop before season two because the first twenty-two episodes are the only ones worth rewatching). I skim through Instagram, but it makes me feel worse, because my timeline is filled with hot #InstaGay strangers from around the world with thousands of followers, smiling effortlessly on gorgeous beaches or rooftops with a view—all so sure of themselves, and their purposes, and their futures.

I have lots of unanswered texts too. But I don't care.

The school called twice. The secretary left voicemails both times with near-identical messages: "Hello, I'm calling for Sky Baker. This is Rose from Principal Burger's office. We noticed Sky wasn't at school today and we're checking in on him. Please call the school back at blah-blah-blah, I don't really care about Sky, but this is my job, and it's not the eighties anymore but I still dress like it is."

That was the gist, more or less.

My mom doesn't call. My brother doesn't either. I'm assuming they must have learned about the Most Embarrassing E-blast to Have Ever Been Sent, though. The entire state of Michigan probably has by now.

Marshall's called three times and texted five:

Um wtf is going on?

Why are you ignoring me?

are you embarrassed or something?

call me!

. . . Okay, dude, whatever.

I'm too ashamed to text him back.

Mrs. Brandstone lets me skip again on Wednesday, and Petey and Ray start delivering my meals to me.

They bring down toast and yogurt before they go to school, and then lamb chops for dinner, quietly leaving the tray outside my room and vanishing without saying a word. Ray attaches sticky notes to my forks that read *18!* for both meals. It took me a few minutes to realize why: Ray remains adorably *way* more into my upcoming eighteenth birthday than I am. I feel guilty, because clearly I can walk upstairs to get my own effing food and stop throwing myself a total pity party down here like this. But still. It's appreciated.

Mrs. Brandstone starts making me leave my bedroom door

open during the day. I think it's her attempt at not allowing me to feel entirely closed off from the rest of the family, even though it's definitely more for her own peace of mind than it is anything else.

At least she isn't making me go back to school, so I'm not fighting this new open door rule. Plus, it means Thelma and Louise will come down and snuggle with me a lot more, which has been nice.

I finally hear from my mom. It's a nothing text, basically. **Heard what hapened @ school**, she writes, careless enough to not worry about typos. **Here if u need to talk. Praying.**

Praying.

Eff that.

I begin The Lord of the Rings trilogy and get excited because I find a stash of extra candy I didn't eat from a trip to LMEP a few weeks ago. I binge while falling down a Galadriel Wikipedia page rabbit hole. Then I start watching some *Drag Race* but fall asleep from a sugar crash, even though it's a really good episode.

Bree hasn't been downstairs or texted. I know I should go up there and break the ice, but I also know she's still upset with me and I don't want to press her too soon.

I miss her, though.

"Do you think Bree wants to talk to me yet?" I ask Mrs. Brandstone during one of her nightly check-ins. "I really am sorry."

She adjusts the belt on her bathrobe, thinking. "She's still a little upset." When she sees my face, she adds, "But don't worry. Bree will come around. All friends fight sometimes." She gives me a half smile and disappears up the stairs.

The pit in my stomach hasn't left since I accused Bree of the e-blast hack. What was I thinking? When the boulder of gay gloom is barreling through your mind, you do things that don't make sense. I wish I could explain that to her now.

By Thursday, things get worse.

Or better.

I can't decide.

The e-blast definitely spread. Far and effing wide. Because of course it did. People must be really worried about me not being at school, judging by the wave of DMs and comments pouring into my social media accounts.

You and Ali are the best, Sky. 🖤 is the first one. From Aubrey Douglas, of all people. I think I've exchanged, like, three words with her since fourth grade? After Aubrey's comes Ryan Giltlen's: *Don't let whatever asshole did this bring you down, dude!!!* he writes. He's a nice guy, but I don't really know him that much either. Random.

Then Dan comments on my most recent Instagram photo: *Thinking of you, Sky.* I imagine him sending it from Sbarro for some reason. It's weird how he was avoiding me and Marshall at all costs that day, but he'd go out of his way to say something nice online. I get it, though. I'd likely do the same. Humans are weird. Plus, since he's another maybe gay dude at RLHS, I'm sure the e-blast pissed him off too.

A few junior girls from Anatomy send me rows of orange hearts at almost the same exact time, so they discussed it beforehand, I assume. This one Drama Club girl, Samantha Buzzdorth, shares a Maya Angelou quote that's vaguely related to my shitshow situation. I'm fairly certain it's misattributed, but whatever. It's the thought that counts.

Teddy DMs me on Instagram too. *Hey Sky, I support you and Ali 100%* 💪, he writes. I roll my eyes with a little smile. Straight guys: Even their emojis have to be tough.

I keep rereading Teddy's message, though. His was especially nice to get; I think because, the more I get to know him, the better I feel about expanding our friend trio to include him? I don't know. I write back, *Thanks, Teddy* 🖤. Wait, no. A heart emoji? Too much, Sky. Way too much. I replace it with a thumbs-up.

Then I delete the thumbs-up and go with a standard smile.

Yeah, that works. A perfectly acceptable smile.

Send.

I roll over, beat Louise in a staring contest, and then scroll through Instagram for a few minutes. But my mind inevitably wanders back to the only person in Rock Ledge whose week has been the same level of dumpster fire as mine.

Although the absolute last thing I want to do is reach out to my crush, who last saw me hurling pancakes across Winter's desk, I need to make sure he's doing okay.

Hey. I message Ali on Instagram. *So. I'm really sry for what happened. This whole thing spun out of control. Anyway, I'm super embarrassed.* 😟

I always fantasized about sliding into Ali's DMs. Never under circumstances like these, though.

Not even ten seconds later, he responds.

Hi Sky High, he writes. The three little bubbles tell me there's more to come. *Crazy, I was just going to message you.*

A brief pause. More bubbles.

It's cool, he continues. *Everyone's been nice. Don't apologize. Not your fault. Why haven't you been in class?*

I think for a minute. How can I boil down everything I've felt since Monday morning into a succinct DM?

Instead, I simply go with: *Just taking a few days to feel better.*

There aren't any bubbles for a few seconds. Then, *Well you should come back soon. You're missed.*

A lump expands in my throat.

You're missed.

Rock Ledge is still awful, to be clear. Maybe not quite as awful as I thought it was on Monday.

I'm over Ali Rashid.

Seriously.

It was a welcome relief, learning from his messages that Ali's been thinking about how I'm doing, just like I've been wondering about him. But, in terms of my crush, something has totally flipped. Now, when I think of him—remembering my shower-dreams, or his Ali Grin, or his knee tap in his basement—I instantly feel like I'm going to puke up Mr. Brandstone's pancakes all over again.

Those eyebrows, and those lashes, and those eye crinkles when he laughs. They're just not the same to me anymore. I've felt uncomfortably powerless being so swept up in my Ali Rashid crush; a part of me had been wishing it'd go away. Just not like this.

But it's good. It's fine.

Whatever.

. . .

Friday night, Mrs. Brandstone comes downstairs for her nightly check-in. She knocks on the door frame, even though—because of the new rule—the door's already open. She's also probably extra sensitive to knocking on doors around me after the bathroom shower-dream debacle.

I pause *The Two Towers* on my laptop.

"Can I come in for a second?"

I move my feet to give her space next to me. It's almost like Louise can sense a heavy conversation is about to happen, because she slides off the futon and shuffles her way upstairs to avoid the awkwardness of it all.

"So," Mrs. Brandstone says, sitting and crossing her legs. She exhales, thinking over her next words, before removing her bright red glasses. "How are you feeling?"

"Okay," I say. Which is the truth. I'm definitely not as upset as I was earlier in the week, but I'm still angry. I'm still never going back to that heterosexual hellscape of a school ever again.

"I'd be hurt if that happened to me too."

"Yeah."

"'Hurt' is an understatement. I'd be devastated."

"Mhm."

"Whoever did that is a lowlife, Sky."

"I know."

"A scumbag."

"Yeah."

"They'll find out who it was. I hope Bree's dad never does, though, because, well . . ." She sighs. "Let's just say the kid's father may end up in the hospital."

I know it shouldn't, but the thought of that actually makes me feel better.

I grin at her. She grins back.

"The school has been calling," she says. "I guess they called your mom, too, and figured out you've been staying here."

I swallow hard.

"It's okay," she says. "I explained the situation. It's fine. And you know what? I'm sorry about all that, too." Her eyes are getting watery, I think, but it's hard to tell because it's so dark in my bedroom. "I've never actually said that to you, but . . . your mom was wrong for reacting like she did over the holidays. You understand that, right?"

I nod.

She collects herself a little. I can tell it's been something she's wanted to say to me for a really long time, and she just peeled it off like a Band-Aid and got it out.

"Do you think you'll be up for school on Monday?" she asks after clearing her throat. "You can't keep missing school this close to graduation."

I pull the blanket up around my chin. "I'm not sure."

Then it's quiet again, but for the muffled sounds coming from the kitchen upstairs. Clare is yelling about something, and one of the dogs is barking like crazy. She makes pizzas on Fridays, and I bet she caught Petey sneaking Thelma and Louise his toppings again.

"Okay." She pats my leg. "We can chat about school more this weekend—"

"How's Bree, by the way?" I blurt.

She smiles. "Bree's good. You two should talk."

"She wants to talk to me?"

"I'd definitely give it a shot. Why don't you come upstairs and have some dinner with us? Clare tried out a new recipe: BBQ chicken pizza. It has your name all over it."

I shrug. She gets the hint.

"Well, what about tomorrow?"

I nod.

She nods too.

"I'll leave you alone," she says, moving to stand up, before remembering something. "Oh, I almost forgot why I came down here in the first place."

She pulls a stack of paper and a brown grocery bag out from behind her. I didn't even notice she walked in carrying anything.

"Bree brought home your classwork for the week . . . ," she says, pushing the papers toward me. It's surprising and nice that Bree would do that for me; maybe she doesn't completely hate my guts, after all. "And someone left this for you on our front porch."

Mrs. Brandstone drops the paper bag onto my lap. Someone wrote *For Sky* on it.

"What is it?" I ask.

"I have no idea."

I give her a look like, *Of course you know what's in it.*

"What?" she says, grinning. "I'm not a snoop, you know."

If anyone is a snoop, it's Mrs. Brandstone.

But I let it slide.

She starts to leave, but turns around when she gets to the door. And it might be because I've been extra lonely down here, but it makes me feel a million times better, seeing her silhouette in the doorway. It's where moms usually stand when they say good night to their kids in the movies, I think is what is it. Or something. I don't know. But knowing she's there, looking back at me in the dark, almost makes me feel like I'm one of the Brandstones.

Almost.

"We like having you here, Sky," she says.

I can't see her face because the light's pouring in around her, but I think she can see mine. And I hope she can see my smile and knows I mean it.

Once I hear her footsteps at the top of the staircase, I reach into the bag and pull out a yearbook. The year 1996 is engraved in big, scarlet letters across the front.

What the—?

I open it up to the first page, and a note drops out. In big, all-caps letters, someone wrote:

PAGE 34. GO TALK TO CHARLIE.
665 DUTCH ROAD, TRAVERSE CITY

Uh . . . huh?

I flip to page 34 and immediately feel my insides filling up with . . . something. I don't know. This overwhelming feeling.

I can't describe it.

There's a black-and-white photo of my dad—a photo I've never seen before. He's sprawled across the hood of an old car, laughing and squinting into the sunlight next to another student. My dad was a senior at Rock Ledge this year, I think.

He was the age that I am now.

The caption reads, *Henry Baker and Charlie Washington.* *"Charlie is the toughest guy I know," Baker says of his friend.*

FIFTEEN DAYS

This whole thing is freaking me out.

Who leaves an anonymous note in an old yearbook directing someone to meet up with an old guy he's never met, an hour's drive away? Serial killers? Deranged exes in horror films? Villains in Batman movies?

All of the above, really.

Even if I did want to meet this Charlie guy, how would I even break the ice doing it? *Hi, my dead dad was your friend in high school and someone—I don't know who—wanted us to meet two decades after the fact.*

I don't even remember my dad. Without the origin story of Mars and a few family photos my mom buried away in basement boxes, there's little evidence he existed. I ate a terrible sandwich with spicy mustard in the church parlor after his funeral, and it gave me the worst stomachache of my life. But that's my only dad-related memory. And my dad wasn't *alive* during it. Does it even count?

The point is, for all intents and purposes, my dad remains a complete stranger to me, which means his still-breathing high school buddies are *definitely* complete strangers to me. Charlie Washington sounds like a shady congressman. Or the guy a small town decides to name its elementary school after. Or a villain in a Batman movie.

Or all of the above.

I find the dude on Facebook. Apparently he's a dermatologist. From his short "about" section and a few browsable pics I can click through without creepily friending him, I see he has salt-and-pepper hair, round glasses with thick rims, and a big smile that doesn't show his teeth.

It's weird to think my dad would have been his age now.

I wake up on Saturday morning feeling a lot better and clear-headed than I have been all week. I don't feel *good*, exactly. But I don't feel terrible, either. I think it's because now I have Charlie Washington to distract me from the dumpster fire that's become my life.

I brush my teeth, change out of pajamas for the first time in four days, and head upstairs, anxious to see Bree again.

She's sitting at the kitchen island.

"Hey," I say hesitantly.

Bree jolts at my voice, nearly spilling her cereal. "Holy crap." She sighs, hand on her chest.

"Sorry."

We're the only ones here, except Thelma and Louise, who both wander over to me and rub up against my thighs, happy to finally see me aboveground again.

"You're alive," she breathes, taking a bite of Raisin Bran and scrolling through her phone.

This is a good sign, because—as last weekend demonstrated—Bree gives the silent treatment when she's *really* pissed. The fact that she's saying anything to me at all means we can iron this out.

Hopefully.

"So," I say, taking a deep breath. Even though I've been anxious to get it over with and say it, apologies are still hard. "I'm sorry."

She doesn't respond.

I just keep going. "I never should have accused you of all the e-blast stuff. It's, like . . . tinfoil-hat-level nutso for me to think *you* had anything to do with it."

Still, no response.

"So, yeah . . . I'm sorry. Really."

She lifts her bowl to slurp some of the leftover milk. "Okay," she says, putting it back down.

More silence. More awkward.

"Okay." I fidget in place, really wishing she'd say something. "Well, I, um . . . can I borrow your car?"

"Why?"

"I need to run an errand."

She drinks more of the milk, pauses, and glances at me suspiciously.

I walk over to a cupboard and start making her a peace offering: a cup of hot cocoa. "How about this," I propose, filling a mug with water, plopping it into the microwave, and hitting start. "You take me to Traverse City—"

"Traverse City?" She howls out a laugh. "I'm not going to LMEP today."

"—and I'll buy you lunch."

She pauses.

Even though the Brandstones have the most chronically over-stuffed refrigerator in the Midwest, Bree can never pass up a free meal.

She thinks. "Define 'lunch'."

"Anything you want in Traverse City."

"Bella's?"

"What's Bella's?"

"That Italian place."

"The place where a plate of spaghetti is, like, twenty-five dollars?"

"Yes."

Is meeting Charlie Washington worth the most expensive plate of pasta in northern Michigan?

I scooped ice cream for tourists six days a week all last summer to help save up for my first semester of community college, but those funds are quickly depleting. I'm probably not going back to school to graduate now, though, eliminating any need for that scholarship or college savings anyway.

"Sure, yes, fine," I decide, transferring her cocoa into a thermos. "Bella's it is."

"Great."

"Great."

"When are we going?"

I hand her the hot cocoa. "Now."

Google Maps has us taking a slightly different route than when we go to LMEP, and our drive along Lake Michigan is beautiful. The sky is empty of clouds, and the water is reflecting all sorts of blues through the bare trees. I remember Winter talking about how the blues are bluer up here. She has a point.

Still, any serene views of the lake are squashed by the massive amount of awkward in the air.

"Why are we going a weird way to LMEP?" Bree asks, breaking the silence.

"Because we're not going to LMEP."

"Um . . . what?"

"I'm going to see Charlie Washington."

"Who?"

"Your mom didn't talk to you about the yearbook?"

"What yearbook?"

"Seriously?"

I just assumed Mrs. Brandstone looked inside the bag and knew the yearbook was there, along with the note. And I also assumed she talked to Bree about it, because this is Mrs. Brandstone; she prods her offspring about *everything*.

"I have no idea what you're talking about," Bree reiterates. "What yearbook?"

"This one." I pull it out of my backpack. Bree glances at it as the sunlight dances across the book's scarlet-and-blue cover. "My mom's?" Her face scrunches in confusion before she turns back to the road. "Why did my mom give you her yearbook?"

"Wait. This is your mom's?"

"Yeah. I've seen it in my parents' room a million times. She graduated in 1997."

I flip to the junior class pages. "What was her maiden name?"

"Graham."

Yep, there she is: teenage Mrs. Brandstone: aka Jennifer Graham. She had bigger hair and a slender face, but the same bright freckles and deep dimples.

This is weird.

"Will you please tell me what the hell is going on?" Bree pleads, increasingly agitated. "Who is Charlie Washington?"

"Pull over."

She does. I fill her in on the anonymous note in the yearbook and the photo of my dad.

"My mom tells me everything," Bree says, staring off in thought, almost offended. Her hands are still at ten and two, even though we're sitting here with the engine off. "Why would she do this without telling me?"

I lift the book up and flop it around to see if more notes drop out. None do, of course. I'm not sure what I expected. I skip to page 34 and search the page for another clue. Something—*anything*—to have this make more sense.

Bree leans over to take a look. "Your dad was hot, by the way," she says under her breath.

"Can you not?"

"Sorry." She takes another look. "I didn't realize my mom and your dad went to school together."

"I didn't either."

"My mom never mentioned it."

"Doesn't it feel like the type of thing your mom wouldn't *stop* mentioning?"

Bree looks at me, eyes narrowed in suspicious thought, before swinging her hot cocoa up for a swig. "What is she up to?"

"I don't know."

Mrs. Brandstone went out of her way all week to make sure I didn't feel forgotten down in the basement. That's the kind of caring parent—the kind of caring *person*—she is. But Mrs. Brandstone is nothing if not a plotter. And my many years of best friendship with Bree taught me that her mom usually has something up her sleeve. Somehow, I've been roped into her newest scheme.

"I'm calling her," Bree declares.

"No!"

"Why not?"

"Because she obviously doesn't want me to know it's her yearbook if she lied about it being left on the front porch, right? Which means she doesn't want *you* knowing, either."

She purses her lips.

"Don't say anything. Please?" I ask.

"Why would she care?" she retorts.

I shrug.

She lets out a sigh.

We sit for a minute in thought before Bree cranks the ignition.

"Also," she says, shifting gears. "Your apology is accepted."

I smile at her. Bree smiles back.

She pulls back onto the road and turns on a playlist. We drive a little bit longer, the sun now high enough in the sky that my right side feels like it's getting sunburned. I'm glad the awkward is slowly escaping the car, like a blow-up pool toy with the tiniest of leaks.

"Two things," Bree says, feeling more comfortable to talk now that we've had a real conversation. She nudges the volume down. "First of all, you have to talk to Marshall."

A wave of guilt blankets my body. "I know."

"He said he's been texting and calling you all week, and you're straight up ignoring him."

"I know."

"He's worried about you."

"I know."

"So you'll call him?"

"Yes."

"Today?"

"Yes."

"Promise?"

"*Yes.*"

"Cool. And secondly, just so we're crystal clear, I never would have gone to prom with Ali if he ended up asking me. Just to say it."

The funny thing is, I kind of forgot about the fact that Ali planned on asking her. "I wouldn't have cared anyway."

"No, it would not be okay," Bree emphasizes. "You adore him—"

"*Adored.*"

"And that would have been the crappiest of crap things a friend could do."

I take a sip of her cocoa. "Honestly. I don't like him anymore."

She gives me a look. "Sure."

"Seriously!" I tell her about how something snapped in me this week, watching Ali stare at the e-blast on Winter's computer screen with that devastated-meets-confused-meets-alarmed expression.

He clearly doesn't like me like that, and that's okay. The spell he's had over my sanity is gone.

I mean it. I'm over Ali Rashid. *I'm over Ali Rashid.* It's weird to think it and know I'm actually telling myself the truth.

I can't tell if she believes me or not, but she changes the subject anyway. "You know who did it, though, right?"

"Did what?"

"The e-blast. The monster who hacked it."

I sit there thinking for a few seconds.

"You really don't?" she asks.

"Should I?"

"It was He Who Must Not Be Named. Duh."

"What?"

"He Who Must Not—"

"No, I know you're talking about Cliff," I clarify. "But . . . did Winter or Principal Burger catch him?"

"No."

"Then why do you think it was Cliff? It couldn't have been him."

"Why not?"

I quickly create my own mental checklist of all the qualifiers needed to be the hacker:

The person somehow got a photo of the promposal wall.

The person somehow accessed Memories to hack the e-blast.

The person somehow got the pic of me and Ali at Ali's party.

Cliff, to the best of my knowledge, couldn't have done any of those things, as I explain to Bree. And come to think of it, I don't know anyone who would.

"But it had to have been He Who Must Not Be Named!" She

turns the music all the way down, certain she's right. "Think about it. No one else in our school is *that* evil. You said yourself he's been a huge dick to you since I've been turning him down. So he hates me, and he hates you because you're my best friend—"

"*Gay* best friend."

"See? And he hates Ali because he's racist as hell. What better way to mess with all of us than hack the e-blast? We're going to get him, Sky," she mutters, a bit maniacally, and more to herself than to me. "I promise."

She could be onto something. Ali *did* tell me at his party that Cliff called him a terrorist just for stepping on his shoelace that one time. Rock Ledge has more than its fair share of MAGA extremists, but no one is as bad as Cliff Norquest.

We finally pull off the main drag along the coastline and drive up this winding hill in the middle of approximately nowhere. This feels like the point in a horror movie when we run out of gas and are murdered in the next hour by some man with a chain saw or by a dead girl's ghost who lives in a hut near the beach. But ideally, Mrs. Brandstone didn't devise a plan to have us hacked to death. I kind of wish big, burly Teddy—with his shot put arms and bodyguard presence—were here to ensure we survive another day.

I grin thinking about his DM on Thursday. And I get a few butterflies, maybe?

That's . . . weird.

Finally, 665 Dutch Road comes into view.

"Day-um, Mr. Washington!" Bree gapes, spotting it through the trees.

The house is humongous, built of gray stones and dark

wood, the green horizon of the backyard disappearing into Lake Michigan's steel blue below. A big American flag is billowing on the front porch, which is surrounded by rock gardens and a bronze fountain that feels more Buckingham Palace than Traverse City. This place would be the nicest house in the Brandstones' neighborhood, hands down. And that's saying something.

"What are you going to say to him?" Bree says, her fingers hugging her cocoa as she leans forward over the steering wheel to peek up at the house's second and third—and possibly fourth?—floors. *"Hello, my friend's mom randomly wants me to meet you?"*

"I'm leaving your mom out of it. I'm selling him a fake yearbook ad instead."

She laughs. "For real?"

"Yeah."

"Well, okay . . . but be careful," she warns. "The last thing I need this semester is a yearbook lawsuit on our hands."

I roll my eyes with a grin. "Relax. I promise it'll be fine. I have a plan."

It's a half-baked one. But it's still a plan.

She's on edge about this whole thing. But so am I. "You sure you want to do this?" she says.

"Yeah."

"Do you want me to go in with you?"

"No."

"What if you get kidnapped?"

"Then that would suck."

"Should we have a signal?"

"Huh?"

"Like, run to the window and wave if you need to be rescued."

"Not too subtle, but sure."

"By the way"—she flicks my arm—"I'm happy we're talking again."

I steal a sip of her cocoa. "Same."

Right before I get out, the front door of the house opens and a humungous St. Bernard comes galloping down the steps toward the car.

I yelp. Bree gasps in elation.

The beast races up to my side of the car, but it's wagging its tail and smiling at us, slobbering all over the place in a super adorable way, so I feel a little less like I'm about to be eaten alive by a monster that lives in Hogwarts's Forbidden Forest.

A man appears in the open doorway; at least, I think it's a man? It may be a tattooed God of some sort.

Bree clearly spots him too. "Um, holy hotness. Is that Charlie?"

"No," I say. Charlie's a handsome older dude, from what I can tell from his Facebook profile, but he's not an inked deity, like whoever is standing up there in the doorway.

Tattooed God Guy is looking toward the car curiously in a white cutoff shirt and purple athletic shorts, his muscly arms and legs covered in jet-black designs. He starts yelling something at us, but we can't tell what.

I unroll my window a tad. "What?"

"I said, the dog is nice!" Tattooed God Guy bellows, cupping his hands around his mouth. "He's big, but he's a lover!"

There's this brief pause.

"Go," Bree says, pushing me out of the car.

I guess I really am doing this.

I step out with Mrs. Brandstone's yearbook. At first, I have it perched against my hip in the gay way, but I snap out of it quickly enough and begin walking more heterosexual up to the front door.

The beast comes forward for pats to the head and to slobber all over my shoes. "Good boy, good boy," I whisper to him, hoping my gentle, gay voice makes it clear I'm no threat.

"What can I do for ya?" Tattooed God Guy asks as I get nearer. He's got a short beard, nice eyes, and a lady-killer smile. His tattoos are distracting blends of morbid, fun, and whimsical.

"Is Charlie around?"

"Huh," he says, shaking his head. "Sorry. You have the wrong house."

"Oh." I stop walking. "Um . . ."

"I'm just messin' with you, bud," he says, grinning. "Charlie's inside. Can I ask what this is about?"

I finally get to the front steps, embarrassed to be out of breath. "This is random, but, ah, I'm in Yearbook class at Rock Ledge High School, and we're—"

"No shit!" Tattooed God Guy bursts. "That's where Charlie's from. I'm Brian." He reaches out for me to shake his hand. I do, and he nearly rips my whole arm off.

You know how people say dogs look like their humans? That's 100 percent Brian and this benevolent beast.

"I'm wondering if Charlie wants to buy an ad in my senior yearbook to help cover our publishing costs," I lie through my teeth. "We're supposed to ask alumni."

I could have been honest. But lying seemed like the way

less awkward choice over telling the truth. And let's be real: I'll probably never see Brian or Charlie ever again after today.

Brian gestures me up the steps. "C'mon in . . . ?"

"Sorry—Justin. Justin Jackson."

"C'mon in, Justin. You too, Bob."

"Huh?"

"The dog."

"Oh."

For being so gargantuan, the house feels cozy and lived-in, with big rugs and full bookcases and warm paintings hung on the walls. The exterior gave off hard-core Republican vibes—billowing American flag on a rich white dude's manicured front lawn? Yikes—but I see a poster leaning up against their coatrack that reads, HATE HAS NO HOME HERE, translated into several languages. That gives me hope that my first impression was wrong.

"I have to get ready for work, but make yourself comfortable in the den," he says, gesturing to the first room off the foyer. "I'll grab Charlie. Charlie!" he yells, turning and leaping up the stairs, two at a time. "A kid from Rock Ledge is here!"

I sit on a worn leather sofa with cushions nearly as wide as my entire futon mattress. Bob follows me in and collapses into a panting, furry brown ball on my feet, which helps me feel less anxious about all this. I reward him with a belly rub for putting me at ease—and also for not killing me outside.

My phone buzzes: **Not murdered yet?** Bree texts.

Nope.

Will you get that guy's number for me?

He's like 35, Bree.

so??????

It smells like pine trees in here, hard-core, but it's fitting. The wooden walls are covered in maps. Lots and lots and lots of maps. Mostly of around here and the Upper Peninsula, but there's also one of Lake Tahoe, and one of somewhere called the Catskills, and then, randomly, Loch Ness in Scotland. There's a big desk in the corner with a computer and art supplies and more stacks of books—

And a small rainbow flag pinned to a corkboard.

"Hi, there," Charlie says, walking in. "Oh jeez, Bob, give him some breathing room, will you?"

He's way less muscly and intimidating in stature than Brian but has the same kindness in his eyes. I couldn't sense that kindness through the Facebook photos. He's wearing a navy suit and mint-colored tie, and seems like a type A perfectionist.

"What's up, Justin?"

"Not too much," I say, shaking his hand.

He drops down into a chair across the coffee table from me, messing with the buttons on his shirt. "Brian says you're from Rock Ledge High School?" He looks equal parts confused and curious.

"Yeah."

"You drove all the way here?"

"I did."

"That's a long way."

"I didn't mind the drive." I point at the wall behind him. "I love these maps."

"Brian and I have visited every location. We love the fresh air."

Between the way he said "we" and the rainbow flag, it's confirmed: Brian and Charlie are definitely boyfriends. Or husbands. Or partners. Or whatever.

Definitely more than friends.

"What can I do for you?"

"So, I know this is random. But I'm in Yearbook class and we're asking alumni to see if they'd be interested in buying ads for this year's book."

"We couldn't do this over the phone?"

That's . . . a very valid point I didn't think about.

I can feel my face turning red. "Yeah, we could have," I say, thinking quickly. "But my teacher has this whole sales spiel she wants us to do in person."

"Ah, I see. A learning opportunity."

"Yeah." I pull out Mrs. Brandstone's yearbook.

"Whoa!" he says. "1996. My senior year." I'm glad he remembers. He shakes his head, beaming. "Nostalgia. What a good sales tool."

He walks over to the desk, throws some papers into his briefcase, and pulls his right foot up onto the computer chair to tie his shoe. His dress socks have penguins on them; they scream "gaaaaay" like my pink collared shirt does, but Charlie seems like the type of guy who doesn't care what his clothes scream—as long as they feel right on him.

"So let's hear this sales pitch," he says.

He's trying to be nice, but I can tell he's under the gun. It's like I barged in right before he has to take off to some important dermatology conference, or sign a mortgage on a third vacation home, or tend to some A-list client who grew a pimple overnight. You know, standard dermatologist duties.

I swallow hard and think through what I rehearsed in my bedroom last night. "We reach out to alumni and show them cool old photos from when they were at RLHS," I say. "If you're interested, you can use a throwback photo from your own yearbook for this year's ad, and we'll give you an awesome discount on a full page."

"That's a neat idea."

"Yeah. Like this one." I brush past Bob to show Charlie the book, flipping to page 34. "Do you remember this photo?"

He takes the book from me gently before squinting down at the pic of him and my dad. "Yeah, I do." He goes silent, but there's this odd glistening in his eyes that suggests there's a story to tell.

"It's a great shot," I say, wishing I could read his mind, hoping he keeps talking. He doesn't. "Who's in it with you?"

"My best friend from high school, Henry."

Best friend.

Not classmate. Not friend. *Best friend.*

"You two were close?" I pry.

"Definitely. This was toward the end of our senior year. And actually, the day it was taken was a really big day for me." He stares at the page in thought for a bit longer before snapping the book shut and handing it back. "Anyway. How much?"

"How much?"

"For the ad."

"Oh." Duh. "One hundred dollars."

"Cool," he says, scanning his desk, I'm guessing for a checkbook. I can't imagine tossing out $100 on a whim, just like that. "I'd love to support the Yearbook class."

Um.

Dang.

I didn't think it'd happen this fast. I didn't even think he'd end up wanting an ad, honestly. Do I really need to sell him a full-page now?

"Just curious," I say before we veer off into a whole other topic. "Why was it a big day?"

"What was that?"

"The photo—you said it was taken on a really big day for you."

He lets out an amused laugh, like the story's not worth retelling. "It had some corny personal meaning, is all—"

"How so?"

He's a little taken aback by my nosiness.

"Sorry," I say quickly. "That was rude. You don't need to explain."

"It's okay."

"It's just, if we want to use that photo in this year's book . . ." Words come spilling out of my mouth to cover my tracks. "It may be cool to have context. You know, if it has an interesting story behind it, or whatever, that might be nice to include."

"Of course." He breathes, a sad smile creeping into his cheeks, a bit unsure of how he can say whatever it is he's about to say. "So, that photo. It was taken the day I came out. I'm gay, and Henry was the first person I told. He was the first person to accept me."

He rolls his eyes, as if it's a silly, embarrassing, childhood secret he never expected to tell a soul. But it rattles me to my core.

The first person to accept me.

Now I know why Mrs. Brandstone sent me here.

"That's probably TMI, Justin," he says, ruffling through his briefcase again. "Apologies."

My eyes are welling up. I almost dash away to find the bathroom, because I can't have a breakdown right here, right now. That'd be a disaster. In the middle of Health class in front of Cliff is bad enough; in a complete stranger's home an hour's drive away is unthinkable.

"Anyway . . ." He laughs. "Look at me boring you with my stories from my good ol' days." His face lights up—like he just remembered something else. "Charlie is the toughest guy I know."

"Huh?"

"Henry's quote in the caption of the photo? 'Charlie is the toughest guy I know'? That's what he's talking about." He nods toward the old yearbook dangling in my fingertips. "He's saying I'm tough because I came out to him that day."

He goes back to his briefcase so nonchalantly, completely oblivious to the bomb he just dropped on me.

"So how does this work?" he asks. "Can I write a check out to the school?" He looks at me, a little bit concerned. He must notice I'm in a state of shock. "Are you okay?"

"Yeah."

"You sure?"

"Yeah."

He smiles. "Do I write a check out to the school? For the ad?"

"Oh, oh, right." I close my eyes and shake my head, swallowing hard.

Keep it together, Sky.

Keep it together.

I can't take money from this guy. I'm not even on our ad-selling team! I could get in serious trouble for doing this. Winter would murder me.

Wait—are the full-page ads even $100?

Breathe.

Just breathe.

"You don't have to pay me yet," I say, steadying my breath. "I–I just realized I'm running late to an appointment. Can I call you in a few days and we can talk about next steps?"

"Sure—"

"Great." I tuck the yearbook into my side and back away toward the exit, nearly stumbling over Bob's paws.

Charlie looks confused. "Do you have my number?"

"We have it on file," I lie again.

"Are you sure everything's okay, Justin?" he asks as I slide out of the den like a pile of goo.

"Yeah! I just—I lost track of time, is all. Thanks, Charlie!"

I jog through the foyer, down the front porch steps, and out to Bree's car.

"First of all, I'm glad you're not dead," she says, turning down a Kacey Musgraves song and starting the engine. "Secondly, who was the hot tattoo guy?"

"Bree—"

"Thirdly, did you get me his phone number? I actually wasn't kidding. And fourthly—"

"*Bree.*"

She stops and gasps, finally seeing the tears that began to fall down my cheeks. "Oh my God! What happened?"

"We have to get back at Cliff."

"Wait, what?"

"I'm not going to let him ruin my senior year."

For the first time this week—or maybe for the first time ever—I know what I have to do. I know what I have to *be*.

Tough.

FOURTEEN DAYS

Bree's inhaling a plate of fettuccine that's $18.00, but I'm too excited to eat my $20 pizza.

"What?" she asks as I stare, her mouth overstuffed with al dente noodles. We're literally the only customers in Bella's because, who else eats lunch at 10:45 a.m.?

"Nothing," I say. "Sorry. I think I'm just . . . still in shock?"

"I would be too!"

"It doesn't feel real."

I finish recapping for a second time everything that happened—more for me than her, I think—and I don't miss a single detail: Brian being incredibly sweet and even more wonderful to look at, Bob stepping in as my impromptu therapy dog, their cool den filled with dope maps, and, most crucially, Charlie's story about my dad and the yearbook photo.

"I can't believe my mom has been sitting on this factoid for *years*," Bree says, dunking her garlic bread in alfredo sauce and shaking her head. "She went to school with your dad, who—can I be real with you?—sounded cool as hell."

"Yeah."

"I know you don't like talking about him, but it sounds like he was an awesome guy."

It's not that I *don't* like talking about him, I want to argue. I just never knew enough about him to have anything to say. Now I do.

"Supporting his gay BFF back in the nineties? What a badass," Bree continues, twirling pasta around her fork and laughing at the absurdity of the morning. "Was it even called 'gay' then?"

Bree goes on a rant about the evolution of problematic vocabulary, but I'm distracted by this *feeling*. A feeling I've never had before.

It's been radiating through my bones ever since we left Charlie and Brian's. It's hard to describe the sensation. But it feels so good. It's warm and comforting. I never realized I'd been missing it until now.

"You realize we have to ask my mom about all this," Bree says. "Charlie, your dad, the yearbook. They could have all been friends!"

"We can't."

"Why not?"

I sigh. "Because, *again*—your mom doesn't want me to know the yearbook is hers. She wouldn't have lied about it if she did."

"So?"

"So . . . let's not say anything to her."

Bree looks annoyed.

"Not yet, at least. Okay?"

"Fine."

"Promise?"

"Yeah, whatever."

There must be a reason why Mrs. Brandstone is being discreet about all this. I have no idea why, but something's telling me we have to keep our mouths shut.

For now.

Plus, I have a more immediate goal in mind.

"How are we getting back at Cliff?" I press, sipping my Coke and feeling completely reinvigorated. Because if I'm going to be the Charlie-level kind of tough my dad would have appreciated, I can't let Cliff Norquest get away with ruining my senior year.

We sit in silence thinking, as the one hungover waiter working this early in the day lights candles at the surrounding tables and turns up the classical music humming overhead. This would be such a romantic getaway under different circumstances.

"We TP Cliff's house?" Bree suggests.

"Think way bigger."

"We *burn* down his house?"

"Okay, not *that* big."

She goes back to her fettuccine. I sip my Coke. We think some more, as the waiter tops off Bree's water.

"Ali," I think aloud.

"What about Ali?"

"Ali deserves to get revenge on Cliff just as much as I do. Let's recruit him to help us."

She nods, chewing a breadstick. "Gwwood idaw."

"Huh?"

She swallows her bite. "Good idea."

"Also, Marshall. Let's recruit him, too."

We split the check—Bree feels guilty about making me pay for it, after all—swing by LMEP because I want to pick something up for Marshall to say sorry, and drive to Ali's house.

We're parked on the street, almost in the exact same spot we were in during our last stalking session, when Mr. Rashid almost caught us, Blizzards-in-hand. That was just a couple weeks ago, but so much has happened between then and now—so much has changed—it feels like decades.

"Want to go up there with me?" I ask Bree.

She's eating my leftover pizza behind the steering wheel and wearing a pair of sunglasses. "Hm . . ."

"Let's go."

"Wait. Do you think it'll be awkward for him, seeing as he was going to ask me to prom, but, like . . . never actually did?"

"Bree," I say, dropping my chin. "Ali saw *the wall*. He saw all our terrible promposal ideas. If anyone should be allowed to feel awkward about all this, it should be me."

She contemplates. "Fair point."

I don't know how I feel doing this. I don't know how I *should* feel. Because I'm over Ali. I think.

No! I *know*. I know I'm over Ali Rashid. (I think.)

Something really did snap in me this week; I don't see him the same way I did Monday morning. But the past two times I've been in the same room as Ali have been so emotionally charged, in such dramatically different ways. Walking up to his porch now, I can only hope my pizza stays in my stomach, unlike Mr. Brandstone's pancakes.

I knock. Ali answers a minute later wearing sweat shorts and a Detroit Lions shirt, Franklin purring by his feet.

"Sky High?" he says, surprised. "Bree?"

I melt a little bit. Because, okay, hearing him say my name still feels like Cupid hit me with a gay-ass arrow. But it's not a shot through the heart this time. It's more like it grazed my shoulder.

He pushes Franklin back inside with this foot, and closes the door behind him. "Everyone in Yearbook has been worried. You can tell even Winter's been all wound up over what happened."

"Can you come over to Bree's?" I ask.

"Right now?"

"Yeah."

"Uh . . ." He glances back inside through the glass in the front door. "Why?"

"We're planning revenge."

"And we're recruiting you to join us," Bree adds.

"Revenge? Against who?"

"The ass who called you a terrorist."

"Enough said." Ali smirks. "I'm in."

Ali slips on shoes and a coat before we jump into Bree's car and head to Marshall's. Ali doesn't ask questions about our plan, and I'm glad, because we don't have answers. Or a plan.

There's a part of me that wants to dig deeper on what I learned about him from his party; his interest in improv, the self-described "nerdy little brown kid" he needed to suppress in order to pull off Mr. Popular, the stories behind the photos of his family hanging in the dining room. But this car ride isn't the time or place.

Instead, we blast Sofi Tukker with the windows rolled all the way down, even though it's starting to rain. The bass is vibrating my insides. Bree is pounding on the steering wheel to the beat. Ali is tapping his foot on the center console and singing along loudly. It's like we're prepping for a battle we know we're going to win.

After we pull into the Jones's driveway, I jump out of the car and dash up to the front door through heavy, cold raindrops. But Marshall steps outside before I can get there.

He doesn't seem happy with me. Like, at all.

"Hey," I say.

"What's up?" He hates my guts. His tone confirms it.

"I'm—"

"An asshole," he spits.

"Yes. But also, I'm sorry."

He doesn't have a retort for that.

"I ignored your texts," I continue. "And—"

"My voicemails."

"And your voicemails."

"And my DMs."

"And your DMs. And that was an effed up thing to do."

"A really effed up thing to do."

"I got you something to say sorry." I hand him a $25 gift card for the theaters at LMEP. "The next three movies are on me, Moe's snacks included."

He takes it from me and scans the text on the gift card before folding his arms. "What makes you think you can buy my forgiveness?"

I think for a second before squishing my face in thought. "Your love of film?"

He shoves the gift card back into my chest. "I know the e-blast thing was terrible. Like, really, epically awful. But seriously—why have you been ignoring me?"

I can tell he truly is confused. And angry. And hurt.

Another wave of guilt washes over me.

"I didn't feel like talking to people. Ask Bree. I didn't even talk to her."

"Why?"

"I was embarrassed."

"About what?"

I pop my eyes open at him. "Did you *not* see the promposal wall?"

He cracks a grin. "Okay, the LOL HELL NO column? That was pretty funny."

"No, it really wasn't."

His grin fades. "Sorry."

"It's just like . . ." I swallow. "I'm gay. But—"

"You are?" he gasps, covering his mouth in fake surprise. "You? *Gay?*"

I roll my eyes. "But I never really talk about it with you. Talk about *gay* stuff. I just . . . I don't know. I assumed the promposal wall would freak you out."

"Dude! Why would it freak me out? Bree told me you two have been working on the wall for a while; I'm honestly kind of bummed you didn't include me. I thought it was epic!"

"Straight guys get freaked out about gay stuff though!"

"Sky." He looks me in the eye and refuses to blink. It's a little intense. "I'm not a random *straight guy*. I'm Marshall. Remember? Your best friend? You can talk to me about anything."

"Okay."

"Even your gay stuff."

"Okay."

"Especially your gay stuff."

"All right."

"Get *gay* with me, Sky."

"Shut up."

We laugh a little, but then fall silent. The bass from a Sofi Tukker song is still vibrating Bree's car and the rain is falling harder, splattering onto the Jones's front porch. But there's a quiet stillness that begins floating between us. Like something more needs to be said.

"I get it." Marshall leans his back against the door, and then gives me the look—the look where I should understand exactly what he's talking about.

Normally, between us, I would.

But I don't. "What do you get?"

"I get why you may not feel comfortable—or even *safe*—being yourself around straight guys." He nods over at Bree's car and grins. "It's sort of the same reason I don't do that."

I look to the driveway. Bree's watching us intensely from the driver's seat, eating my leftover pizza. Ali is dancing in the back to the song, oblivious to the outside world.

"Uh . . . driving while under the influence of pizza?" I ask.

"No. Why I don't blast my music driving around Rock Ledge."

I glance back and forth between Marshall and Bree. I'm even more confused. "What?"

He sighs. "I don't think you see all the small things I do every day to avoid . . ." He struggles to find the right words. ". . . to avoid a mess."

"I'm not following."

He shakes his head, frustrated. "Dude. Do you think people would react the same way to *me*"—he gestures to his face—"blasting music driving through town the way they do with Bree? How do you think the *police* would react? Why else would I avoid turning up in the car?"

"Oh."

"Yeah."

Valid point. Very valid point.

Suddenly, Mr. Jones's constant worrying about Marshall every time his son leaves the house makes a lot more sense. Bree and I are stupid for not having realized this before—especially being his best friends.

What else am I not seeing?

Like, Marshall doesn't know I walk *straighter* with my books held the *straight* way when I pass Cliff in the school parking lot, to avoid a mess. That's one of my small things. Which of Marshall's other small things remain invisible to me?

"My point is," he continues, "I get why you'd feel guarded around me sometimes about gay stuff. But you shouldn't. That's all."

I smile, nodding. "Okay."

"You're my best friend."

"Ditto."

I expect him to shove my shoulder, or slap my back hard like I see him do sometimes with his track friends, or make a dumb joke to cover up the most serious interaction we've ever had. But he doesn't. He pulls me in for a hug instead.

"I'm sorry I ignored you this week," I say into his ear. "I was being dumb. You're right. You're not just another stupid straight guy—you're Marshall."

"I'm sorry some idiot hacked the e-blast and wrote that about you."

"Aw!" Bree yells through the rain, opening her window as we break apart. "Why aren't you guys always this nice to each other? More of this, please!"

"Where did you get the pizza?" Marshall yells.

"We were at Bella's," I answer.

He hands me a piece of cinnamon gum—the *true* confirmation that we're officially good. "Yeah, your breath reeks of garlic. But Bella's? The place in Traverse City?"

"Yeah."

He squints at the car, then turns back to me. "Why is Ali dancing in the back seat?"

I pop the gum into my mouth. "C'mon."

FOURTEEN DAYS

This is a view I never thought I'd see: Marshall and Ali, sitting on my bedroom futon, staring up at my promposal wall in all its horrifying glory. Ali's face is somewhere between confused and awestruck. Marshall is trying his hardest not to crack up.

"Just say whatever you need to say," I breathe. "C'mon, get it out."

Marshall sighs. "No wonder you never invited me down here," he says. "I saw the e-blast, but it's . . . it's so much better in person."

I glance at Bree, who's standing on the other side of the promposal ideas, back leaning against the wall. She shrugs at me sheepishly.

"To be clear, I'm definitely over you now," I emphasize to Ali. "No offense."

"None taken, Sky High," he says, eyebrows furrowed as he reads the list. "Prom or Pistons? I didn't see that one in the e-blast pic. What was that idea?"

"Oh God," Bree exhales, rubbing her forehead.

Ali gasps. "Wait . . . how did I miss Megan Fox Drag in the

e-blast? You were going to ask me to prom in drag? As *Megan Fox*?"

"As you can see, no," Bree clarifies, pointing out that it's in the column LOL HELL NO. "These ideas were *supposed* to be funny. Don't flatter yourself."

"I probably would have said yes to that one, actually," Ali says, winking at me. "Also, what's SpongeBob SquarePants sponge cake?"

"That's it." I move to block the wall from their eyes.

Marshall and Ali grunt in disapproval.

"We've got work to do," Bree says, sliding over to help block the wall with me. "We need to figure out how to get back at He Who Must Not Be Named."

"He who must not what now?" Ali asks.

"Cliff," I say.

"He's been in love with Bree, but she keeps rejecting him," Marshall explains, picking Louise's hair off his sweater. "She refuses to say his name."

Ali turns toward her. "For real?"

Bree turns red.

"Okay, so," I say, moving us along, because I know Bree hates talking about it. "Here's our theory. Cliff has been super pissed that Bree won't give him the time of day. Messing with the e-blast was his way of messing with *her* via *us*—her gay best friend and you."

"A brown dude," Ali confirms.

"Exactly."

"There's a slight issue with this thinking, though," Ali says, rolling off the futon and onto the floor to pat Louise. "Cliff couldn't have hacked the e-blast. He's not in Yearbook."

"He wasn't at Ali's party to take the picture of the two of you on the sofa either," Marshall chimes in. "And how would he have gotten a photo of this wall?"

"That's what we have to find out," Bree says defiantly. "Because it was him. It *had* to have been him."

Ali and Marshall glance at each other and mutually agree to go along with the theory. At least for now.

"Let's start with the photo of this wall," Ali says. "Has Cliff ever been down here?"

Bree lets out a cackle. "Definitely not."

"Who's been down here since you two started writing down the promposal ideas, then?"

"Petey and Ray . . . ," Marshall says softly.

Bree laughs again. "Those two can't figure out how to work the garage door code, let alone hack Memories."

"They obviously wouldn't have done it," I state for the record, remembering how nice they've been to me all week delivering food, and Ray's adorable *18!* birthday reminder sticky notes.

"Clare?" Marshall moves on.

"Clare *is* capable of hacking an e-blast," I say, looking at Bree.

"But what would her motive be?" Bree says. "Her only two goals in life are cooking with Hannah Hart and hooking up with Donald Glover."

"Plus, Clare doesn't have it out for me. Right?" I want to confirm.

"Of course not."

"I assume your parents are innocent?" Ali asks.

Bree glares at him.

"Just checking . . ." He bites his lower lip in thought. "Who else?"

We all go silent.

"No one, really," Bree says, frustrated. "You two are the only friends me and Sky have had over in months. No one's been down here because of the construction."

"What about the workers?" Marshall asks, shrugging.

"What workers?"

"I thought your dad was paying people to do the drywall and flooring in the rec room."

"It's supposed to be a *man cave*," Bree clarifies, rolling her eyes. "But yeah, good call. There's been, like . . . four dudes that used to be down here a lot working, but I haven't seen them in a while." She looks at me. "Have you?"

I think. It's been a long time. One of them almost caught me watching porn in my Grinch pajamas around New Year's, I remember in horror. But I don't have much certainty besides that.

"It's been at least a few weeks, I think—unless they've been coming when we're at school."

Bree pulls out her phone and dials a number.

"Who are you calling?" Ali whispers.

"Bree?" I hear her dad say on the other end of the line, *Sports-Center* blasting in the background, as she puts the phone on speaker.

"Hey, Dad."

"Where are all you kids?"

"In Sky's room downstairs."

"Uh-oh." There's a long pause. *"Is Sky keeping it cool around Ali?"*

I bury my face in my hands. Ali and Marshall let out sharp laughs.

"Dad! You're on speaker."

"Oh hush, Sky knows I'm poking fun. Right, Sky?"

"Yes, Mr. Brandstone," I say through my fingers.

"See?"

"Too soon," Marshall mumbles under his breath as I lift my head again. "Too soon."

"Anyway," Bree says. "Who's been working down here?"

"Down where?"

"The basement."

"What do you mean?"

"Who are the workers who've been doing the walls and floors and stuff for the man cave?"

"Oh. A few of Jerry's employees."

"Who's Jerry?"

"My friend, Jerry. Jerry Wing. He owns that little construction business on Brown Street, near the Shell station."

"Does it have a name?"

"Does what have a name?"

"Jerry's construction business, Dad, please keep up."

"I don't know. You'd have to ask Jerry."

"Thanks. That's all."

"Clare made clam chowder if you're hun—"

Bree hangs up.

Marshall pulls my Mac onto his lap. I plop down next to him on the futon.

"What are you looking up?" Ali asks.

"Who this Jerry person is."

Marshall goes to Mr. Brandstone's Facebook profile—the last time Mr. Brandstone posted on his wall was four months ago, a status that just reads *Damn it, Spartans!*—clicks on the friends tab, and searches "Jerry Wing."

"'Owner of Wing Construction,'" Marshall reads aloud after landing on Jerry's profile. He clicks on Wing Construction's business page, as Bree sits on my lap to see the screen too.

"Any familiar faces?" Marshall says, scrolling down the business's profile. There are photos of Wing Construction's modest storefront on Brown Street and a dozen awkward, pointless selfies of Jerry, who apparently loves wearing visors.

"Wait," Bree says, pointing at one of the thumbnails. "Click that one."

A bunch of workers are in the pic, smiling next to a big hole in the ground they presumably dug.

"Those two guys have been over here a lot!" she says, glancing at me. "Right?"

"Yeah," I say, leaning forward to better see their faces. The one who almost caught me with porn looks about sixty years old— likely *not* someone who'd be involved in a high school e-blast hack—but the other is a beefy, tall dude with a long, red beard, who looks a little bit older than us. "That's them."

Marshall hovers above Red Beard and clicks on the tagged name.

Rence Bloomington.

Rence has one mutual friend with Marshall, too: Clare Brandstone. Bree gasps, picking up her phone again—this time to call her sister.

"*What?*" Clare answers.

"Who's Rence Bloomington?"

"*Who?*"

"Rence Bloomington."

There's a pause. "*The redhead who's flooring our basement?*"

"Yeah. Is that how you know him? From working over here?"

"*He graduated a year ahead of me.*"

"Are you friends with him? Like, in real life?"

"*Not really.*"

"Oh, oh!" Marshall squeals, pointing to the computer screen. He searched for the name "Norquest" amongst Rence's friends, and two names popped up: Denise and Cliff.

Denise and Cliff Norquest.

"Waaaaait," Bree says, grinning giddily while staring at the screen. "Clare, who's Denise Norquest?"

"*Are you downstairs right now?*"

"Yes."

"*Bree. Seriously? You're such a lazy ass. I'm about to hang up—*"

"Wait! This is important! Do you know Denise Norquest?"

"*Yeah. She's Rence's cousin.*"

We all exchange looks.

"*Why?*" Clare asks.

"Do you know who Cliff Norquest is?"

She pauses. "*Isn't he the idiot on the wrestling team?*"

"Yes."

"*Yeah, that's Denise's little brother.*"

"I didn't know Cliff had an older sister!" Bree mouths at us. "So you're telling me that Cliff Norquest is Rence's cousin?"

"Seeing that's how being a family works, yes."

"Oh my God."

"What the hell is going on, Bree?"

"It doesn't matter."

"Come upstairs. I made clam chow—"

Bree hangs up.

"Duuuuuude." Ali gapes.

"Whoa," Marshall says, slowly shaking his head. "It actually *was* Cliff Norquest."

"Shhhhh," Bree says, holding up her finger while dialing yet another number.

"Bree," her dad scolds through the phone a second later. *"You've got to knock this off!"*

"One final question! When was the last time the guys from Jerry's place were over here working?"

"I don't know, Bree. Why don't you come upstairs and have a conversation like a normal person?"

"It's been a while, right?"

"Yes, a few weeks. They'd been coming just about every day, but we had to pause because your indecisive mom's rethinking the space across from the steps again. Did I tell you what she wanted to do there? She's pushing back on the man cave idea and—"

"Dad, focus."

"All right, okay. Let me think . . . their last day was a Tuesday, I remember that. And it would have been . . . it would have been the Tuesday two weeks before last? . . . Yeah, that's right. It would've been then."

"Wait." Bree closes her eyes and shakes her head. "Say that again."

"*Their last day working was the same day Petey puked up Clare's shrimp scampi at swim practice. That would have been two weeks before this past Tuesday.*"

"Okay, so that means . . ." Bree glances up at the promposal wall. "Last Tuesday, the countdown would have been at . . ." She pauses to think. "Eighteen days. And two weeks before that . . ."

"Thirty-two days." Marshall finishes her math, staring at my computer.

He pulled up the hacked e-blast with the two photos. I recoil, because I haven't seen it since the blueberry pancake puking incident. "The last time they worked down here," Marshall continues, showing the computer screen to me, Bree, and Ali, "the countdown would have been at thirty-two days. And look . . ."

There it is. The evidence is staring back at us in plain sight. The promposal wall countdown stood at thirty-two days in the hacked e-blast photo. That makes sense too—the Prom or Pistons idea Bree came up with most recently isn't on the wall in the photo.

"*Bree?*" her dad asks after we're stunned into silence. "*What's wrong? Are you going to come up and have some clam chow—*"

She hangs up.

"I told you!" She clenches her fist and shakes it in the air triumphantly, like she just ran the winning touchdown. "I *told you* it was Cliff!"

"Rence must have snapped the photo of the wall while Sky was at school," Ali recaps to himself aloud, "and shared it with cousin Cliff."

"That's it, right?" Marshall says, closing my laptop. "We tell Winter on Monday? We bring him down?"

"No, no, no," Bree says, now pacing with her head hung low in thought. "If we're going to turn in evidence, we have to have all our *T*s dotted and our *I*s crossed."

"You mean all our *I*s dotted and—"

"Yeah, yeah, whatever."

I imagine my mental checklist from before of all the qualifiers the hacker must have met.

~~The person somehow got a photo of the promposal wall.~~

The person somehow accessed Memories to hack the e-blast.

The person somehow got the pic of me and Ali at Ali's party.

One down, two more to go.

I'm excited—but also mortified. A complete stranger wandered into my room in order to humiliate me. Who does that? Did Cliff ask him to? Were the two of them scheming behind my back since I moved into the Brandstones' and Rence figured out I'm the gay kid his cousin hates? Either way, it's a scary thought.

And I'm ready for revenge.

"Can I just ask: What's gotten into you, Sky High?" Ali smirks, probably sensing my thirst for blood. "Bree said you've been in the dumps all week because of the e-blast. Clearly something's changed."

"Yeah," Marshall agrees, throwing a pillow at me. "That must have been really good Bella's pizza. I can see the fire in your eyes. You want Cliff's head on a spike."

I hesitate to divulge everything about our morning in Traverse City, because it's so rare that I talk about my dad. But I don't want to keep any more secrets from anybody. Enough is enough.

I exhale, long and slow, before diving in.

I tell them about Mrs. Brandstone's yearbook and Charlie.

About how I don't know much about my dad at all, but—for whatever reason—something burst inside me, learning he once thought his gay best friend was the toughest guy he knew. About why I need to be tough too.

I look up from the floor after talking my head off. "Sorry."

Bree, Ali, and Marshall are all giving me the same warm smile.

"Don't be sorry," Bree says, tearing up a little.

"We'll get him," Marshall says, throwing another pillow at me playfully. "We'll make your dad proud."

"Bree!" Mr. Brandstone belts down the staircase. "We're putting away the chowder! Get up here if you want any!"

"Okay!" Bree yells back. "We'll be right there!"

We sit in silence for a minute. Although no one's saying anything, I can tell each one of us is soaking in the task we just created for ourselves. The task to bring down Cliff Norquest.

"So . . . Clare's clam chowder is actually pretty good," Bree finally says softly. "Is anyone hungry?"

"Duh," Marshall says, standing and stretching.

"Yeah," I say. Bree ate the rest of my pizza, so I'm kind of hungry too.

"Hold up," Ali says. "That's it?"

"What do you mean?" Bree sighs.

"We're just leaving it at that?" Ali gapes. "You promised me revenge, Brandstone. That's why I came over here. Revenge on Cliff Norquest."

"Do you have anything in mind?"

"After chowder," he says, brushing Louise's hair off his pant legs with a grin, "we need to go get white shirts and some markers."

TWELVE DAYS

Bree pulls into the school parking lot Monday morning so we can burn this place down for good. Not literally. Obviously. But it feels like that's what we're about to do.

"Are we out of our minds?" I ask for probably the tenth time since Saturday, glancing down at my shirt—which is *way* gayer than the pink collared one I wore to Ali's party. That one's not even close.

"No," Bree reassures me, also for the tenth time. She laughs, a little too mischievously for comfort, sipping her cocoa. "Okay, a little out of our minds. We have one foot in our minds and one foot out."

I groan.

"But what's that one quote?" she says, the car lightly bumping the guardrail in front of us. "Well-behaved women rarely make history? Well, we're making the history books, Sky."

I panic, reaching into the back seat to grab one of Bree's oversized Rock Ledge Rams hoodies to slip on over my shirt. "Just in case—"

"No!" She rips the hoodie out of my hands. "Just in case *what*? You're doing this, Sky. *We're* doing this."

"I think I'm going to puke."

"And if you do, I'll be there to hold your hair."

"What if Ali backs out at the last minute?"

"He won't."

"What if Marshall backs out at the last minute?"

"Marshall definitely won't."

"What if Cliff—"

"Everything is going to be fine."

"How do you know?"

"You missed all last week, dude." She smiles at me. "Everyone is on Team Sky now."

I inhale deeply and stare straight ahead at the heterosexual hellscape I swore all last week I'd never step foot in again.

Everyone is on Team Sky now.

"Okay." My muggy breath sticks to the inside of the windshield as rain splatters against the outside glass. "Let's go."

We start passing students in the parking lot. Nothing weird happens. No awkward eye contact or glances down at my shirt or Bree's.

"You okay?" Bree whispers as we near the entrance under her umbrella.

"I think so."

Then we walk inside.

First hour starts in ten minutes, so the hallways are at peak crowdedness. There seems to be a magnetic pull directing people's eyeballs toward us. And those that notice us *definitely* notice our shirts, too.

No turning back now.

"Sky!" this guy named Roy yells. "Welcome back!"

"Yaasss, Sky," a girl—I think she's a sophomore on the debate team—hisses in approval as we pass. "Love the shirts, y'all."

How does she even know my name?

I smile at her in thanks.

"Still all right?" Bree whispers, nudging me in the ribs. More stares, more grins, more nods in approval.

"Yep," I say, nudging her back. I think I'm telling her the truth.

My heart is racing, my palms are sweating, and a faint voice in my head is urging me to run back to Bree's car and wait there until the school day ends. But a louder voice—my dad's, I'd like to think, even though I don't remember what it sounded like—is telling me it's going to be okay. "I'm tough too," I whisper to myself.

"Huh?" Bree asks.

"Nothing."

Just as planned, we pop into the boys' bathroom near the photography room—the one no one ever uses.

"Ali?" I say, my shaky voice echoing off the empty stalls and tile floor. I don't see anyone else in here.

"Marshall?" Bree follows up.

There's a second of heart-stopping silence, then—

"Hey," Ali answers from behind one of the mint-green stall doors.

Bree and I glance at each other in relief. At least one of them didn't back out.

"Thank God," I breathe.

"Why do you say that?" Ali asks.

"I didn't know if you'd follow through."

"The shirts were *my* idea, Sky High. You think I'd flake?"

He emerges wearing his too.

Marshall barrels through the bathroom door a moment later, slightly out of breath. "Sorry I'm late. My dad made me clean up my room before I left." He pulls off his rain jacket, revealing his shirt as well.

All four of us are doing this. It's really happening.

Holy eff.

We turn to face the mirror together, standing side by side. There's my slender frame dwarfed by Ali's bulkier build, his thick, full eyebrows next to my sandy browns. To my left, Bree's bushy hair falls down her chest, blocking out a little more of the letters than what's visible on the rest of ours. Then there's Marshall, proudly standing on the other side of Bree, being the best straight guy friend a gay boy could ask for.

Our stark-white shirts read DAYS LEFT: 12 written in permanent marker across the stomach—just like the wall's countdown reads in the Brandstones' basement this very second.

Across our chests, however, are slightly differing messages.

My shirt reads GAY FOR ALI in red.

Bree's and Marshall's shirts read GAY FOR SKY in blue and green.

And Ali's reads I'M NOT A TERRORIST. BUT I AM GAY FOR SKY in purple.

If Cliff thought he'd shut me up—shut *us* up—he was dead wrong.

"I can't believe this is happening," I say, goose bumps shooting down my arms.

"I can," Ali retorts, flashing an Ali Grin. He puts his arm around my shoulder and holds up his phone to snap a pic of the four of us.

"We have to hustle," Bree says, glancing down at her phone.

Marshall gives my shoulder a shake, like he's amping up the quarterback before the biggest game of the season. Ali lets out an excited shriek.

The four of us march to the C-wing, where Cliff is always hanging out with his friends before first hour. We don't mean to part the crowd, but it sort of just happens.

Someone starts clapping, which is kind of hilarious, but also makes me feel very badass. A few others actually, genuinely gasp. A small handful of freshmen laugh, kind of in a shocked way. But most just stare, little smiles sprouting across their curious faces.

"Get 'em, Sky."

"Daaaamn."

"Holy . . ."

"I'm gay for you too, Sky!"

I spot Dan standing near his open locker. He nods as we pass, not afraid to make eye contact with me now.

Ainsley and Teddy are waiting expectantly near a drinking fountain. Marshall must have given them a heads-up about our plan, because their first hours are on the other side of the building—they wouldn't be here unless they wanted to see this go down.

"Woot-woot!" Ainsley yells, slapping Marshall's butt as he walks by. "Love it!"

"Looking good," Teddy says, nodding at me and Bree.

Butterflies. Again.

Teddy-related butterflies.

I don't look at Cliff as we approach. He's certainly not worth acknowledging. But I know he sees us and our shirts. I can hear it in his speechlessness.

I've never felt as tough as I do right now.

TWELVE DAYS

I thought things might settle down before Yearbook in the afternoon, but they definitely don't. The whole class is gathered around me, Bree, Marshall, and Ali like it's a freaking press conference. They might as well have mics held up to our mouths. It's kind of great, though. It's not like we weren't asking for it.

"I am obsessed with these shirts."

"Who came up with the idea for the countdown? Marshall?"

"You're all bonkers."

"So, Ali." Dustin York grins devilishly. "Are you going to say yes to Sky when he asks you to prom in twelve days? Is that what's happening here?"

"The shirts are *symbolic*," I answer quickly, shaking my head. "Ali and I aren't going together. The shirts are supposed to send a message: Whoever hacked our e-blast isn't going to shut us up. That's it."

"And every day we'll be wearing new shirts with the countdown on them until the Senior Beach-Bum Party is here," Marshall says with a smirk. "So you all better get used to them."

Everyone laughs excitedly.

"Who messed with the e-blast, anyway?" Christina chimes in. "Do we know which idiot did it yet?"

"Principal Burger is investigating," Winter says, striding into the classroom. "Everyone settle down."

The herd breaks up, shuffling to their respective computers.

"Welcome back, Baker." Winter nods, bending low so only we can hear as she walks by. "Quite the interesting choice of wardrobe, you four."

"My color matches my aura," explains Ali, pointing at the purple letters scrawled across his chest and batting his eyes. He's decided to sit next to me, Bree, and Marshall today. That's a first.

"Oh!" Bree jumps and motions for us to lean in to hear her better over the chitchat and grinding of chairs against the floor. "Someone should talk to Carolyn today!"

"Why?" Marshall asks.

"Because she was with Sky and Ali when they were in the basement at the party—when someone took the photo," she answers, looking over at me. "You mentioned that, right?"

I forgot I told Bree about that. But judging by Carolyn's level of drunkenness that night, Carolyn may have forgotten that too.

"The shirts are fun and all," Bree continues. "But we need to stay focused on Operation: Pin It on He Who Must Not Be Named. Carolyn is a valuable asset in gathering more evidence."

"Can we come up with a more succinct title?" Ali asks.

"Huh?"

"'Operation: Pin It on He Who Must Not Be Named'? That's, like, fifty syllables long, Bree."

Bree ignores him. "All I'm saying is, someone needs to see if Carolyn knows anything about the pic."

"Um, that'll have to wait," Marshall mutters, turning his phone toward us.

There's an Instagram post shared twenty minutes ago from Carolyn—hair disheveled, sprawled out in bed next to a pile of used tissues—with the caption, *I didn't know it was possible to feel this terrible. #ThotsAndPrayers #SeasonalFlu #Homesick* 🤢. It's kind of hilarious, considering Carolyn posts Facetuned, duck-face selfies 99 percent of the time.

"Damn," Bree says. "Is it rude to show up at her house when she's sick?"

"Seriously?" Marshall tilts his head at her. "You'd do that?"

"Kidding," Bree assures, turning to her computer. "Sort of."

"Let's just text her and ask if she saw anyone take a photo of me and Sky," Ali says, pulling out his phone.

"No!" Bree pushes it down. "We can't leave a text trail."

"Huh?"

"We don't want this getting back to He Who Must Not Be Named, right?" Bree lowers her voice. "Not that I don't trust Carolyn, but we have to be smart. We can't leave any evidence that we're onto him."

"I mean. We could call her," Ali says.

Bree just grimaces.

Marshall nods. "Asking in person seems like a safer bet."

"We have to be patient—as difficult as it'll be." Bree sighs. "Carolyn won't be sick forever."

I'm laughably behind on my Yearbook deadlines after spending an entire week moping around with Thelma and Louise. But finding the ability to focus on anything other than Operation: Pin It on He Who Must Not Be Named is pretty close to impossible. Before I know it, the bell is ringing, and I've hardly put a dent in my work.

Winter calls me over to her desk. Marshall, Bree, and Ali leave without me, fielding more questions about the shirts on their way out.

"I wanted to check in on you," Winter says, rolling up the sleeves of her sweater.

She says something else, but my brain goes numb for a second when I see a text pop up on my phone. A text from Gus.

Hey, it reads. We should talk soon.

Damn.

Gus heard about the e-blast. He's already heard about these shirts, too, probably. Even though he abandoned me and my mom and moved downstate after high school, Gus is still ensnared in the Rock Ledge gossip. Some people may physically leave this town, but they're still attached to the grapevine, no matter the distance. Gus is one of those people.

There's no way he'd be texting me if he hadn't somehow been affected by the e-blast or these shirts. I'm practically dead to him—unless my existence becomes an inconvenience.

"Baker?" Winter asks after I stay silent. "Everything okay?"

"Oh yeah," I say, forcing a smile and pocketing my phone. "Sorry, what did you say?"

"I just asked how you're holding up."

"Last week was the worst."

"I bet."

"But I'm okay."

"You sure?"

"Yep."

"Okay. So, the shirts . . ." A smile creeps into her cheeks. She pauses, hoping I'll jump in with an explanation.

"The shirts are sending a message to whoever did it. They're not going to shame me into hiding away for the rest of my senior year."

"Okay." Her eyes zoom in on my chest. "I like that message."

"Thanks."

"Principal Burger promised me he'll get to the bottom of it."

"I'm sure he will," I say sarcastically. Because Burger is an idiot who couldn't pick Ronald McDonald out of a lineup.

She smirks before turning to a spreadsheet on her computer. "I'm going to ignore the deadlines you missed last week, by the way."

"Oh, thank y—"

"But," she cuts me off. "You'll need to hustle to make up for it. Blank pages in our yearbook? Not an option."

She shuffles papers around, revealing a big-ass stain on her desk. I inhale in horror, staring down at the sprawling purple spot. "Is that from . . . ?"

She lets out a rare laugh. "Yes."

"I'm so sorry."

"It's okay. Cleaning up pancake puke is surprisingly not the grossest thing I've had to do working at this school."

I'm mortified.

And she can tell. "I need to get a new desk anyway, Baker. Don't worry about it."

She hands me a proof of one of my assigned yearbook

pages. It's absolutely destroyed by copy edits in red pen, and I'm somehow both annoyed and grateful that Winter seems to still have the same high expectations for me that she had two weeks ago.

"Cross the finish line of your senior year strong," she warns in her usual tone. "You owe it to yourself."

I nod in compliance.

"Glad to have you back, Baker."

I never would have guessed it a week ago, but I'm glad to be back too.

Riding a wave of newfound optimism, I decide to call Charlie's work office between classes and leave a message apologizing for what I did. Even though he's only slightly less of a stranger to me than, like, the theater ushers at LMEP, leaving him in the dust Saturday was beyond rude. He seems like a genuinely sweet guy who deserves better than my abrupt departure, and I'm fairly certain my dad would agree.

His office is easy to find on Google.

"Dermatology Center of Northwest Michigan," the receptionist answers.

"Is Dr. Washington in today?"

"Are you a returning patient?"

"Um, more like . . . a friend." Wait. I'm not a friend. Who am I to Charlie? "Er, family friend. Sort of."

The receptionist laughs.

"He and my dad are friends," I finally articulate.

Are friends. It's a little surreal referring to my dad in the present tense. But *the doctor is friends with my dad* surely sounds better than *the doctor used to be friends with my dad, who died more than a decade ago.*

"Can I have your name?" the receptionist asks.

"My name. . . ."

"Yes."

"Justin Jackson."

"One moment, Mr. Jackson."

Oh. The receptionist is . . . actually connecting me to Charlie? When has a doctor ever been available?

"Hi, Justin." It's Charlie.

"Hey," I reply.

My brain is scrambling. I'll dive right into the apology. "Sorry about running off on Saturday."

"Not a problem. Was everything okay?"

"Yeah, I forgot about an appointment."

"Been there. Almost forgot my eight thirty patient this morning, actually."

The line falls silent for a second.

The only logical next step is starting where we left off.

"Are you still interested in the full-page ad?" I ask.

"Of course."

"I can swing by and we can talk the details, if you want."

"That sounds great. It's quite the trek for you, though. Would you prefer to plan it out over the phone or e-mail?"

I think about their warm den, Bob's fluffy fur, the kindness in Brian's and Charlie's eyes. "It's okay. Are you free this evening? I'll be in Traverse anyway," I lie.

"Tonight works great."

After school, I ask Bree if I can borrow her car. She's more open to it once I promise to fill the tank.

"Are you finally going to ask Charlie about my mom?" she asks, handing me the keys and lifting the Crockpot lid to check on Clare's corned beef and cabbage. "I bet they had a secret love affair before he came out, or something. How crazy would that be!"

"Keep it closed!" Clare scolds Bree from the couch over an episode of *Nailed It*. Bree rolls her eyes, but puts the lid back on the Crockpot anyway.

"No, I don't think so," I answer.

"Why not?"

I motion for her to keep her voice down; Mrs. Brandstone could be lurking around any corner. I just assume Mrs. Brandstone *is* lurking behind every corner.

"Because, for the millionth time," I whisper. "We're not supposed to know the yearbook is your mom's, which means—"

"Yeah, yeah, I get it. Why are you going back there anyway, though? To stare at Hot Tattoo Guy? What's his name again? Brian?"

The question catches me off guard.

"You want to learn more about your dad," she answers for me, sneaking another peak at Clare's corned beef. Clare doesn't notice this time. "I would want to learn more too, if I were you. I get it. Just be back by a reasonable hour, Justin Jackson."

"Okay, Mom."

"Bree!" Clare spots her. "Keep the lid closed!"

One hour and three Marvel theories podcast episodes later, I pull into Charlie's driveway. Bob comes barreling out the front door again, like I'm his long-lost human returning home from war.

"Robert, settle down!" Charlie bellows from the front porch. Today he's wearing a light blue suit with a tan tie. Dr. Washington knows how to dress. "Nice to see you, Justin. Come in, come in."

Bob and I trot up the asphalt together and into the house. The cloudy day makes the foyer dimmer and chillier than last time, but Charlie's made up for it by lighting candles and playing some cozy piano music over a sound system that can probably be heard in every room. From the smell of it, there's something delicious cooking in this kitchen too.

"Brian made beef stew before he went to work," Charlie says, apparently reading my mind. "Want some?"

"I'm okay, thanks. What does Brian do for work?"

"He owns Traverse Tats down on Front Street."

"Tats as in . . . tattoos?"

Charlie laughs. "Yeah. Makes sense, huh?"

I nod, remembering Brian's bulging, inked forearms and calves.

"He's covered!" Charlie continues. "Absolutely addicted. He just finished one and is already planning his next."

"What's it going to be?"

"A cactus behind his knee." Charlie rolls his eyes, smiling. "Whatever makes him happy."

I take off my shoes and coat—I changed shirts to avoid any weird questions about what in the world GAY FOR ALI and DAYS LEFT: 12 might mean—and follow Charlie farther into the house. We get to the kitchen, Bob panting at my side, and it's even nicer than I expected.

There's this huge window above the sink that looks out over the lake. It feels like we're floating along on a cruise ship. A dozen expensive-looking copper pots and pans are dangling above a massive stove with a million burners, white cupboards with infinite storage lining the surrounding walls. A big granite island—twice the size of the Brandstones'—anchors the middle of the room, dotted with items reflecting Charlie's and Brian's contrasting lives: a thick medical book, tattoo sketches, a pile of colorful neckties, graphite pencils.

"Sorry about the clutter," Charlie says, pushing things to the side to make room. He catches me staring at the fridge, which is covered in crayon drawings. "Brian thinks his niece is the next Georgia O'Keeffe."

I nod, only 80 percent sure I know who Georgia O'Keeffe is. "Oh, I assumed those were Brian's handiwork."

He lets out a hearty laugh. "Brian sticks to coloring *people*, not paper. Are you sure you don't want any stew?"

"Yeah, thanks."

"Suit yourself." Charlie helps himself to a bowl and breaks off a big chunk of crusty bread before joining me at the island. "I dug these out of the basement," he says, pulling over a shoe box I hadn't noticed, and reaching inside. It's filled with old pictures. "Think I could use a few of these in the ad, along with the photo from 1996? I'm getting a full page, after all."

"Absolutely." I pull the box closer. "Can I take a look?"

There are baby photos, class pics, and snapshots of his family, all bent, discolored, and flaring at their edges. Charlie was an avid tennis player, I learn from a series of posed portraits— stacked in ascending age—featuring him and his racquets. His salt-and-pepper hair used to be just pepper, too. I don't know why, but it makes me giggle. Fortunately, Charlie doesn't notice.

"Does the high school still hold Ram Ragers?" he asks, holding a pic near his eyes with a grin on his face. "The big bonfire parties next to the football field?"

"I don't think so."

"Too bad. Those were fun. Oh! What about nugget Fridays?"

"Nugget Fridays?"

"They don't have chicken nuggets every Friday in the cafeteria anymore?"

I shake my head.

"What a travesty." He pulls out more photos and splays them across the island far away from his bowl of stew, eyes glossed over in this weird nostalgic trance.

I don't really know what to say while he's so distracted by his past life, so I open my laptop and sign in to Memories. "Do you want me to mock up what the ad could look like using one of our templates?"

"Sure," he says, breaking off some bread, eyes still glued to his photos. "Wow, Melissa Johnson looks completely different now. . . ."

"Who?"

"Sorry, no one you know," he mumbles, chewing a big mouthful. "Just an old classmate. I think she moved to Cincinnati."

He glances up at me.

I don't know what expression I must be making, but I think it unintentionally suggests he should rein in his enthusiasm for his glory days. "You know, high school really did suck." He scratches at his five o'clock shadow. "It's easy for me to look back at those years fondly *now*. But it was terrible when I lived them."

I smile, clicking around in Memories to look busy.

"That's the danger of nostalgia," he continues, spooning more stew. "Your mind wants to relish in a sugarcoated past that never actually existed."

The kitchen goes quiet, except for the piano music playing overhead and Bob begging for some beef stew of his own. He's just as bad as Thelma.

"Anyway." Charlie walks around the island to stand by my side, sliding glasses onto the tip of his nose. "What's this template look like?"

"You can include pictures here," I say, pointing to empty boxes on the spread, "and, if you want, you can write a message over here."

"Neat."

"But it's just a template; we can customize whichever way you want."

"I wish Brian were here," he says, squinting at the screen, sort of confused, crow's feet deepening. "Brian's better at this creative stuff. I'm just the boring skin doctor."

Skin doctor. That's right. I knew a dermatologist was a skin doctor. Duh. But I kind of forgot until just now.

I wonder if Charlie would ever look at Mars for me?

I'd have to get over my fear of being shirtless anywhere but by myself in the bathroom. And I'd probably have to reveal my true identity, should I ever become his patient. There's no getting around that; a fake ID is much harder to pull off when it comes to health insurance.

But I remember when I was younger, the dermatologist at the

clinic telling my mom about options to minimize or cover up the scarring. I can't remember if it was a specific procedure, or special ointments, or what, but any kind of treatment was way out of my mom's budget anyway. Charlie could give me some advice.

I'm about to bring it up, but one of the photos catches my eye: a polaroid with my dad.

I tense up.

"Where was that one taken?" I ask.

Charlie glances at the photo I'm pointing to. "This one?" he says, dragging it over with his fingertip. "This was . . ." He pauses for a second, staring up at the ceiling in thought. "Chicago, early 2000s. I think I must have been . . . twenty-three or twenty-four?"

It's a group photo. My dad looks legitimately happy in it too. Not the kind of fake happy everyone flaunts only when the camera flashes. But this real, liberated type of happy I've never seen on him in the few family pics my mom keeps around. He's an entirely different person.

He's wearing a shirt with a rainbow on it too.

"Did you go to Chicago a lot when you were younger?"

"I lived there. I went to undergrad and med school in Evanston. I couldn't wait to escape Rock Ledge."

"You have no idea," I say. "Well . . . obviously you *do* have an idea."

He laughs.

"That's the same guy from the 1996 yearbook photo," I say nonchalantly, hoping my acting skills are up to par. "Henry, right?"

"Oh yeah, Henry." He lifts the photo closer. "Talk about someone who wanted to escape Rock Ledge."

"What do you mean?"

"Henry always wanted out, but he never got the chance. Married young and settled down fast."

I nod along, trying to look like I'm listening to a story about a stranger—not the sobering love story of my parents. This is all so strange.

I'm sitting here, mocking up a full-page ad I'm not even sure I'll be able to place in the yearbook, claiming to be someone named Justin Jackson, listening to high school stories about my dead dad from his best friend, who has no idea who I am.

"He loved visiting me in Chicago, though; we always had a blast. He was such a great friend, Henry. I miss him." Charlie puts down the photo and picks up another—one in which he's wearing a Rock Ledge High band uniform and playing the saxophone. "Anyway. How about this one from band class? I think it was my junior year. I look like a total dork in it, but I might as well embrace my inner Steve Urkel, right?"

"Yeah," I say, struggling to place who Steve Urkel is. I turn my attention back to my computer, feeling a little bit closer to the dad I'm just now beginning to know. "I think that pic works great."

Henry Baker wanted to escape. In his own way, my dad was a Rock Ledge outsider too.

TEN DAYS

By Wednesday, the school starts to get the sense that the four of us aren't messing around. Because for the third straight day, me, Marshall, Bree, and Ali wear our gay shirts.

And we have ten effing days to go.

For the record, I really *don't* know what's going to happen when the clock—er, our shirts—strike zero. A few people in Yearbook think we've devised some master scheme for the Senior Beach-Bum Party. The joke's on them, though.

"Wait, *are* you going to ask Ali to prom?" Marshall whispers into my ear as we leave Trig, Ali just steps behind us. Our shirts are still drawing smiles, high fives, and curious stares; Ali is too distracted by the attention to notice we're talking about him.

"No," I whisper back, like Marshall should know that by now. "Well . . . I'm probably not going to. I don't think. Right?"

"I—"

"That's not the point of the shirts."

"True."

"The whole point of our shirts is to shove it in Cliff's face."

"Right."

"I'm not letting some asshole ruin my life."

"Exactly."

"But *should* I ask Ali?"

No. No, I shouldn't. I'm over him.

But what if people expect me to, now that the e-blast hack happened? It feels like everyone's been rallying around the two of us as if we're an unlikely rom-com pairing that'll end up happily ever after. This whole thing's starting to feel bigger than just *me* and what *I* want to do for prom.

"Do you want my honest opinion?" Marshall asks.

I nod.

He checks to make sure Ali is still out of earshot. "You deserve to go to prom with someone who sees you like you used to see Ali," he says with a shrug. "And that's . . . probably not Ali." He cringes. "Sorry."

Cliff and his crew totally ignore me in Health class. Again.

He couldn't even look me in the eye while passing out graded papers for Mrs. Diamond, the freaking coward. But honestly, it's great. Being invisible to him and his cronies may be my favorite part about wearing the shirts. An invisibility cloak for racist assholes, if you will.

It's obvious why he wouldn't dare confront me too. Just like Bree said on Monday, *Everyone is on Team Sky now.* Cliff won't pick a battle he knows he can't win.

And he won't win this one.

The downside to Health, however, is that I learned Carolyn is still sick and out of class. Bree's joke about visiting her on her deathbed to ask about Ali's party is seeming less like a bad idea by the hour.

I'm late to Yearbook because I had to make up a pop quiz during lunch for Mr. Kam from the week I missed. When I walk into Winter's, I immediately sense that something's up, though. The whole class is gathered around Bree.

Ali turns to me, a weird look on his face. "Yo, we have an issue."

I slide through everyone to find out what's going on.

"Did you see it?" Bree asks, annoyed.

"See what?"

She hands me her phone.

Victor Bungle—our annoyingly type A, brownnosing, judgmental class president—posted a photo on Instagram. The pic itself is relatively normal. Well, relatively normal for Bungle at least; he's standing on the football field wearing a fake, toothy smile and a Rock Ledge Rams shirt, like it's a stock image photo shoot.

"So?" I say. "What am I missing?"

"Read the *caption*."

I scroll down.

Attention, Senior Rams:

Something is making big waves this week, and as your class president, I feel the need to address it.

As many of you know, a few students have been wearing controversial T-shirts to school proclaiming that they're "gay" for others. What started as a mean-spirited prank involving the Yearbook e-blast has now evolved into an even uglier mess that, quite frankly, is starting to poison the fun of our senior year, just as the Beach-Bum Party and prom are right around the corner.

As your president, I think it's important for all of you to know that I do not condone these four individuals' shirts.

To be clear: I am a proud supporter of the gay community. What happened with the e-blast was unfortunate. But to the students making a mockery with your "countdown" apparel: Do you really have to flaunt your sexual orientation for the world to see?

I don't strut around saying I'm "straight for ABC"—why do you feel the need to remind us you're "gay for XYZ"?

Enough already.

I sincerely hope this shirt-wearing distraction comes to an end so that ALL of us seniors—gay, straight, and otherwise—can finish our high school experience as Rams, happy and drama-free.

Sincerely,

V-Bungle

I stand there gawking at the screen, wondering if I should be laughing or enraged by the absurdity of what I just read. "What a little . . ."

"Be nice, Baker," Winter warns from behind her desk.

"Be nice? He just shat all over us with this stupid post," I say, glancing around at everyone else. "'I do not condone their shirts'? Who does he think he is? A congressman releasing an official statement?"

"Basically," Marshall mocks, sitting back in his chair and sighing. "It's Victor Bungle. He's a—"

"Jones, you be nice too." Winter cuts him off as well.

"Are you seeing the comments, though?" Bree asks through gritted teeth.

I skim through. Holy crap. "So many people are eating this up."

"Don't stress," Erica Pott says, shrugging. "Who cares? It's a stupid Instagram post."

"*I* would care," Christina speaks up. "I already checked, and most of the people commenting in support don't even go here, though. It seems like it's a lot of parents, weirdly enough."

"Parents?" Bree squeaks, getting hot. "What the hell is wrong with these parents?"

"Is anyone else pissed he brushed off the e-blast hack, too?" Marshall stands up. Everyone's anger is ticking upward, like we're the Yearbook Mob, ready to grab pitchforks. "Like, he called the e-blast hack a 'mean-spirited prank.' That's it? A prank?"

"It was racist, homophobic harassment," Ali chimes in. "That's what it was."

"Exactly." Marshall points at him in agreement. "As class president, he should be more upset about the e-blast hack than our shirts. That's the *real* controversy."

"Well?" Bree asks, glancing around. "What should we do?"

"Alert Instagram?" Dustin suggests.

"But it's not *harassment* harassment."

"Should we tell Principal Burger?" Christina asks. "Would he do something about it?"

"Doubt it."

"Wait." Bree is clicking her pen maniacally, deep in thought. She has the same look in her eyes as she did in my bedroom figur-

ing out which construction worker snapped the pic of the promposal wall. "It's the end of the year, and we still have funds left in
our class account. . . ."

The room falls silent as heads turn to Winter, who looks up
from her computer while crunching on a carrot. "And?"

"*And*," Bree continues, "there's probably enough money left for
nine days' worth of plain white shirts for a class of twenty-five
kids. . . ."

Winter's eyes glide back to her computer, as her lips curl into a
smile she's trying hard to hide. "Your call, editor-in-chief."

TEN DAYS

Bree has to stay after school for a bit to finish up some Yearbook stuff. Usually I'd either make Marshall take me back to the Brandstones' or—if he has track practice, the weather's decent, and I have a new playlist to listen to—I'd walk. But today I weirdly don't mind hanging out at RLHS after the last bell rings.

And believe me: That's definitely a first.

I snag a pop out of the gym vending machine and head to Bree's car to hang out on the hood because it's a nice day and my endorphins aren't in the dumpster. A bunch of people stop to talk to me about my GAY FOR ALI shirts and Victor Bungle's obnoxious post, which went viral around school in just a few hours.

"His post was *asinine*, Sky."

"I support you and Rashid, Baker!"

"Victor's an idiot."

"Don't stop with the shirts, bro, I love it."

"I heard the whole Yearbook class is going to wear countdown shirts too. Is that really happening?"

I woke up in the same body, in the same town—but somehow, this isn't my life. This *can't* be my life. Jocks who didn't know my name a few weeks ago are now going out of their way to assure me they have my back? Freshmen nervously complimenting my shirt, like I'm locally famous enough to be intimidating?

Me? My life? No. Couldn't be.

This is bonkers.

"Hey, Sky," Teddy says, wandering up to Bree's car.

Butterflies.

No. I cannot be getting butterflies!

You'd think my Ali obsession would have taught me a lesson in crushing on unavailable straight boys. But apparently my tingling insides didn't learn a thing.

He's got on supershort shorts and a long-sleeve Rock Ledge track shirt that almost fits his bulky, skyscraper torso like a crop top. My guess is our broke athletic department ran out of his size. "How's it going?" he asks.

"Great," I say, sitting up on the hood and shielding my eyes from the sun with my hand. "Marshall's already on his way to practice."

"I know," he says, resting against the passenger-side door.

Teddy came over here to talk? Just to me?

"Oh, okay, cool," I say, clearing my throat and trying to sound a little less gay. Which, come to think of it, is ridiculous, considering my shirt *literally* points to the fact that I'm into a dude. I take a swig of my pop. "What's up?"

"In the car on our way to the movies, you mentioned you liked *To All the Boys I've Loved Before*, right?"

The question totally throws me. I tense up a bit. "Yeah."

He cracks a smile and pulls out his phone, tapping the screen. "I came across this and thought of you." He shows me the screen.

It's a Twitter account called No Context: To All the Boys I've Loved Before.

This time, unlike in the back seat of Bree's car, I can't hide my excitement. I squeal, nearly choking on my Coke.

"Yes!" I snatch the phone from his fingertips, laughing. "I saw this a couple months ago and was *dying*."

The premise of the account is pretty stupid, to be honest. It's just screengrabs from the movie turned into memes that are especially hilarious out of context. But it's the kind of Internet-stupid stuff that I'm constantly DMing Bree; it's basically how we communicate.

Honestly, it's downright shocking that Teddy—shot-putting, chest-bumping Teddy—would also eat this up.

"I especially love that one," he chuckles, pointing to a meme that combines a Peter Kavinsky quote with a pic of Baby Yoda.

I snort—and immediately cover my nose with my hand, turning pink.

"You need to see the sequel," Teddy says. "I'm telling you."

"Yeah?" I say—as if I haven't rewatched it three times already. "It's good?"

"*So* good." He takes his phone, adjusting the straps on his backpack. "I've got to run to track practice."

"And then you'll just *keep* running when you get there," I try—and fail miserably—at making a joke.

"Huh?"

"Never mind." I shake my head.

He laughs. "Later, dude."

"Bye."

He jogs off to the track while the butterflies in my stomach do nosedives.

Teddy is a fan of *To All the Boys*? He just went up roughly 10,000 percent in my book.

The parking lot eventually empties out. After snagging a hoodie out of Bree's back seat, I jump back up onto the car and stare at these wisps of white clouds hovering above. They feel just barely beyond my reach.

Just a few days ago, I was hiding away in the Brandstones' basement, refusing to leave. I thought my life was over. Or, at the very least, I thought my senior year was over—whatever was left of it. I didn't think I'd ever be able to return to RLHS, or look Ali in the face, or be more open about gay stuff with Marshall. But I did all those things.

And it feels . . . *good.*

I don't think I believe in God or an afterlife, so it's bonkers to imagine the whole hilarious Hollywood cliché of my dad looking down on me and being all proud, or that he's somehow working behind the heavenly scenes to make all this happen, or whatever. I'm being ridiculous, even letting my mind wander down that road. But it's like he somehow knows what's going on. It's weird. I miss him, is what it comes down to. It's strange missing someone you hardly even knew though. I guess I miss the dad I've been learning about since meeting Charlie.

"Is that how you got your name?"

I bolt upright, clutching my chest. Now it's Dan standing next to Bree's car.

"Sorry," he says, embarrassed and shrinking further into his hoodie. "I didn't mean to scare you."

"It's okay," I say, running my hands through my hair and trying to look less startled than I am. "W-What did you ask me?"

He squints into the sunlight. "Is that how you got your name? Like, after the literal sky?"

"Um." I look up again. The wisps of clouds have already disintegrated. "I don't know, actually. My dad named me, I'm told."

He nods but doesn't saying anything back.

"She's working on Yearbook stuff, but she should be out soon," I note, assuming Dan's looking for Bree.

"I know."

Marshall's *and* Bree's new besties are going out of their way to talk to me today?

It gets quiet. And then it gets awkward.

"So," I continue. "How's it going?"

"I'm good. How about you?"

"Pretty good, pretty good." More silence. More awkwardness. It's getting kind of unbearable. "Can I . . . help you out with some—"

"I'm wondering—launch—GLOW?" he word vomits in a rush.

"Huh?"

"Sorry—*again*." He buries his face in his hands, flustered and overwhelmed. I'm just now realizing he's nervous as hell. "That came out way too fast. I wanted to ask if you'd help me launch GLOW here? Like, at school?"

"What's GLOW?"

"Gay, Lesbian, or Whatever."

"What?"

"Gay, Lesbian, or Whatever. GLOW."

"Oh." I've never heard of GLOW before.

"It's a group for LGBTQ students. It's like Gay-Straight Alliance, but less emphasis on the straight."

Oh. Dan's telling me he's gay.

"I'm honored," I laugh. "Of course I'll help you start GLOW. That sounds amazing. And also, welcome to the gay club—er, the *openly* gay club, anyway."

He bites his lip. "Actually, I'm not gay. I like girls."

"Gotcha. So you're bi?"

"No, I just like girls. I'm a trans guy."

Wow, way to royally mess this up, Sky.

"Sorry," I say, shaking my head, embarrassed. "I feel like an idiot."

"It's okay." He cracks a smile. I can see the relief spreading across his face. "He/him pronouns still work great, just so you know."

"Awesome." I scooch over to give him room to sit on the hood. "Thank you for telling me. I'm happy you did."

I really do feel like an idiot, though.

What's the expression my mom used to say? "Assuming makes an ass out of you and me," or whatever? I'm definitely feeling like a giant ass right now for deciding—without ever having a real conversation with him—that Dan was in the gay boat with me. I think it's the timid and slightly terrified energy he gave off; it reminded me of myself, when I get caught up in walking the straight way down the hall, or sounding less gay, or carrying my books like a guy is supposed to. We've both been struggling to bury our otherness beneath the surface, but I shouldn't have assumed our otherness was the same.

"Are you out to anyone else?" I ask him.

"I mean, I'm out to everyone, technically, but everyone assumes I'm cis," he explains, joining me on the car and pulling his hood away from his face. The sunshine strikes his olive cheeks and chin. "I came out at my last school. It was a mess. I couldn't be there a single second more, so I bounced."

"I'm sorry," I say. "People suck."

"They really do."

"So Rock Ledge is sort of like your fresh start, huh?"

"Maybe? I'm *trying* to make it my fresh start, at least." He pauses. "It's like, it's great being seen as the guy I really am, but no one knows I'm trans, so I've kind of traded one closet for another. You know? I still get weird looks from people—like they're trying to figure me out. It's as if they think the new kid has a secret." He shrugs.

Dan's describing *me*. And I feel awful about it.

Marshall and I had speculated about his sexuality in the food court and judged him for ignoring us. Why did I jump to conclusions before letting Dan tell me his own story? I wish I could go back to January and be there for him from the start.

"Well." I try to find the right words. "You don't owe anyone an explanation. If you feel like telling someone you're trans, go for it. But if you don't, it's none of their business anyway."

"Oh yeah? Do you have a lot of experience coming out as trans?"

"No, I—I'm just trying to support you—"

"Sky, I know." His lips crack into a smile. "I'm just messing with you."

Dan crosses his feet and tugs at the drawstrings of his hoodie.

I catch a whiff of the fragrance he's wearing, which reminds me of grapefruit, as he lets out an almost silent sigh. I hope he's exhaling at least a bit of the burden he's been carrying around since moving to Rock Ledge.

"Does Bree know?" I ask him.

"Yeah, she does," he says. "But no other students do. Maybe don't tell anyone? At least for now."

I do the thing where I zip my lips shut with my fingertips.

We sit for a minute soaking in the nice breeze and the chirping birds and the dwarfing sky above. I have questions, because I've never met an openly trans person before. Hell, I've barely met any out gay people. Like, when did he know he was trans? And *how* did he know he was trans? I never had a big, gay epiphany moment—where I, like, saw John Boyega on a red carpet and thought, *Yep, that's for me!* It was a slow revelation kind of thing. I wonder if it was the same way for Dan. But now's not the time for me to pry.

"Those gay shirts you've all been wearing are incredible, by the way," he says, breaking the silence. "Ten days. The Beach-Bum Party, right?"

"Yeah."

"Are you actually going to ask Ali, though? Isn't he straight?"

Before I respond, the school doors creak open across the lot, and Bree appears carrying her bags and books. She spots us sitting together and hustles over with a big smile.

"I told him," Dan says as soon as she's within earshot. I can hear the relief in his voice.

Bree's face melts into pure elation. "Yay!" She throws her books onto the hood of the car—they immediately slide off onto the asphalt—and wraps her arms around Dan's middle. "Feel better?"

"Totally," Dan says, cheeks still flushed.

Bree climbs onto the car and nestles into the space between us, before looking up at me. "I told you Sky is a good one."

My heart swells a bit.

I haven't always been one of the good ones. Especially when it comes to Dan. But I'll do better.

The three of us sit a bit longer, getting our first sunburns of the year and enjoying the freedoms of an empty parking lot. Bree recaps everything we know about the e-blast hack and its aftermath—how Rence Bloomington had to have been the one who took the photo of the promposal wall and passed it on to Cliff; how everyone in Yearbook will also be wearing gay countdown shirts in solidarity after Victor Bungle's ridiculous post today; how Cliff and his cronies have been ignoring us all week, and why that's honestly the best part of all this.

Dan is following along excitedly, watching Bree's mile-a-minute lips meander through each plot point, trying to keep up. I like him, I decide.

I really like him.

Because if being gay in ass-backward Rock Ledge is like running a marathon, being trans must be like finishing one of those triathlon races where you run twenty-six miles *before* biking and swimming another million more.

Dan is the epitome of tough. And I can appreciate tough.

NINE DAYS

After a day of preparing and buying supplies, Yearbookers have commandeered the Brandstones' basement with handfuls of markers, mounds of brand-new white T-shirts—bought in bulk, courtesy of the remaining class funds—and lots and lots of glitter. Too much glitter. Thelma will be sparkling like a four-legged angel for days.

Except for a corner where there's some construction equipment, most of the main basement area is still empty of any furniture or storage, so it's the perfect spot for twenty teenagers to fan out with art supplies. Mr. and Mrs. Brandstone don't seem to care one bit—or they're *really* good actors, which seems more probable.

"Again, thank you." I overhear Winter near the bottom of the basement steps, Bree's parents standing nearby. "I planned on doing this in my classroom, but Bree invited all the kids over here before I even knew about it."

"Yep." Mr. Brandstone sighs, sipping from his bottle of beer. "Sounds like Bree."

Winter footed the bill for a few giant sub sandwiches, chips, and soda. Dustin hooked up his Spotify to speakers, and some people are dancing and singing along. Petey and Ray keep peeking down the stairs—curious why a swarm of high schoolers has taken over their home, but too intimidated to actually come down the steps—and Clare has texted Bree several times for us to keep it down (apparently there's a *Chopped* marathon on).

My bedroom door is closed, of course.

I don't want the promposal wall becoming A Whole Big Thing, even though everyone's already seen the pic of it in the e-blast. I wouldn't really care if someone wandered in there, but it's not like I want to show it off.

"Wait, who do we say we're gay for?" Christina asks the room, a pink marker in her hand. "Ali? Sky? Or do I have to pick a girl because I'm a girl?"

Bree and I look at each other.

"I don't know." Bree shrugs, popping a potato chip into her mouth. "Whoever you're kind of gay for."

The class starts buzzing in side discussions.

"Can it be a famous person?"

"Does it have to be someone at our school?"

"What about if we keep it to just our Yearbook class?"

"Let's stick with seniors?"

"Everybody!" Marshall announces, standing on the tips of his toes. "Write down whoever you want to write down—classmates, politicians, musicians, boys, girls, whatever!"

"There are no rules to this!" Ali follows up, wandering around with his hands crossed behind his back, gazing at people's work like an art critic. "Just be gay for someone—or some*thing*."

I'm kind of relieved.

Because on one hand, it would have been flattering to have every Yearbooker being gay for me on their shirts. But all that extra attention for the next eight days would have been brutal for a 70 percent introvert like me.

A lot of people are going gay for public figures like Seth Rogen, Michael B. Jordan, and Michelle Obama, or superheroes like Batman, Storm, and Iron Man. A few people are choosing other Yearbookers, who reciprocate the favor on their own shirts. A couple are even choosing teachers, which could get a little dicey and borderline inappropriate, but that's not my problem. Some are putting the same name down on all the remaining shirts before the Beach-Bum Party; others are mixing it up with a different person each day of the countdown.

But the point is, Yearbookers have my back. Mine *and* Ali's. And it's amazing. At one point, Ali and I catch each other's eyes across the basement and grin, both feeling the love. We both may have gotten screwed over by Cliff—but now we're fighting back.

I don't have much to do because I already made my remaining shirts, all GAY FOR ALI. I'm mostly just moseying around, eating chips, and poking fun at everyone's terrible handwriting skills alongside Dan. Even though he's not in Yearbook, he decided to come over and help everyone else with their ideas.

"Gay for . . . Joe Jonas?" says this guy, Tim, bouncing his shirt idea off Dan.

Dan thinks for a second. "I think you're more of a Nick guy."

"You know what?" Tim nods slowly in agreement. "You're right."

See? This is why I love Dan.

"This is so great, Sky," Mrs. Brandstone says proudly as I pass, standing with her mug of evening decaf coffee, watching everyone work. She asks me something else, but I spot Teddy bouncing down the stairs and immediately zone out.

You know when you see someone you've been around a dozen times before, but you feel like you're just *now* seeing them for the first time? That's me.

The butterflies are more like a full-on stomach roller coaster.

Teddy's wearing this badass beige suit with a maroon tie, like he wandered off the red carpet for the DuVernay film and came straight to the Brandstones' basement. His thick, wavy hair is styled back and parted to one side—a totally different look than the big, mangled mop I'm used to seeing post-track-practice.

I'm not the only to notice either.

"Damn, Teddy!" Christina bellows across the room.

"Who are you trying to impress?" Dan teases him with a smile.

The whole class breaks out into "ooo's" and "ow-ows!" Ali rushes over to give him a fist bump. Marshall whistles seductively, and Mr. Brandstone starts to slow clap, spilling his beer. Teddy turns the brightest shade of red I've ever seen on a human face.

"How'd you come up with it?" Mrs. Brandstone asks.

I forgot she was talking to me.

I quickly peel my eyes away from Teddy. "Come up with what?"

"The idea for the shirts."

"Oh, it was Ali." I nod toward my former crush, who's helping Dustin spell out "George Stephanopoulos" on a shirt. "He came up with the whole 'gay for' thing."

"They're clever."

"Yeah."

In the chaos of this surreal week, I almost forgot that Mrs. Brandstone is responsible for this. Like, *all* of it, really. If she hadn't given me her yearbook, I never would have met Charlie. I never would have gotten tough, gone back to school, or wanted revenge on Cliff. And I definitely never would have agreed to wear these shirts around school.

Now is the time to go there. To confess I know the yearbook is hers, to find out why she couldn't just be up-front with me from the get-go.

"You graduated from Rock Ledge, right?" I prod, taking a step closer toward her.

"Sure did," she says, sipping her coffee. "Feels like a lifetime ago. Treasure it while it lasts, hon."

"What year did you graduate again?"

She's grinning, watching Christina mark up a shirt that she says will read GAY FOR FRENCH FRIES in gold glitter. "1997. Long before you and Bree were crawling around."

"So, you went to school with my dad, then?"

That gets her attention.

She turns away from Christina's french fries shirt, adjusts her red glasses. "I did."

"How come we've never talked about that before?"

She inhales long and slow, before letting it out at an equal pace. "I didn't know if you wanted to."

"Why wouldn't I?"

"I didn't want to risk making you uncomfortable."

Well, now I *am* uncomfortable.

"Sorry," I say. I'm not sure why I felt the need to apologize. "I'll start talking about him more, I think."

"You don't need to on my behalf."

"I know," I say. "But I want to."

She smiles. "You know, I—"

But Marshall hollers at me from across the basement.

My eyes dart between him and Mrs. Brandstone.

"Go ahead," she says, smiling and nodding in Marshall's direction. "We'll chat later."

I zigzag through a myriad of bodies strung out across the floor to Marshall and Bree, who are hovering above Teddy sitting cross-legged, a pile of shirts in front of him.

"Tell him it's fine if he makes a shirt, will you?" Marshall asks me. "He's being all weird about it."

I look down at Teddy; his face is still glowing red from all the catcalls he got a minute ago. "Why wouldn't it be fine?" I ask.

"I don't know." Teddy glances around, a hesitant smile on his face. "This is a Yearbook thing. I'm intruding."

"Hardly." I sit down across from him and steal a bite of Bree's sandwich. "I know we can be a cultish group, but the more the merrier. And he might make a shirt too." I point to Dan, who's laughing with Dustin on the other side of the basement.

"*But*," Bree says, ripping her sandwich out of my hands and taking a bite too, "if you make one, Teddy, you have to commit. You have to make a shirt for every day leading up to the Beach-Bum Party."

"Who says?" I ask.

"I don't make the rules." She shrugs.

"You literally just made up that rule," Marshall jabs.

She shrugs again.

Ainsley arrives at the bottom of the stairs a minute later, overwhelmed at the sight in front of her. She says hi to Ali and steals a swig of his pop before zigzagging her way toward us through the bodies on the floor.

"Hey, everyone," she says, hugging Bree and pecking Marshall on the lips. "Um, this is *amazing*. It's like a shirt-making factory down here, and Ali's the floor manager." She grins. "The whole school is going to lose it."

"Principal Cheeseburger probably will too," Bree adds, grinning mischievously.

"Tell Teddy he should make one," Marshall says to Ainsley. "He doesn't want to because he thinks it's a *Yearbook* thing."

"Teddy, you should definitely make a shirt," Ainsley confirms.

"Even if I'm not in the class?"

"I'm not either!" she argues. "But I *am* a little bit gay for Camila Cabello, and I plan on making a shirt that says so."

Marshall and Ainsley start to float off into their own little world, as expected.

"So, what's with the suit?" Bree asks Teddy.

Teddy glances down, like he forgot what he was wearing. "Oh, I had a recital tonight."

"Recital?"

"I play piano."

Teddy? A musician?

I never would have pegged him for a pianist. But then again, I never would have pegged him as an avid fan of rom-coms. I'm learning in real time just how wrong stereotypes can be.

"How'd it go?" Bree asks.

He scrunches his face. "Not great."

"I'm sure it wasn't *that* bad."

"My palms get real sweaty when I'm nervous," he says, flashing his hands at me and Bree, his green eyes widening. "And my fingers slip all over the keys."

"Hashtag relatable." Bree nods. "Every time I have to present something in class, I turn into a gross, sweaty mess."

"Right?"

Teddy is getting flirty with Bree, I think. And between that and sitting next to Marshall and Ainsley, I definitely feel like the big, gay fifth wheel again—just like we're back in the dining room at Ali's party. But this time I don't have Franklin the cat to distract me.

Thelma is around here somewhere, though. I stand up to leave, but—

"Sky?" Teddy speaks up as I'm drifting away, flattening out the shirt with his apparently sweaty palms. "What goes where again?"

I sit back down.

Mr. Brandstone calls for Bree because someone spilled a two-liter of Sprite and he wants help cleaning it up before Louise drinks it all and makes herself sick. Now it's just me and Teddy sitting face-to-face.

I'm suddenly . . . nervous, I think?

Yep, nerves. The butterflies are back.

"There are no hard and fast rules," I clarify. "But if you do it like most everyone else, put the countdown in black marker here. If this is your shirt for tomorrow, it'll read DAYS LEFT: 8."

"Right here?"

"Yep. And then, in the color of your choice—"

"I like orange."

"—in orange, write who you're gay for across the chest."

He squints at the shirt in thought, biting his lower lip, before looking up at me. "Who's a good person to put down?"

His eyes are so *green*. I've never noticed how much they pop. It's like the insides of two kiwis staring at me.

"Um." I look around at the rest of the class. "It can be anyone. A lot of people are using celebrities. Cassy put Michelle Obama. Dustin, being Dustin, put down Mr. Zemp. Christina is gay for french fries."

He laughs. "I'm going to keep it simple and stick with you—the founder of Rock Ledge's gay movement."

"Oh yeah?"

"Yeah."

He hunches over the shirt to get to work, and I get a whiff of his cologne or his shampoo or something. It makes my heart pound a little bit faster. Just like with Dan's, the scent fits him.

"There," he says, straightening back up and looking down at the floor proudly.

GAY FOR SKY is scrawled across the chest of the shirt in bright orange letters.

"Perfect," he says.

"Perfect," I agree. "Also, um . . . thanks for messaging me after the whole, you know"—I gesture at the chaos around us—"the whole e-blast mess." I didn't plan on bringing it up right now, but it just started spilling out of me.

"Oh." He's turning red again. "Of course."

"It was really nice of you."

He smiles.

I smile too.

"Teddy! Settle a bet for us!" Ainsley yells, giggling and motioning for him to come over. "Marshall thinks there are ten planets in the solar system."

Teddy rolls his very green kiwi eyes while grinning and scooches away to Ainsley, his gay shirt in-hand.

I'm not entirely sure what happened, but I'm irrationally excited that Teddy isn't too much of a straight guy to be gay for me. At least on a T-shirt.

NINE DAYS

D amn it!" Christina belts, her high-pitched voice slicing through the music and chatter in the Brandstones' basement like a butcher knife. I jolt and turn her way, along with everyone else. She starts to laugh, but also looks completely devastated.

"What?" Ali asks from across the basement.

She holds up her shirt so we all can see that it reads GAY FOR FRANCH FRIES.

The basement erupts in laughter.

"You all suck," she yells, giggling along too.

"What are *franch* fries, Christina?" Dustin prods.

"Bite me," she says, whipping out her sparkly, bedazzled phone to take a pic of her gay shirt fail.

"Are franch fries just french fries, but dipped in ranch?" Ali prods.

"Screw you."

Wait. Hold on.

Her bedazzled, sparkly phone. . . .

The Monday Christina took out the same sparkly phone in Trig to show Marshall her Memories account comes rushing back. She couldn't log in that day—the day of the e-blast hack.

"Christina!" I belt out, way too loudly.

"Whoa. I'm right here, Sky, no need to screech."

I scooch over to where she's sitting.

"If you're about to tear into my franch fries shirt too," she warns as I get close, "I will see myself out—"

"No, no," I say, lowering my voice. "Remember when you had your Memories issues in Trig? Like, you couldn't sign in or something?"

"No."

I sigh. "Think. We were working in small groups in Kam's class, and you came over to Marshall to see if he could fix—"

"Oh right." She nods. "Yeah, that was weird."

"What happened, exactly?"

"I tried signing in that morning, but the system had locked me out. I ended up having to create a new password. I think it said something like—" she thinks "'Your account operated on an untrusted computer,' or something like that."

"Had that ever happened to you with Memories before?"

"Never."

"Yeah, same." I bend in closer to her. "Do you realize that was the same Monday of the e-blast hack?"

Her jaw drops. "Are you saying . . ."

"I *don't know* what I'm saying. But that seems strange. Right?" I glance over to Ainsley and Marshall, who are now disgustingly cozied up with each other, their arms and legs tangled up in knots. "Hey, Marshall."

He looks over.

"Emergency meeting," I whisper-yell, attempting to avoid anyone else noticing. "Hurry."

Me, Christina, and Marshall slip away into my bedroom.

"Oh my God, the wall!" Christina says, grinning, staring at the promposal ideas. "It's even more glorious in person."

"Yeah, yeah," I mutter, flipping open my laptop and signing in to Memories.

"I meant it as a compliment, Sky!" She plops down next to me on my futon, ruffling my hair. "Adorbs. Truly a work of art."

"I was in the middle of an amazing cuddle session before being so rudely interrupted," Marshall jabs, closing the door behind him and crunching on some chips. "What's this *emergency meeting* about?"

"Remember when I couldn't sign in to Memories that one morning because someone on an untrusted computer or whatever signed in to my account?" Christina asks.

"Sure."

"*That* was the same morning of the hack," I add.

Marshall stops eating his chips. "Oh."

"Yeah."

"Could that mean something?" Christina asks, bouncing on the futon. "What does it all *mean*, Marshall?"

"Untrusted log in," he says, more to himself than to us. "I think you'd get that notification when a different computer or phone you don't normally use signed in to your Memories account. That's why you got booted and had trouble logging in. Wait a minute!" Marshall's face lights up as he falls onto the other side of me, dragging the computer onto his lap. "I can't believe I forgot about this. Memories has sort of, like, a log-in sheet thing, where you can see what day and time every user in our class signs in to Memories and when they sign out." He clicks around in different boxes for a minute or so, until a spreadsheet finally appears. "Aha!"

"Whoa," I breathe, looking down.

"I didn't know Memories had this!" Christina says, craning her neck to look.

"It has a treasure trove of useless features—many of which Winter doesn't even know about," Marshall says. "But every now and then, one comes in handy."

He starts scrolling down, going further back in time. I notice that during the school week—and especially during the hour of Yearbook class—there are a bunch of names signed in to the system. But on weekends, the log-in sheet is almost entirely blank— except for our type A editor-in-chief, Bree—because no one is spending their Sundays cranking out yearbook spreads in Memories. Makes sense.

But then we get to the weekend right before the e-blast hack.

"Look," Marshall says, pointing to that Saturday—the day after Ali's party, when we went to the DuVernay movie and Bree was in a foul mood. There's only *one* name appearing on the login between that Friday evening and Monday morning.

"'Christina Alpine,'" I read.

"Huh?" Christina gapes. "What the fuck?"

"User Christina Alpine logged in to Memories that evening at 7:12 p.m." Marshall looks from the screen to her.

"That's horseshit," she says, straightening back up, looking confused as hell. "There's no way I would be working on Yearbook stuff on a Saturday night. Literally. Zero chance of it."

"What were you doing that Saturday?"

She thinks. "The day after Ali's party . . . oh! I was at Tana's. She had a chill get-together. We all baked cookies, shared a blunt, and watched *Billy on the Street*."

"And you're sure you never signed on to work while you were at Tana's?"

She laughs. "Seriously? You guys. I barely work on Yearbook stuff while I'm *in* Yearbook, let alone when I'm stoned and . . ." She gasps. "Wait. Oh damn . . ."

"What?"

"Oh my God."

The door creaks open and Bree's face appears. "Oh, here you are," she says, walking in. "Why are you all in here—"

"Close the door! Close it!" Marshall squeals, motioning for her to come in.

She does. "Okay, okay, calm down." Bree reads our faces. "What happened?"

Christina stands slowly. "Cliff Norquest," she mutters.

"I knew it," I say, my stomach dropping.

"Wait, what?" Bree panics, glancing around at the three of us. "What'd that idiot do now?"

"I was at Tana's," Christina continues, "and Cliff randomly showed up uninvited with his awful friend who wears cowboy boots . . . what's his name? Brendon!"

"Pastures?"

"Yes. Brendon is friends with Mary, which is why they showed up, I guess. Anyway. It doesn't matter." She thinks for a second. "Cliff said he heard a rumor there was a really bad photo of him on the wrestling yearbook page. And I assured him there wasn't, because I was assigned that page, so I, *of all people*, would know."

"Fact check: correct," Bree says. "I just edited the wrestling page today. There's not even a picture of Cliff on it, except for the team photo. But hold up—what's going on?"

"So," Christina ignores her and continues, "Cliff gets all worked up over it, claiming I'm lying and demanding to see the page for himself. To shut him up, I signed in to my Memories account using his phone to show him the spread really fast . . ." Her face scrunches into pure guilt.

"Why wouldn't you use your own phone to sign in?" I ask.

"Because we were in the kitchen, and my phone was in the den downstairs. It just seemed easier to use his."

"Okay, for real," Bree pleads. "What the hell is going on?"

"We have more evidence it was Cliff," Marshall answers. "Now we know *how* he did it—hacked the system, leaked those photos."

"But wait. How does my story mean Cliff did it?"

"It's another sign pointing to him," I say.

"A big one," Marshall adds. "You can only edit the e-blast in Memories, and the timing on the log-in spreadsheet seems to sync with your story. You probably used his phone to sign in and show him the wrestling page at about seven p.m., right?"

Christina thinks. "Yeah, that checks out." She looks over at me and Bree. "I'm so sorry."

"*That's* why you were having log-in issues on Monday morning in Trig," Marshall notes with a satisfactory grin. "It's a security measure. Memories makes you sign in and change your password if an untrusted computer or phone—in this case, Cliff's—accessed your account."

Holy eff.

I cross off another item on my mental checklist.

~~The person somehow got a photo of the promposal wall.~~

~~The person somehow accessed Memories to hack the e-blast.~~

The person somehow got the pic of me and Ali at Ali's party.

"I wish I had remembered all this sooner," Christina says, defeated.

"It's okay!" I say, standing to jump up and down, feeling a little bit like Veronica Mars. "This is good news, franch fry. We're one step closer to nailing Cliff."

"Now we know *how* he hacked the system and *how* he got the photo of the promposal wall in the first place," I explain.

"Stupid Rence Bloomington," Bree spits angrily.

"All we need to figure out is how he got the picture of Sky and Ali at Ali's party—then he's a goner," Marshall says, turning to Christina. "This all stays top secret, though, okay?"

Christina nods, excited to be in the know. "Of course."

The bedroom door bursts open. Ali is standing there, mustard spilled all down the front of his shirt. "Oh, *this* is where the party's at," he says, looking around. "What did I miss?"

EIGHT DAYS

I was certain at least a couple of Yearbookers would chicken out. But every last one of them, plus Ainsley, Dan, and Teddy, end up wearing their gay shirts on Friday. The whole school is buzzing over it. It's like, if the four of us made waves on Monday, today's a full-blown tsunami.

I overheard Mr. Kam complaining to another teacher that Principal Burger is getting a ton of calls from faux-concerned parents. Rumor has it that one of the religious student groups—yeah, we have, like, five of them at RLHS—wants to launch a petition. (Demanding what? No one is exactly sure.) Even the student Newspaper staff is running around getting quotes from Yearbook kids for a piece on the e-blast and the Victor Bungle drama. And if the Yearbook and Newspaper kids are working together? You know shit's getting real.

Between the shirts and getting one enormous step further in Operation: Pin It on He Who Must Not Be Named (Bree never did offer up a more succinct name), I'm on cloud nine.

Me, Bree, and Marshall always eat lunch in the hallway outside Winter's, but today we want to make sure we flex our shirt solidarity in Victor's face. We decide to sync up with Ainsley and Teddy and claim a spot in the cafeteria for once, only a few tables away from where our brownnoser class president habitually pounds cheeseburgers with the rest of the self-righteous student council.

"Should we go confront him?" Bree asks us, staring at Victor with a look that suggests he dognapped Thelma.

"No," I say firmly.

"Why not?"

"Yeah, why not?" Marshall says with a burp, surprised I'd rather Bree not start World War III in the middle of lunch.

"Let our shirts speak for themselves," I urge, popping some Cheetos into my mouth. "The shirts are messing with Cliff, aren't they?"

"Maybe," Bree mutters, eyes still glued, unblinking, on Victor like a cheetah stalking her prey. "I haven't seen He Who Must Not Be Named all week. I think he's hiding from me."

"Cliff is usually marching around these halls screaming for attention," Teddy says, biting down on a pickle. "But he's been keeping a very low profile lately."

"See?" I wave my hand in front of Bree's face to take her attention away from Bungle. "Cliff has been avoiding me, too. And now Bungle knows his stupid post won't shut us up either."

"Yeah," she says, slowly prying her eyes away from Bungle's table. "You're probably right."

She's not looking at him anymore, but I can tell she's still distracted. I decide to shift subjects. "Anyway, Petey asked if we'll play *Smash Bros.* with him after school. A chill Friday sounds great after how nuts this week has been. We can order Mario's or ask Clare if she'd make her nachos. You down?"

"Can't," she says, tapping at her phone. "I'm going to Dan's."

"He's gay, right?" Marshall blurts, licking mashed potatoes off his spork.

Ugh. Here we go. We might as well be back in the LMEP food court again.

I know Marshall doesn't truly care about Dan's sexual orientation, but the continued speculation is all the more irritating—especially after Dan opened up to me about what he's been through.

Bree rolls her eyes. "Marshall, just . . . don't."

"Don't what?"

"Speculate," I answer for Bree. "You did this same thing in the food court. Remember?"

He drops his chin at us. "Guys, c'mon. You know I don't care. I want Dan to feel comfortable being himself, is all."

Our table falls silent.

Bree seems flustered. I'm trying to bite my tongue to stop the conversation from spiraling into a bigger fight. Teddy and Ainsley both seem very preoccupied with their sandwiches.

"I'm sorry, Bree," Marshall says softly. "Honestly, I didn't mean to sound like an ass—"

"It's fine," Bree says, avoiding eye contact.

The bell rings. Bree immediately stands and slips into the crowd pouring out from the cafeteria. I nearly spill my Cheetos everywhere trying to catch up to her.

"Hey." My hand lands on her shoulder. "You okay?"

"I'm fine." She's speeding down the hall and won't look at me.

"Marshall doesn't mean anything by it," I say. "He doesn't get why it's rude to ask those sorts of questions."

"It's more than rude. It's intrusive."

"You're right."

"The last thing Dan needs right now is dudes like Marshall gossiping behind his back about who he really is."

"Totally. But hey—" I tug her sleeve. "Are you sure everything's okay?"

She stops dead in her tracks, turns, and buries her face into my shoulder. "Yes, I'm sorry. It's just"—she comes up for air—"Dan's gone through so much since leaving his last school behind. Now he's trying to find his place here, and it's just been . . . it's been a lot."

"I bet."

"I hate that he can't just be himself free of judgment. You know?"

"I definitely do."

Her eyes catch mine. "Of course you do."

"Do you want me to talk to Marshall about it?"

"No, it's fine. I'm not mad at him. I'm just . . . yeah, it'll be okay." She brushes some Cheeto dust off my shoulder with a half-hearted smile. "I'll see you in Winter's."

She darts off.

Bree and Marshall must talk it out—or Bree bottles it up for another time, which she does a lot—but, either way, they're laughing with each other over some classic Vine videos in class a half hour later.

Something's definitely up, though.

Because the three of us get into beefs all the time, no big deal. But Bree seemed especially rattled over Dan.

In Winter's class, Marshall bends in my direction but keeps his eyes on the Memories spread he's working on. "If you don't end up playing *Smash* with Petey, want to go to LMEP after school with me and Ainsley?" He slaps a filter onto a photo of the freshmen honor roll group to make their teeth whiter. "We're seeing the new Bourne."

Playing the role of third wheel would make watching Matt Damon leap between rooftops for two hours even more unbearable, so I decline. But I propose driving with them there so I can take Marshall's car to visit Charlie, who lives close-ish to the theater. I have to finish up his yearbook ad anyway. I could sneakily learn more about my dad again too.

Hell, maybe I'll work up the courage to ask Charlie for his advice on Mars.

Marshall agrees and doesn't even make me chip in for gas.

After school, we run back to his house so he can grab the LMEP gift card I gave him. (He mentions that he'll buy my snacks at Moe's through the end of the year; I think he feels guilty for accepting the gift card from me after we talked things through.) We're about to pull out of Marshall's driveway when the garage door opens and Mr. Jones appears in his yardwork attire, rake in hand.

"Damn it," Marshall sighs from the driver's seat. "Get ready, everyone." He rolls down his window as his dad approaches. "Yeah?"

"How's everyone doing?" Mr. Jones asks, bending in half to see inside the car. His glasses slip down onto the tip of his nose. I have total déjà vu from the night of Ali's party.

"Great." Ainsley smiles.

"Good," I reply.

"Headed to the movies?"

"Yep," Marshall says quickly. "No, we're not drinking, yes, we're buckled up, and yes, I'll be back by curfew."

"You're finally getting good at this—right as you're about to leave the nest," Mr. Jones says, grinning and reaching inside the car to pat Marshall on the back of the neck. He turns to me riding in the back seat. "Hey, Sky."

"Hey, Mr. Jones."

"I like those shirts you've all been wearing."

I tense up. Those shirts? Those *gay* shirts? Marshall's dad likes those *gay shirts*?

"Oh," is all I can think to say. "Thanks."

"It's about time someone puts this town in its place. I'm glad you, Bree, and . . . what's the other kid's name?"

"Ali Rashid."

"Rashid, that's right. I'm glad you're all standing up for yourselves. You won't regret it."

He gives me a wink before standing back up straight, tapping the hood of the car, and reminding Marshall to drive the speed limit.

I'm speechless.

Never in a million years did I think I'd hear a pep talk like that coming from tough-as-nails, polo-shirt-wearing, manly man Mr. Jones.

It's about time someone puts this town in its place.

I can't stop smiling the whole way to Traverse City.

After Marshall and Ainsley jump out at LMEP, I drive to Charlie's, where Bob comes galloping down the driveway to greet me like I'm a regular.

"Hey, Justin," Charlie says as I step into the foyer. "New car?"

"I wish," I say, slipping off my boots. "I don't have my own car. It's just a friend's."

Brian gets home from work a few minutes later, and we end up at the kitchen island again. Charlie pulls out more photos to sort through, even though I thought we picked the final five he wants for the ad the last time I was here. He mostly likes wandering down memory lane, is what I think it is.

Brian's playing bartender and makes the two of them some fancy-ass drinks with gin and what I think is mint, and Adele's playing gently over the speakers. I kind of feel like I'm invading their Friday night date plans or something, and they're being nice and accommodating. Third Wheel Sky, at it again.

"So, how's school going?" Brian asks me.

I almost answer honestly—diving into the e-blast hack, and the promposal wall, and the gay shirts, and figuring out how Cliff pulled it off—until I remember that here, I'm not Sky Baker.

"Same old, same old," I lie instead as Justin.

"I almost asked if you wanted one," Brian says, pointing to his glass and laughing at himself. "You've got what, another three years before you're twenty-one?"

"Yep, unfortunately."

"Yikes."

"We have water, pop, lemonade . . . ," Charlie says, scanning the inside of the open fridge.

"Lemonade would be great, thanks."

My phone buzzes on the countertop.

It's another text from Gus. My stomach flips.

I forgot to respond to his last one. Okay, I've been *telling* myself I keep forgetting to respond. I'm really just dreading it.

hey I'll be in town next week, Gus writes this time. want to grab dinner at Denny's with mom on thurs?

"Everything okay?" Charlie asks, sensing something's up.

I write back sure to Gus and pocket my phone.

"Yeah," I say, rolling my eyes with a forced grin. "Just my brother."

"It looks like you saw a ghost," Brian says.

"We have a complicated relationship."

"No further explanation necessary," Charlie says, nodding. "Unless, of course, you *want* to talk about it. Then I'm all ears."

I laugh, sort of awkwardly, desperate to change the subject. "Nah, another time. I did want to ask you about a medical thing, though."

Charlie peels his eyes away from a stack of old photos, his face hardening with seriousness.

"Not like a *medical* medical thing," I clarify. "Just, like—how does it work to, um, book an appointment with you? At the dermatologist office?"

"I could help you arrange one. Why, what's going on?"

Nerves creep up my spine. "I have this burn scar from when I was a kid."

"Oh yeah?"

"It's pretty ugly."

"Are you on your parents' insurance?"

I don't even know if my mom *has* insurance. I haven't been to the doctor in years.

Charlie sees that I'm struggling to answer. "Don't worry about it. My office can work something out. I could also take a peek at it now, if you don't want to go through the hassle of an appointment."

"Jeez, Charlie," Brian mutters. "Put him on the spot, why don't you?"

"It's fine," I say. "It's just—I haven't shown him to anyone in a while."

"Him?"

"Er—" God, I'm an idiot. My cheeks are getting red. "Yeah, it's sort of weird, but I have a nickname for him. For my scar."

Charlie smiles. "What's the nickname?"

He's a dermatologist. He sees scars all the time, I bet. He's probably seen a lot worse than Mars. I should just do this now.

So I take a deep breath and pull my shirt collar down, revealing the god-awful pinkish splotch covering a chunk of my chest.

"His name is Mars."

"Mars? I like it."

Charlie comes closer to look.

Something happens, though.

His demeanor changes. Like, immediately. He looks all serious, like there's something wrong, or . . . I don't know. It's not what he expected to see? Then he glances at Brian, who doesn't seem to share the same look of concern.

"What?" I ask, kind of panicked. "Does it look bad?"

"No," Charlie says quickly, his confused face melting away into its normal, smiley self. "It doesn't look bad at all."

"What's up with the name Mars, though?" Brian asks, pouring my lemonade, oblivious to the flash of apparent horror that gripped his partner.

"It looks like Mars, is the general idea," I say. "Like, the planet."

Brian's mouth pinches up like it's the cutest thing he's ever heard, before sliding my lemonade toward me across the counter.

"I've seen plenty of scars like Mars before," Charlie says. "I'll set you up with an appointment at my office, if you want. Don't worry about the insurance stuff."

"Sure," I say, nodding. "Thanks."

Brian suggests moving into the den to finish up the ad because it's less chilly in there, so we start collecting the photos to change rooms.

But really, what the heck just happened there?

Because Charlie definitely saw *something*. Does Mars look way worse than even I imagine he does? Is there something else wrong with him? Do I have cancer? Am I *dying*?

"I'll meet you in the den," I say, slipping away to their lavender-scented bathroom off the kitchen.

Standing in front of the mirror, I pull down my shirt collar again to double-check Mars for . . . I don't even know! An abnormality? A second head growing out of the scar tissue? What am I not seeing?

Uh-oh. That boulder of gay gloom that races down the mountain in my mind, crashes in spectacular fashion, and throws me into a mental breakdown? I feel it starting to pick up steam.

No. I can't do that here.

Not here, Sky.

It's just a freaking scar. Yes, an ugly, big one. But still. Just a scar.

Charlie's the doctor, not me, though. Why did he freak out for a second?

I could have imagined it. Maybe what I saw as confusion and alarm was really just his *thinking* face—the way he looks whenever he's examining a new patient, or something.

I tend to overanalyze things, I know. This could be one of those times.

I take a deep breath and pump the brakes on the boulder as best I can.

I imagine giving Louise a belly rub. *Inhale.*

Laughing in my seat at the movies between Marshall and Bree. *Exhale.*

Listening to Winter tell us about her travels when she was younger. *Inhale.*

Once the boulder comes to a complete stop, I turn on the faucet for a second to make it sound like I actually used the bathroom, and leave for the den. But I hear Charlie and Brian hissing back and forth right before I turn the corner to walk in.

"No, it's definitely him," I hear Charlie whisper.

"Are you sure?" Brian replies.

"I'd bet my life on it. It's Sky."

Eff.

Eff, eff, *eff.*

I take a step away from the room and press my back into the wall, pulse racing, mind spinning. Just like that, the boulder is barreling down the mountainside again.

"What are you going to do?" Brian asks after silence grips the room in a choke hold. "You can't bring it up tonight . . ."

"I can't *not* bring it up, though."

Mars gave me away.

It had to have been Mars.

Charlie must have seen him when I was a kid or something. I don't know. I look a lot different from when I was in elementary school, so it makes sense Charlie wouldn't recognize me after all this time. But Mars? Mars hasn't changed at all. Except for expanding as I've grown, he's always looked basically the same.

The boulder crashes.

My eyes begin to water. My heart is pounding in my fingertips. I can't be here. I'm too embarrassed to show my face again.

I creep back into the kitchen, gather my computer and bag, and carefully glide back through the foyer to leave.

"Justin?" I hear Brian ask as I'm closing the front door behind me, and I sprint to Marshall's car.

SIX DAYS

I can't stop thinking about Charlie and Brian all weekend and how royally I effed it all up. I should have just been honest from the start: honest about Mrs. Brandstone's yearbook, honest about my name, honest about my dad.

Honest about everything.

"Why aren't you with my sister?" a suspicious Clare asks me on Sunday night, wrapped up comfortably in her pink unicorn hoodie.

We're on opposite ends of the living room sofa eating the banana bread she just pulled out of the oven, and watching *Buffy* reruns. Well, she's watching *Buffy*—I'm staring down at a phone notification pestering me about a missed call from Charlie. There's no way I'm calling him back. "Embarrassment" doesn't even begin to describe the somersaults my stomach takes every time I relive Friday night's awkwardness in my head.

Bree's doing homework at Dan's, I explain to Clare, and Marshall's helping his dad retile their bathroom.

"Wow," she says, looking at me like I'm the most pathetic thing she's ever seen. "You three really do lead boring lives."

Mrs. Brandstone, sweaty and stressed, walks into the kitchen and drops big paper grocery bags onto the island countertop.

"Where's Bree?" she asks too. I guess me and Bree really are at that level of inseparable where seeing one of us without the other immediately raises alarm. I explain what I just told Clare. Mrs. Brandstone can sense something's up.

"Everything all right?" she asks, unloading an unjustifiably large number of corncobs from the grocery bags.

I should talk to her about Charlie and her yearbook, now that the secret's out. But I'm so ashamed from lying to them about it—and, in retrospect, running away from their house for a *second* time—I don't want to bring it up.

"Yeah, I'm fine," I lie. "Just sort of have the Sunday blues, is all."

I toss and turn all night. But Charlie and Brian are only responsible for some of my nighttime anxiety, really.

I'm mostly dreading dinner with Gus and my mom. Because what is there to talk about? I have nothing to say to them.

"Big news, Sky High!" Ali appears at my side as we're leaving Trig on Monday. He's wearing his latest GAY FOR SKY shirt, and I'm wearing my latest GAY FOR ALI one. It's weird how normal this whole totally abnormal thing has become.

The countdown's at five days today.

Five effing days until the Senior Beach-Bum Party.

"Carolyn is finally back," he continues, swinging his overstuffed backpack onto his back. "I asked her if she remembers anything useful about my party."

Oh shit, that's right.

Between everything else going on, I basically forgot about the Carolyn factor. She's been sick for a week, after all.

"What'd she say?" I ask, rubbing my eyes.

"Jeff Blummer!"

"The pothead?"

"Yes!"

"What about him?"

"Jeff was sitting on the sofa across from us in my basement! At least, that's what Carolyn remembers. I know she was borderline blackout that night, but she might be onto something?" Because we're in the hallway surrounded by people, he's desperate to stifle the excitement beaming from his big hazel eyes—like he's won the golden ticket to Willy Wonka's Chocolate Factory but is trying to keep it a secret.

"That's crazy."

He stops walking, which makes me feel like I should stop walking too. "Why aren't you more excited about this?"

"I am," I lie. "I'm just tired."

He eyes me suspiciously. "Well, meet me and Bree near the D-hall doors at lunch if you're up for it."

"Up for what?"

"We're going to corner Jeff and demand answers," he says, like it should have been obvious.

This is going to be awkward as hell.

I almost don't meet up with Bree and Ali because the dread of a family dinner with my mom and Gus is simmering in the back of my mind all morning, laying a wet blanket over what should be an exciting day. But not going would probably result in Bree harassing me about what's wrong, so I decide to join.

"Where does Jeff eat lunch?" I say, glancing around D-hall.

"Where do you think?" Bree nods out the door window, toward the parking lot.

"The same place he gets high all day long," Ali adds.

We slip out and jog across the front lawn so as to not get caught for skipping, and spot Jeff's rusted, ridiculously old minivan parked crookedly near the tennis courts. Sure enough, he's sitting in the driver's seat next to his friend Sam.

"Can we hop in for a second?" Bree asks, knocking on the window.

"I don't sell anymore," Jeff says, sucking up a lime-green beverage in a large Taco Bell cup.

"We don't want to buy anything," Ali assures him. "We just want to ask you a few questions."

Jeff looks at Sam. Then looks back at us. "You're not cops, are you?"

Bree exhales. "Jeff, we've gone to school together since third grade."

He lets us climb into the back. It's trashed with mounds of fast-food wrappers, and reeks of weed. It's like Jeff is *trying* to be a walking, talking real-life stereotype.

"You were at my party a couple weeks ago, right?" Ali asks.

"Uhhh." Jeff sucks from his straw. "Who's party?"

"Ali's," Bree says, irritated. "Ali Rashid's. The guy who just asked you the question. The guy literally sitting right here."

Jeff glances back at us, notices our shirts, and smiles. "Sweet fashion statement." He hiccups. "Is anyone gay for me?"

"Do you remember being in my basement that night?"

Jeff licks his lips in thought. "I think you have the wrong dude, dude—"

"Jeff." Bree's getting impatient. "You let me, Sky, and Marshall in the front door. Do you remember anything from that night? Like, *literally* anything?"

He scrunches his face, sucks from his straw again. "Wasn't there a cat?"

"Yes, Franklin," Ali says. "Franklin's my cat."

Jeff smiles. "Yeah," he says, nodding in delight. "I remember Franklin."

"Can we see your phone?" Bree asks.

"For what?"

"Someone took a photo from the party they shouldn't have. I just want to make sure it wasn't you."

He shrugs, handing it over to Bree. "I don't have anything to hide. Don't look at my dick pics, though."

Bree opens his photos app and scrolls up—past several collections of nearly identical bathroom selfies and a ton of recipes screen-grabbed from a food blog—until she sees pics with time stamps from about two weeks ago.

"Aha!" she screams, tapping the screen.

A photo enlarges; it's the one of me and Ali sitting on the sofa in the Rashids' basement—the one that had *It turns out the terrorist is a fag, too* photoshopped across the top.

It's *the* photograph.

Carolyn was right.

"What the hell is this?" Ali yells, taking the phone and flipping it so Jeff can see. "Why did you take this photo?"

Jeff stares at it for a good five seconds, wearing the most confused expression I've ever seen on a face. "Wait, I can explain."

"You better," Ali roars.

Jeff rips the phone out of his hand. "Calm down, man!"

"Explain why you took that photo, and we will," Bree says.

Sam starts laughing in the passenger seat. Not because of what's going on, I don't think. He's just higher than a kite.

"Listen, listen," Jeff breathes, closing his eyes to remember more clearly. "Some dude borrowed my phone that night. He said the basement was too dark for his camera to pick up the shot, and he didn't want his flash to go off, so he wanted to try mine." Jeff opens his eyes again and looks to Sam. "What's that one guy's name again?"

"What guy's name?" Sam asks between laughs.

"The one guy."

"Which guy?"

"You know, he had that shirt on."

Sam laughs even harder. "I don't know, man."

"What did he look like?" Bree asks.

Jeff takes another suck through his straw. Lime green comes shooting up from the cup. "He's got blond hair . . ."

"Okay, blond hair."

"And superwhite teeth."

"Blond hair and white teeth."

"And he's on the wrestling team."

The three of us exchange looks.

"Okay," Bree says, literally on the edge of her seat. "Blond hair . . . white teeth . . . on the wrestling team . . ."

"Oh!" Ali perks up. "Brendon Pastures?"

Jeff smiles and points. "That's him."

"Brendon asshat Pastures." Ali shakes his head. "I remember thinking it was strange he crashed my party all by himself and didn't even seem like he wanted to be there."

"And remember?" Bree says excitedly. "Christina mentioned Brendon was with Cliff the night Cliff crashed Tana's get-together and used her Memories account on his phone." She turns to Jeff. "Can I see your phone again, Jeff? I just want to check a couple more things."

He hands it back to her.

"Brendon probably texted the photo to Cliff that same night," Bree whispers to me.

First, she searches Jeff's contacts. No "Cliff" or "Brendon" is saved in there, though. She dives into his recent text messages, scrolling all the way back to the dates surrounding Ali's party, but Jeff only had five text exchanges that weekend: a boring convo about ham sandwiches with Sam; everyday interactions with his mom and his dad; very uncomfortable sexts with someone saved in his phone as "Kylie Jenner's Twin"; and a contentious back-and-forth over America's preparedness for a nuclear attack with someone dubbed "Hiccup."

"Who is Hiccup?" Bree asks.

Jeff slowly opens his mouth to respond, but—

"You know what? Never mind."

On the cusp of defeat, Bree slowly moves to hand Jeff's phone back to him, but then her face lights up. "Wait!" She taps Jeff's e-mail app, goes to the sent folder, and scrolls back to the night of Ali's party.

"Yep!" she says, grinning mischievously. "Look. Brendon e-mailed himself the photo."

She shows me and Ali. Brendon e-mailed the pic to BPastures101@gmail.com that night.

"I bet he tried covering his tracks by e-mailing the pic instead of texting—because a sent e-mail is easier to miss on your phone than a sent text," Bree says, thinking aloud. "And, because it was too dark in the basement for his own camera to get the shot, he made sure to use a pothead's phone, because *of course* a pothead won't care or remember. No offense, Jeff."

"None taken," he says, smiling, eyes closed.

We start jumping out of the car.

Jeff wakes back up. "Say hello to Franklin for—"

But we close the van door behind us before he can finish.

"How much time do we have left before lunch ends?" Bree asks as we walk across the lawn. I'm struggling to keep up.

"Five minutes," Ali answers.

"Oof, let's go quick."

I follow a determined Bree zigzagging her way through the cafeteria, where she finds Carolyn eating macaroni with a group of sophomore boys who are all obsessed with her.

"We owe you," Bree says, plopping down at her table, smiling from ear to ear.

Carolyn—bright-eyed and fully recovered from the cold that kept her home last week—perks up. "Why, what did Jeff say?"

"He had the photo on his phone."

"Stop it!" She gapes. "I knew it! I remember him hanging out on the couch near you two, that little creep."

"But," Ali cuts her off. "We figured out Brendon took it and e-mailed it to himself that same night."

"Brendon Pastures?"

"Yep."

"That little . . . ," Carolyn breathes, both pissed and impressed. "So now what? Are you going to tell Winter how it all went down?"

"It wasn't Brendon, though."

"But I thought you just said it was. . . ."

"It was He Who Must Not Be Named," Bree explains.

"Who?"

"Cliff Norquest," Ali clarifies. "All the other evidence points to him. Brendon probably texted or e-mailed the photo to Cliff the night of my party. Brendon is an accomplice—not the ringleader."

"Sneaky bastards," Carolyn mutters. "So y'all just have to prove Brendon gave Cliff the photo?"

"Ideally, yes."

She bats her hand at us, like it's no big deal. "Don't worry, babes. I got you."

Bree looks confused. "What do you mean?"

Carolyn smirks. "I have Econ with Cliff, and he hangs out with his d-bag friends in the front of the class whenever we watch movies in there—which is, like, every day. He always leaves his phone out on his desk in the back of the class. I don't think it even has a passcode."

"Not the brightest bulb," Ali says.

"Right? Girls send him nudes, and they just pop up for everyone to see. It's so nasty. Anyway, yeah. I got you."

"Wait a minute," Bree says. "Are you saying you'll break into

Cliff's phone to see if Brendon sent him the photo?"

"It's not *breaking in* if he just leaves it out, now is it?"

They all exchange devilish looks as the lunch bell rings.

"Carolyn, you're a beast."

"I know," she says, as we all disperse for next hour. "Also, can I make a gay shirt too? I'm having hard-core FOMO."

Bree nods with a smile.

After we squeeze our way through the masses huddled near the cafeteria doors, Bree corners me on our walk to Yearbook. "Is everything cool with you?"

I nod and try to look perfectly fine.

She's not convinced. "You've been so quiet today."

I want to tell her about Gus and my mom, but I also don't want to ruin her excitement over the latest development in Operation: Pin It on He Who Must Not Be Named.

"I'm good," I say, attempting a genuine smile. "I swear."

FOUR DAYS

Tuesday morning, Principal Burger officially hits his break-ing point. The secretary comes over the loudspeaker in Mr. Kam's class as we're wrapping up first hour, asking if me and Ali can come to the office. I know this can't be good.

"Do you think Burger caught Cliff?" Marshall whispers, cau-tiously optimistic, as I gather my things.

"Definitely not," I answer. I hate to sound like a Debbie Downer, but this has something to do with our gay countdown shirts, I just know it. And—not to brag—walking into the office and reading the room, I immediately sense that I'm right.

Winter and Victor are waiting for us with Burger, who's sitting behind his crowded desk, a massive deer head floating above him next to a diploma from a school I've never heard of. It smells like mothballs and sweat in here. After four years at RLHS, this is my first time setting foot in the principal's office. Somehow, it's exactly as I imagined.

"Boys," Burger acknowledges, gesturing for me and Ali to take the seats next to Victor.

Winter, leaning against the back wall with her arms folded

across her chest, nods at us, confirming she's on our side. Thank God.

"We've got to settle this shirt thing out," Burger says, the condescending grin on his face indicating he's not taking any of this seriously. He leans back in his creaky chair, the fluorescent light's reflection shifting spots on his balding head. "These shirts you've all been wearing are becoming a distraction."

"A distraction from what?" Ali asks.

"Learning."

"How so?"

Burger narrows his eyes on him. "I don't appreciate the tone, Mr. Rashid."

"Can I say a few words?" Victor speaks up, raising his hand.

"No. Now," Burger barrels onward, "Ms. Winter told me she allowed the Yearbook class to make these shirts for the remainder of this week, so no one here is in trouble. But I wanted to bring everyone together so that all of us can find common ground and work toward a solution."

"What's the status of your investigation?" I pipe up.

"Pardon?"

"I thought you were looking into who hacked Memories and sent out the terrible e-blast."

"Well, we don't know if any systems were *hacked* per se. But yes—I've been looking into who's responsible."

"And?"

"Pardon?"

"And what have you found? Who's responsible?"

If me and a few other seventeen-year-olds are inches away

from finding the final piece of evidence to sink Cliff, certainly a principal's investigation—with the entire school's resources at his disposal—should have nailed the criminal days ago.

Burger leans forward again, the chair extra squeaky this time. "I don't appreciate your tone either, Mr. Baker."

"Now can I say a few words?" Victor repeats eagerly.

Burger holds his gaze on me just long enough for everyone to feel uncomfortable before giving Victor the go-ahead.

"First of all, as my viral post noted, I am not homophobic, but—"

"Objection," Ali chides, turning to Victor. "You are."

"This isn't about Sky being gay," Victor protests.

"Your *viral post* begs to differ," I mutter.

"Boys, let him finish," Burger interjects.

"All I'm saying is, I get it," Victor continues. "It's obvious you want attention and these shirts provide both of you with that. But you're making the Senior Beach-Bum Party all about *you* and *your* promposals at the expense of every other senior. The beach party and prom are about us coming *together*. Is this how you want our senior class to remember you?"

"Sure," I say quickly.

"Yup." Ali shrugs.

Victor, frustrated, looks to Burger.

"Boys," Burger scolds. "Let's be honest here. The shirts do come across as a little . . . *much*."

There's something about the way he says it.

Much.

I already have the dinner with my mom and Gus to worry

233

about, and the whole debacle with Charlie is still simmering away in the back of my mind, putting me on the brink of meltdown mode. This is the last straw.

The boulder begins bouncing down the mountain in my mind. This time, it's not so much a boulder of gloom, though—more like a boulder of *rage*. There's no way I can stop it.

Honestly? I'm okay with that.

"You know what?" I snap. "We *are* doing this to get some attention, Principal Burger. Because someone sent out an e-blast that called *me* a faggot and called *him* a terrorist, and this school has done absolutely nothing about it."

"Where was your viral post about *that*, Bungle?" Ali demands.

"Boys, boys." Burger closes his eyes, throttled. "Let's cool it. Sky, we don't need that kind of language—"

"What kind of language?" I ask.

Ali pounces. "You mean the homophobic and racist language that was spread throughout this school and prompted exactly *no* response from you or your office?"

"Ms. Winter?" Burger sighs, turning purple and calling for backup. "Can you chime in here?"

Winter places a hand on both my shoulder and Ali's. "My students are frustrated, Principal Burger."

"I can see that."

"And for good reason."

You could cut the tension in the room with a knife.

"You told me you'd be looking into who was responsible for the e-blast," she continues. "But it's been more than two weeks, and you've given me no updates on the situation."

"Well. . . . " Burger, surprised by Winter's rebuttal, stumbles, a single bead of sweat trickling down the bridge of his nose. "I'm sorry things like this take time, but I have other responsibilities, of course."

"Surely protecting two of our students targeted with hate speech is toward the top of your priority list?"

Burger goes silent before cracking a malicious grin, realizing he won't be leaving this battle unscathed. It's gloves off for him, too.

"Here's the dilemma," he says, eyes darting between the four of us. "I have thirty-something messages on my phone from concerned parents wondering what's going on with these so-called gay shirts spreading like wildfire among the student body. I have over two dozen seniors requesting private meetings with me, alarmed that their prom seems to be—and I quote one of them directly—'going gay.' And I have—"

"What?" I blast. "Going *gay*? That's the dumbest thing I've ever heard."

"Can you blame them?" Victor jabs. "If everyone's proclaiming their gay crushes for prom, it implies our senior prom is, in fact, getting pretty gay."

"And so what if it is?" Ali yells. "Who the hell cares?"

"Ali." Winter taps his shoulder to calm him down.

"I care!" Victor roars. "I care when people are shoving their sexual preferences down other people's throats and ruining prom for the rest of us."

"*Again.*" Ali bends closer toward Victor. "Where was this outrage from our senior class president when someone dragged us in the e-blast?" He turns to Burger. "And as far as your thirty-something phone messages from concerned parents—clearly you haven't listened to them, or else you'd know that three of them were from my mom and dad wondering what you're doing about their son being called a terrorist in an email sent to hundreds of—"

"Enough!" Burger rises from his chair, which bolts backward and slams into a dusty bookshelf. The deer antlers—now appearing right above his head, making them look like his *own* antlers—are trembling from his outburst. "Here's what we're going to do. Victor, delete your post about their shirts. Got it?"

"Sure," Victor says, shrugging. "Whatever."

"And you two," Burger spits. "Enough with the shirts. They're no longer allowed under school dress code."

"May I ask how the shirts break dress code?" Winter pushes back calmly.

"They've become a distraction from learning. I'm no longer allowing them—for you two, or any of the other Yearbook students."

"With respect," Winter says, still cool and collected, "I won't be enforcing that ban in my classroom. As long as a bully is running around this school unchecked, I won't be policing the shirts my students choose to wear in protest."

The room falls silent.

Burger inhales, trying desperately not to explode again. "I'm *this* close to saying to hell with this whole ridiculous Senior Beach-Bum Party. It's April. There could still be *snow* on the ground anyway."

Victor clears his throat, bends closer toward Burger's desk, and lowers his voice. "Sir, you, ah . . . you can't *technically* do that. It's at a public beach and it's organized by the seniors independently of the school. So, ah . . . *technically*, it's not a school-sponsored ev—"

"Well!" I swear the veins in Burger's head start visibly pulsating. "We might have to cancel prom, then!"

Victor gasps.

"Not for everyone," Burger adds. "Just for those who continue to wear the shirts. Enough is enough."

"Principal Burger." Winter smiles. "Surely we can figure this out without taking prom away from students?"

"Ms. Winter." Burger returns the smile, but maliciously. "How about this? Unless you plan on chaperoning your *own* prom for your *own* Yearbook class"—he lets out a sharp chuckle—"you'll need to enforce the ban."

"Well," Winter sighs, thinking. "Okay, then."

Burger blinks. "Okay you'll enforce the ban?"

"Okay I'll be chaperoning my own prom for my Yearbook students," she says, patting me and Ali on our shoulders. "Let's go."

FOUR DAYS

In Yearbook, Winter tallies a vote: Should we have our own Yearbook Prom or not?

Not a single student votes against it.

"Settle down, settle down," Winter says over the room's buzzing. "You're all sure about this?"

I thought there might be some second-guesses from some, but there's not. The entire class cheers in approval.

"It seems like we're doing our own prom, then," Winter confirms, looking surprised by the words coming out of her own mouth. "We have to get a few things straight, though."

"Pun intended?" Ali says, to laughs.

"We used up our remaining class funds for the shirt-making party at the Brandstones'," Winter explains. "So we have to think frugally. The total cost should be covered by each of you pitching in just a few dollars if this is what you want to do."

"Easy," Bree says. "The biggest prom expense—by *far*—is venue. We can use my basement. Tons of room for dancing."

"Ask your parents *first* this time, Brandstone," Winter warns. "I don't want your mom and dad to kill me."

"I'll be in charge of finding a DJ," Dustin says, to nods, because most people agree he has good taste in music. "I know some people who'd do it, free of charge."

"My dad can cater appetizers, on the house," Christina adds. Her family owns a burger joint for tourists downtown.

"Great." Winter sits on the end of her desk and hunts for a pen and paper to jot down notes. "What are some other things we need to be thinking about?"

I raise my hand.

Winter points at me.

"Well." I clear my throat. "I think, like, yeah, the idea of Yearbook Prom is great, and I'm glad we're all stoked about doing our own thing." Everyone gets quiet and turns to me, unsure where I'm going with this. "But let's not forget *why* we're doing this: because Burger had a problem with our gay shirts."

"And he doesn't seem to care about the e-blast hack in the first place," Ali adds. "Like, at all."

"Right. Let's make sure we keep that in mind while planning this. It should be a prom for *everybody* at this school—especially gay and trans and other queer students—"

"And Black and brown kids!" Ali pipes in again, raising his hand. "All, like, four of us, anyway."

"Exactly. Everyone should know they're welcome and that they can be themselves. I think that's important."

My cheeks are burning.

I didn't mean to get all serious in front of everybody, and I hope I didn't come across as condescending or preachy. It just slipped out. Most people seem on board, though.

Especially Winter, who's beaming. "I think that's an excellent point, Baker."

After school, Ali, Marshall, and Ainsley decide to come over to Bree's to plan Yearbook Prom stuff over hummus and pita. Everyone's dotted around the kitchen stuffing their faces and excitedly mapping out how it will all go down, but—as invested as I want to be—I'm only half there in my head. Because most of my mind is still obsessing over dinner with my mom and Gus. I just can't shake it.

"Earth to Sky," Bree says, snapping her fingers in front of my face. She laughs at herself. "Earth to Sky," she mumbles. "That's kind of funny."

"Huh?"

"I suggested rainbow-colored streamers for obvious gay reasons," she says, flashing her computer screen—filled with photos of dozens of bright party decorations—my way. "Yea or nay?"

"A rainbow theme might be a bit too cliché."

"If we're thinking about photos, that'll be a color overload, clashing with people's dresses and suits and stuff," Ainsley adds, sucking hummus off her fingertips.

"True, true," Bree considers, chewing on the end of her pen in thought.

The doorbell rings. It's probably Dan.

Everyone over at the house knows he's a trans guy. He asked Bree to fill us in, and she sort of just word vomited it out right as Ali coincidentally dropped a spoonful of hummus onto the floor.

No one cared, of course, because this group is solid. Ainsley and Ali each said something to the effect of "Huh, cool," while

Marshall yelled "Oh, nice!" and dunked his pita in Ali's spilt floor hummus, horrifying the rest of us. Now I bet Marshall understands why Bree got upset with him in the cafeteria.

Bree thought it'd be a good idea to include Dan in our Yearbook Prom discussions, considering we're trying to make it especially welcoming for LGBTQ kids, which was smart. I'm the only out gay kid we know, after all—the responsibility to queer this dance up can't solely rest on me, right?

"We pass out mini rainbow flags at the door?" I suggest to Bree over my shoulder on my way to the foyer, appreciating the rainbow sentiment she suggested. "I like where you're going with it."

I get to Bree's front door and swing it open—

But it's Teddy standing there.

"Oh," I say, surprised.

Butterflies, butterflies, *butterflies.*

He laughs. "Hello to you, too."

He's wearing sunglasses and extra short shorts again. Also, his tank top really shows off his muscles. Just saying.

"I didn't know you were coming over," I say.

"Marshall invited me."

There's this awkward pause.

"Sooo." He rocks back and forth on his sandals, hands in his pockets. "Can I come in?"

"Oh, duh, yeah." I move aside, blushing. "Sorry."

He smells like whatever cologne or shampoo or deodorant he was wearing at the shirt-making party, and it's still delightful.

"There he is," Marshall says happily when Teddy appears at my side in the kitchen. "What took you so long?"

Teddy circles the kitchen, sharing hugs and fist bumps with everyone. "Yearbook Prom, eh?" he says, taking a seat and diving into the hummus. "First, shirts, now your own prom? Damn. What are we thinking?"

Bree flashes him her computer screen, where she's created a rough blueprint of the basement—where the DJ and dance floor will be, the area for food, and the spot where people will take pics with a backdrop.

"Dig it," Teddy says. "Especially the food. What's on the menu?"

"Christina's dad is catering, on the house."

Teddy nods in impressed approval. Then he puts both fists knuckles-down onto the countertop and leans forward, propping himself up a bit and craning his neck to see into the Brandstones' sprawling backyard. Doing so makes his shot-put muscles pop even more.

Again, just saying.

"You can see Lake Michigan from your backyard?" he says like a giddy toddler, staring out the window. Teddy is from normal Rock Ledge—not 1 percent Rock Ledge—and I know the effect Bree's house and subdivision can have on kids like us.

"We have shared beach access with our neighbors."

"The Brandstones are *fancy*," Ali jokes.

"Maybe we can extend prom into the backyard if it's warm enough?" Ainsley suggests. "Actually . . . can we walk down there tonight before the sun sets? It's so warm out today."

"Totally—to both ideas," Bree says. "Climate change has its perks."

There's another knock.

I jog to the front door again and let Dan in. He's got on a snug purple shirt and a shiny golden watch.

"I'll never get over how big this house is," he says, flipping his baseball hat backward and pulling off his leather boots.

"Right?"

"What do Bree's parents do again?" he asks, following me toward the kitchen. "Er, is that a rude thing to ask?"

"I don't think so? But either way, I don't even know."

"Hey." He touches my shoulder before we get back to the group. "Do you know if Bree told everyone? About . . . me?"

"Oh yeah. They're all totally cool with it." I smile. "Except for Teddy."

"Teddy?" He scrunches his face. "He has a problem with it?"

"No, no, sorry," I whisper. "I just meant—I didn't realize Teddy was coming over, so I don't think Teddy knows yet."

Dan nods. "I'll tell him later."

I lead him into the kitchen, feeling a little nervous *for* him, to be honest. But everyone's chill right from the get-go. Bree wraps him up in a hug before pulling up a chair. "Join our pita party."

After a few minutes of hummus and discussing the DuVernay film—Teddy makes the mistake of referencing a quote from the movie, which launches Marshall into a monologue about the story's surprise ending, to the annoyance of everyone—Bree refocuses on her computer.

"What do you think about this?" she says to Dan, moving the screen to face him. "I'm torn. Should the photo area go here? Or here?"

Dan bends over to check out her blueprint. "I don't have an opinion, really. But is there only one bathroom?"

Bree looks to where he's pointing. "In the basement, yeah. Guys' will be downstairs, and girls' will be upstairs."

"If I were you, I'd have both be for everyone," Dan says. "What's the point of assigning girl and boy labels to two single-stall bathrooms?" He looks around at everyone, turning pink. "Not to be nitpicky."

"Yes!" Bree punches him lovingly on the shoulder. "You need to be my prom-planning coordinator."

Dan cracks a grin and rubs the area where Bree hit him. I've been on the receiving end of her happy punches too—they hurt more than you'd think.

"What other dope prom ideas do you have up your sleeve, Dan?" Marshall asks with a grin. "You're quiet, but I bet there are some good ideas floating around in that head of yours."

Dan's pink glow gets rosier.

"Yeah," Bree says, pushing her computer across the counter toward him. "Let's hear it."

Dan laughs and looks back at the screen. "Hm, well . . ." He bites his lower lip in thought, clicking through Bree's long list of notes. "Paris?"

"Huh?"

"You want the backdrop for our prom photos to be the Eiffel Tower?" Dan shakes his head in playful disgust. "Bree."

"What?!"

"That *is* a bit . . ." Ainsley scrunches her face, hesitant to criticize. "Cliché. Plus, we have to be frugal as hell, remember? A Paris backdrop sounds pricey."

"Agreed," Marshall says quickly—as if he's been bottling it up for decades.

Bree looks around at all of us, a bit hurt. "So you all hate it, huh?"

"I love you, Bree, but I have to agree," Teddy says, dunking his pita. "Rock Ledge could not be less Parisian in any possible way."

"How about"—Dan thinks for a second, placing a comforting hand on Bree's shoulder—"we go the group shot route?"

"How so?" Bree asks.

"If we want this prom to be inclusive for LGBTQ students, I don't think most LGBTQ kids in Rock Ledge would have significant others to bring anyway," Dan says. "The overt romance stuff may land flat."

"True," I add.

"We could buy a bunch of super cheap props—oversize sunglasses, feather boas, those sorts of things—and let people have fun with them in front of the camera?"

Bree punches him again.

"Ouch!"

"Sorry!" she squeaks before jotting down his idea. "I got excited. I love that."

After Dan throws out a few more fantastic suggestions—like having a sign-up sheet for GLOW set out for interested students—Ainsley brings up the beach again. We slip on our shoes and wander out through the backyard toward the water.

To get there, we have to follow a dirt path through a small patch of woods. On a sunny day like today, none of us mind the walk, though. The trees are still bare from winter, but the air feels full and sticky like June. You can hear the white noise of waves crashing up against the earth—a sound that, even after hearing it all my life, I still can't get enough of. When we turn a final bend and see the deep blue of the lake straight ahead, Marshall and Ainsley take off running like kids at recess. By the time we catch up, they've planted themselves on a long, dead tree trunk laid out across the sand.

"You can smell spring coming," Ainsley says, eyes closed, hair blowing in the breeze.

"I wish it'd hurry up," Marshall says, digging a hole in the sand with his foot. "This weather better stick around for Beach-Bum!"

They dissect all the drama happening—Ali rehashes our scandalous meeting with Winter and Burger for the millionth time so Dan can hear it from the horse's mouth, Marshall fills Ainsley in on the latest developments with Carolyn and Jeff, and we all take turns talking about how much we hate Cliff.

But I'm mostly quiet because thoughts of my mom and Gus just won't quit. They're relentless. Every few minutes, their concerned faces burst back into my consciousness, bringing a wave of anxiety with them. It's driving me nuts.

I decide to deploy a tactic Winter brought up in class one time. People do better in job interviews when they envision the process beforehand, she explained. Like, if you can imagine yourself sitting there—responding to the questions, going back and forth with the interviewers—it apparently helps you feel more confident when the real thing comes along.

So I think about the restaurant where we're meeting. I try to predict how they'll be dressed, what they'll look like. I go over the small talk they'll probably bring up, and the awkward questions they'll inevitably pose too—about being gay, about the shirts, about the e-blast. I imagine listening to my mom's awkward

Church Speak, because she'll definitely get all biblical on me. I need to be prepared.

I don't know, though. Rehearsing the dinner in my head may be making my anxiety worse.

"I say we take a swim," Marshall yells, taking off his shirt and ripping me away from my thoughts. "Who's with me?"

"No one has bathing suits," Ainsley points out, like he's lost his marbles.

"So? Go in your underwear," Marshall says, like it should be obvious.

Bree shakes her head adamantly. "I'll keep my clothes on, thank you very much."

"I'm going to sit this one out," Dan says, smiling and staying put on the tree. "I'm not a big swimmer."

"Boooo," Ali taunts him playfully. "What about you?" He looks at me. "You're in, right?"

I pretend to contemplate, even though the answer is an absolute no. The thought of introducing Mars to the world four days early is truly terrifying. "Tempting, but I'll stay here with Dan."

"Oh, come on!" Teddy yells, pulling off his tank top.

"I won't accept no as an answer," Marshall says, grabbing my hand and pulling me up off the tree. Ainsley starts giggling as we play tug-of-war with my right arm.

This is a nightmare.

"Okay, okay," I yell in surrender. "But let me go grab towels for us first so we don't freeze to death."

"Fair point."

I hate this.

I wander back up to the house and honestly think about just staying here. None of them have ever seen Mars. How grossed out will they all be?

I am not prepared for this. But I should try to be tough—even if tough is the last thing I'm feeling right now.

I slip off my shirt and stare back at my reflection in the bathroom mirror. There's Mars. Ugly-ass Mars. I get this whiplash of déjà vu again—this time, the morning Mrs. Brandstone walked in on me shower-dreaming about Ali. The countdown was at thirty days.

I steady my breath, grab a stack of towels, and head out to the beach, a nauseating sense of dread slowly filling up my gut. I throw one of the towels over my left shoulder to hide Mars from view.

About halfway to the water, I see a silhouette coming toward me. The sun is low in the sky behind whoever it is, so I can't distinguish a face until they're just a few yards away.

It's Teddy.

"Hey," I say, relieved the towel over my shoulder is there.

The sunset's lighting up half his face in this orangish-pink glow. He already jumped into the water, it looks like, because drops are collecting on the tips of the wavy, dark hair dangling over his forehead and peppered across his torso, glistening alongside noticeable goose bumps. It's like I'm in another one of my shower-dreams.

"Here," I say, throwing one of the towels at him. "Looks like you need this."

"Thanks." He starts drying off, shivering as he goes. "The water is freezing!"

"Well, duh." I smile. "You know it's April, right?"

"I was headed up to the house to see if you needed a hand with the towels," he says. "You were taking a while."

"Sorry. I'm a slowpoke."

He studies my face for a second. "Is everything all right?"

"Yeah, why?"

He grins—it's a very specific Teddy Grin. But who knows if it's reserved just for me. Ali's Grin wasn't. I learned that the hard way.

"I noticed you've been quiet," he says. "Not that it's any of my business."

No one knows about my dinner Thursday night. And I've wanted to keep it that way. There's so much exciting stuff happening this week with the gay shirts and Yearbook Prom planning, I didn't want my personal baggage spoiling everyone's fun.

But I should let it out. At least to one person.

"I'm seeing my mom for the first time since she kicked me out of her house for being gay," I spill.

His Teddy Grin disappears.

"Sorry," I say. "I know that's . . . kind of heavy."

"Don't apologize." He steps closer toward me. "How are you feeling about it?"

"Ah," I kind of laugh, because I can't even parse through the messy, overwhelming answer to that question lying with my own thoughts at night, let alone have the ability to articulate it in a surreal moment like this. "I'm not really sure."

He reaches out and touches the side of my arm. His fingers are cool from the water. "I'm sorry that happened to you."

"It's not your fault."

"I know. But I'm still sorry. Your mom's missing out."

249

I don't know what to say. "Thanks," I finally get out.

He glances back toward the beach, his hand still pressed against my left arm. "Dan just told me."

"About him . . . ?"

"Being trans, yeah. And that you helped inspire him to tell us."

Wait, what? "He said that?" I ask, tingling on the inside.

"Yeah. That's huge." He smiles. "Screw your mom. You're making a difference to a lot of people in Rock Ledge, even if you don't know it."

He pats me on my arm using the same hand, and the towel draped across my chest—the towel covering Mars—falls to the ground.

I immediately pick it back up, but it's too late.

Teddy spots it.

Teddy spots Mars.

"Hey," he says, staring at my chest. "That's badass."

Badass?

Mars is many things, but I never thought of him as badass.

"What happened?" Teddy asks nonchalantly—like he's asking about what I had for lunch today and not the most humiliating thing about me.

I try to steady my voice, like I'm not completely and utterly mortified. "It's a burn scar from when I was a kid." My face is turning the same shade as Mars, I think. "I got it in a car accident. I've had it forever."

He raises his left arm high up in the air, revealing a scar near his armpit. It's way smaller than Mars, and much lighter, too.

But maybe a scar is just a scar.

"Shard of broken glass," he explains, pointing at his own battle wound. "Six years old. St. Patrick's Day." He laughs. "That's all you need to know about that."

I smile.

We turn and head back to the beach together.

I want to cover up Mars again. But I fight the urge, and I fight it hard. Teddy apparently thinks Mars looks *badass*, which is hard to believe. But the fact that he said it has to count for something.

TWO DAYS

Bree drops me off at the restaurant on her way to take Ray to one of his tutoring sessions.

"Good luck," she says as I step out the passenger side door.

"Good luck," Ray repeats.

"Thanks," I say, smiling at him in the back seat.

Bree gives me a look like, *You got this*, before driving off.

I'm glad I finally caved and told her about the Mom/Gus dinner too. I should know by now that my problems always feel much less overwhelming—or at least more manageable—once I fill Bree in as well.

I go in and seat myself in the nearly empty room. A nice waitress gives me orange juice. Five minutes go by. Then ten.

They're late, of course, which I should have expected. I'm getting increasingly upset with myself—sitting here in the booth, scrolling through Instagram like an idiot—for actually showing up on time, thinking my mom and Gus would do the same. For actually showing up *at all*.

I should have known better.

"Refill?" the waitress asks.

I don't remember taking a single sip, but the juice is gone. "Sure, thanks."

My mom and Gus changed restaurants super last-minute to this empty diner that smells like wet carpet, in the middle of nowhere a whole town away. I'm not sure why; the location is way less convenient for all three of us.

"Hey," the waitress says, pouring juice straight from the carton. "You're the kid from Rock Ledge."

"Uh . . . yes?"

She stops pouring and looks up at me. "The kid with the shirts."

"Oh. Yeah." I glance down, nervous.

Before I left, I made sure my zip-up hoodie hid my gay shirt underneath, because I know it'd make my mom that much more uncomfortable. But it's still completely covered. The waitress must recognize my face.

"Cool." She smiles and leaves.

That was weird.

I think the main reason I've been dreading today is because I'm not sure what I want to come of it. What does Gus think about all this? Will my mom apologize? Will she double down on her insanity? Will she ask me to move back in with her—but only with conditions?

I don't know. I'm scared to find out.

Finally, I spot Gus's truck pulling into the gravel parking lot and crunching to a halt right outside the window I'm sitting next to. He steps out of the truck in a pair of baggy light-blue jeans and a green backward hat, greasy hair poking out from the sides.

And his girlfriend steps out too.

What is she doing here?

He waves at me, but the two of them take a minute to finish their cigarettes before coming inside.

"Yo," he says, plopping down into the booth and snatching up his plastic menu. He's twenty minutes late, but I know he won't be apologizing. "How's it going?"

"Good."

"You remember Chelsea."

"Yeah," I say, nodding at her. "How are you?"

She pushes her hair back, revealing her freckled neck and chest. "Good, you?"

I shrug. "Can't complain. Where's Mom?" I glance back out to the parking lot. "She didn't come with you?"

The waitress appears. "Can I get you two something to drink?"

"Water is fine," Gus says.

"Do y'all have milkshakes?" Chelsea asks.

"Yep."

"Butterfinger?"

"We don't have Butterfinger, no."

"Malt?"

"We have chocolate, vanilla, and strawberry."

"What about Oreo?"

"We just have chocolate, vanilla, and strawberry."

"Hrm." She scans the menu. "What about mint chocolate—"

"*Jesus*, Chels," Gus hisses. "They have chocolate, vanilla, or strawberry. Just pick a flavor."

Chelsea eyes him angrily. "Water is fine."

The waitress walks away.

Gus scans his menu, flipping it from front to back several times.

"Remember what Dad used to get here all the time?" he asks nonchalantly, eyes moving across the appetizers.

The question feels like a concrete block dropped on my head.

"We came here with Dad?"

He looks up, confused, as if I should have known. "Yeah. Every Sunday." He turns the menu, pointing in the apps section. "Mozzarella sticks. He *always* got mozzarella sticks."

"Cute." Chelsea yawns.

"How come you never told me this?" I ask.

He shrugs. "I thought you knew."

Gus doesn't get it. He never has.

He doesn't understand how our three-years age difference means everything. Before Dad died, Gus's brain was old enough to start storing Dad memories, documenting our Sunday stops at the diner, absorbing his mannerisms, the way he spoke. Gus doesn't understand that while Dad's like a friendly ghost who visits from time to time, my memory draws complete blanks. I don't feel anything.

Well, until Charlie.

I contemplate bringing Charlie up to Gus—because he may remember Charlie from our childhood—but Gus changes the subject.

"Anyway," he says, stretching out one arm along the top of the booth. "You're graduating soon."

"Yeah."

"How does it feel?"

I shrug. "Fine."

"Just fine?"

"Yeah." I shift in my seat, wondering how much Gus already knows about the countdown shirts, and my promposal wall, and Yearbook Prom. "I'm looking forward to it being over. Is Mom on her way?"

"I was the same way," Chelsea says. "High school is the worst."

"Are you going to community college?" Gus asks.

I stare at him.

He stares back.

Why doesn't he want to talk about Mom?

"Yeah," I finally answer. "Well, hopefully. I applied for a scholarship."

"Cool. Way less expensive than going to—"

"You heard I'm gay, though, right?" I blurt. "I assume Mom told you what happened over the holidays? And you heard about what's been going down at school? The Yearbook e-blast, my promposal wall that leaked . . . ?"

Gus and Chelsea stare at me.

It gets real awkward, real fast.

"Just thought I'd clear the air," I say after they stay silent. "It's been a while since we last talked."

"Yeah, I heard about all of it," Gus says, nodding. "Mom filled me in on your fight. But it's not like I didn't know before."

"What do you mean?"

He looks at me like I'm an idiot. "Sky, c'mon."

"What?"

"You've always been prancing around," he laughs. Chelsea laughs too. "You never had a lot of guy friends."

"Marshall's a guy."

"You hate sports, you listen to gay music. The jeans you wear? It wasn't difficult."

When Marshall pokes fun at me for gay stuff, it doesn't feel like this does now. I want to throw my orange juice in Gus's face and get the hell out of here.

The waitress comes back with their waters. "You guys ready to order?"

"Question," Chelsea says. "What kind of ranch do you have?"

"Ranch?"

"Yeah."

"I didn't know there were different kinds."

"Is it, like, the runny, thin kind? Or the thicker kind?"

"Um . . ."

"Can you bring out a little sample so I can taste?"

"It's the thinner kind, I think."

She deflates. "We'll need another minute, then."

The waitress slips away.

I stay silent, staring out the window in search of my mom's car, getting antsy.

"I didn't mean it like that," Gus says, noticing I'm pissed. "I just mean, I wasn't that surprised you were gay, is all."

"I've got gay friends," Chelsea butts in, as if I give a rat's ass about her opinion on any of this. "It's no big deal, hon."

I want to throw my orange juice in her face, too.

"Where's Mom?" I ask Gus again.

He doesn't say anything.

"Gus," I say louder. "Seriously, where is she?"

"Sky."

"Is she coming or not?"

"Calm down, dude."

"Tell me what's going on or I'm leaving."

We get into a mini stare-down. My ears burn, more and more rage bubbling up inside me with every second Gus avoids telling the truth.

"Fine," I warn, before sliding my butt across the booth to leave. "I'm out of here—"

"She's not coming."

I stop. "What?"

"She's not coming."

"I heard you; it's just . . . Why not? I thought that's why you wanted to get dinner. I thought that's why we're here—so me, you, *and Mom* could talk about everything."

"It was."

"Well, what the eff happened?"

"Why do you say that?" he jabs.

"Say what?"

"'Eff.' You're seventeen years old. You can swear."

"Why do you care?"

"Because you sound ridiculous."

"Guys," Chelsea intervenes, raising a menu between us for a second. "Let's all take a deep breath . . . inhale, exhale . . . good. Everyone, relax."

I look back out the window.

Maybe he's wrong. It was a miscommunication. My mom's going to pull into the parking lot any second now.

But do I even *want* her to?

I don't know. I don't know how I feel about anything right now. All I know is that I'm angry.

"So that's it?" I say. My voice cracks a little.

Gus is playing with his spoon and avoiding looking me in the face.

"Mom's just . . . she's not showing up? Did she say anything to you about it?"

He digs into his coat pocket and pulls out a pamphlet that's been folded in half a few times. "She was planning on coming. Dinner was her idea." He pushes the pamphlet toward me. "But she changed her mind today."

"What's this?" I ask, picking it up.

"Just open it."

"'New Beginnings'?" I read, unfolding the glossy pamphlet. It looks like the brochure to an outdoor summer camp or something. All the images feature photoshopped teens with unrealistically white teeth playing volleyball, and eating ice cream, and—yep, there it is—reading the effing Bible.

I toss the pamphlet aside. "Are you serious?"

"What?"

"It's one of these culty Christian summer camps, Gus."

He shrugs. "I don't know what to tell you."

"Are you on her side?"

"I'm not on anyone's side."

"Do you think I should go to this place?"

"Dude," he cuts me off. "You're basically homeless, right?"

"No, I'm staying at Bree's."

"So, yeah, basically homeless."

I want to flip the table. "*No*, I'm living with the Brandstones."

"Look. She said that if you go to this retarded summer camp thing—"

"R-word, hon," Chelsea mutters.

"—if you go to this camp, you can move back in with her. She'll even pay for it, and you know how broke Mom is. Isn't it worth it?"

I knew it. There would be conditions.

No apologies, no change of heart.

Just conditions.

"I don't know," Chelsea says as I'm trying to keep my cool, tapping her nails against the table and sucking her water through a straw, looking at the pamphlet. "Call me crazy, but this camp looks kind of fun."

I can't with her.

I honestly just can't.

"Chelsea," I snap. "Please just . . . don't."

"Don't what?" she asks.

"Please, *please* stay out of this."

"Hey!" Gus roars. "Don't talk to her like that."

"Or what?"

"Or I'll beat your faggot ass, that's what."

It's like everything hits pause. The word feels like a dagger.

It hurt really badly when I read it in the e-blast. But this time, it stings worse. Much, much worse. You wouldn't think it, right? You'd think the word written in an e-mail that hundreds or thousands of people see would be a bigger deal. But it's not.

I stare at him, and he stares back. It feels like an eternity passes before I can look away again.

"You have to go," the waitress says to us out of nowhere. I realize the few other customers in the restaurant are all staring.

"Okay," I say, scooching out of the booth and tossing the camp pamphlet onto the table, along with a five-dollar bill. "Later, Gus. Say hi to Mom for me."

ONE DAY

Everyone will expect an answer from me at school today because the countdown stands at one. One effing day.

"What, exactly, is happening tomorrow?" people like Christina, and Dustin, and Carolyn, and *everyone* will ask, expecting either a thorough answer or a promise that, whatever my plan is, it's going to be spectacular. "How are you going to prompose to Ali at the beach?"

I've been wearing countdown shirts the past two weeks, revving everyone up about some climactic moment on the shores of Lake Michigan like I'm announcing a run for office. I dragged the whole Yearbook class into this charade too. And then the whole school.

I can't *not* do something worthwhile. Right? People are counting on me to take a stand, to speak out—to somehow turn this surreal, lemons-to-lemonade situation into something meaningful.

People like Dan and Teddy.

"Hey," Bree says outside my bedroom, knocking softly on the door. "Can I come in?"

"Yeah."

It swings open.

There she is, standing in the doorway next to a curious, concerned Louise—how do dogs always know when you're down in the dumps?—Bree's shirt reading GAY FOR SKY and DAYS LEFT: 1. The artwork is extra special today too, written in huge bubble letters that are filled with yellow glitter, because 1) it's my favorite color, duh, and 2) I'm a Hufflepuff.

"Feeling any better?" she asks, dropping onto the futon, already knowing my answer.

She picked me up yesterday from the gas station I walked to after leaving the diner. On the ride back to the Brandstones', I gave her a play-by-play detailing the whole debacle: Chelsea's weird thick-ranch fetish, my mom flaking and sending a culty Christian summer camp brochure in her place, and, of course, Gus's f-bomb.

"Eh," I answer. "But I like your shirt, though."

"You're coming to school today."

"Eh."

"The countdown is at *one*, Sky."

"Eh."

"The school needs you."

I actually laugh out loud at the ridiculousness of that notion—but then remember what Teddy said: that I'm making a difference. I should at least try. Try to be tough.

So I stand up—but still groan in protest.

"There you go." She grabs my final GAY FOR ALI shirt off my dresser and throws it at my chest. "Meet me at my car in five."

"Wait," I say as she's walking out. "Do you think your parents will want me gone once you move to California?"

"Why are you bringing that up *now*?"

"I don't know. Just . . . 'cause."

I can't stay here forever, after all. Bree will be gone soon. I *will* end up at that culty Christian summer camp, if it means I'm not living on the literal streets.

"Of course you'll be able to stay here," she says like it's the dumbest question in the world. "My parents are obsessed with you. They'd let you stay here until your, like, thirtieth birthday. Now get dressed."

I breathe a little bit easier on the way to school after hearing that.

I've gotten kind of used to the stares and the smiles and the whispers behind my back the past two weeks, wearing my gay shirts. But just as I suspected, today hits a fever pitch.

"How are you going to prompose, Sky?"

"So wait—Ali's gay? Or is this all just a stunt?"

"If I go to the beach party late, will I miss your promposal? I have a dentist appointment in the morning, and then my sister has a soccer game, but I should be there by three."

"Don't worry, Sky. Ali will definitely say yes. I think so. I hope so."

"Are you, Ali, and Bree a throuple? I heard you, Ali, and Bree are a throuple. . . ."

I sidestep most of the questions, successfully avoiding having to give any clear responses. But it sort of feels like my resistance to answer is fueling even more speculation over the promposal that will never come to be.

It seems stupid in retrospect that I wouldn't have talked to Ali about what would happen at the Senior Beach-Bum Party. But when we first decided to make the shirts, the clear understanding between us was that a promposal wouldn't be happening. It's always been about the message the shirts sent.

But now that this has all taken on a life of its own—a life much bigger than me or Ali ever anticipated—I'm thinking it'd be smart to have a plan in place.

Or else, I'm setting myself up for a disaster.

Bree, Marshall, and I eat lunch in the second-floor science wing instead of outside Winter's classroom in the busier part of school, so I can avoid the onslaught of promposal and beach party questions.

"Does anyone know where Ali is?" I ask. Ainsley and Dan are making up tests, and Teddy had a meeting with a track coach. I'm grateful it's just the three of us. Don't get me wrong—the others are great. But we're the original three.

"He said he's going to Improv Club," Bree answers, sipping a La Croix.

I choke on my Cheez-It. Bree shoves her drink into my face for me to take a sip and avoid death.

"Why is that so surprising?" Marshall asks after I get back to breathing normally again.

"I didn't even know we *had* an Improv Club," Bree adds.

I didn't tell Bree or Marshall about Ali's secret desire to join. Not that either of them would have thought anything of it. It's just, that conversation in his basement still feels personal and special to me, even though he's no longer an obsession of mine. Just a friend. Actually, it probably feels personal and special *because* he's no longer an obsession, but a friend.

I take another swig of Bree's La Croix to clear up my throat. "I think Ali would be great in improv, is all."

They both give me a look, knowing there's more to the story, but decide it's not worth interrogating me about it, with everything else going on. Bree goes back to her sandwich and Marshall pulls out his phone.

"Dude, you're legit famous," he says, scrolling with a grin on his face. "People are posting pics in their gay shirts. And there's a hashtag circulating too."

"Shut up!" Bree scooches across the floor to see Marshall's phone. Her jaw drops. "Oh my God. There are fifty-seven posts under the hashtag #GayForSky! And none of them seem to be trolls."

They both look up at me, giddy.

"This is *wild*," Marshall says, shaking his head.

"Can I have an autograph?" Bree grins.

I nod and play along, pretending to sign an autograph with an imaginary pen and paper.

But they're both way more thrilled about all this than I am. I can't fully shake what happened yesterday.

Because as soon as this all dies down tomorrow, Bree and Marshall will get back to planning their freshman years far away from Rock Ledge. And I'll be stuck here, "basically homeless," as Gus put it. I know I should be thinking more optimistically. It *does* feel cool to have so many people at school rallying around me.

But yesterday sucked.

On our walk to Winter's class, I decide to ask Marshall about

Teddy. Because I'm still, like, 90 percent certain he's straight. But when he saw Mars at the Brandstones' beach, there was something about the way he touched my arm. And his wanting to come check on me at the house. And how he looked all proud of me after I told him about my dinner plans with my mom and Gus. And that charming grin of his.

I don't know, actually. I'm more, like, 70 percent certain he's straight. Er, 60 percent.

50 percent?

"Hey, um, which girls are tickling Teddy's fancy, by the way?" I ask. It comes out just as awkward and creepy to Marshall as it sounds to my own ears.

He squints at me. "Did you say 'tickling Teddy's fa—'"

"I just mean, who is Teddy into? Is he dating anyone?"

Marshall shrugs as we walk down steps, still scrolling through the GayForSky hashtag. "Why?"

"Has he ever said anything to you about, like . . ." I try to hint at it without being ridiculously obvious.

Marshall looks up from his phone. "Huh?"

"Has he—"

"Holy crap!" Bree yells, shoving her phone in front of us and nearly falling down the stairs. "Holy *crap*."

"What?"

"Carolyn got him. She freaking got him."

Marshall's phone buzzes. Mine dings as well.

Carolyn texted all three of us a note and a picture.

GUILTY! LMAO, her text reads. you bitches owe me (jk jk) xoxo 🖤.

She sent a screenshot of a photo Brendon e-mailed Cliff at 1:39 a.m. the night of Ali's party. A photo of me and Ali sitting on the sofa.

The photo of me and Ali sitting on the sofa.

Me, Bree, and Marshall look up at one another, frozen on the staircase, completely stunned.

That's it. That's the last piece of evidence we need.

~~The person somehow got a photo of the promposal wall.~~

~~The person somehow accessed Memories to hack the e-blast.~~

~~The person somehow got the pic of me and Ali at Ali's party.~~

"Let's go," Bree commands, turning to race to Winter's class.

"Wait." I grab her by the shoulders. "Should we get Ali first?"

"No! He's playing improv, or whatever. C'mon!"

I rush down the steps behind them and dash the length of the hallway to the Yearbook room, through a group of sophomores in gay shirts and two Cliff Cronies, who quickly dodge out of *our* way. And that's kind of cool.

"Hey!" Bree bellows, coming to a halt in the doorway.

Winter, eating lunch at her desk, drops her banana in surprise.

"Sorry! But we have to talk to you."

She motions for us to come in, mirroring our urgency. We close the door behind us.

"It was He Who Must Not Be Named," Bree breathes, fanning herself.

"Cliff Norquest," Marshall clarifies. "Cliff hacked the e-blast."

"We know because Rence Bloomington—who is Cliff's cousin—has been helping renovate my basement, which is where Sky's been staying because his mom kicked him out for being gay, but you already knew that." Bree pauses to inhale. "We have proof that Rence was working at my house *the same day* the promposal wall photo was taken. How do we know? Because the countdown on the wall in the e-blast photo matched. It makes perfect sense." The words are spilling out of her like she's rehearsed them—which, knowing her, she probably has.

Winter tries to get a word in. "Brandstone—"

"We know Cliff was able to log in to Memories to hack the e-blast because he manipulated Christina the day after Ali's party," Marshall explains. "She told us. The Memories log-in sheet backs me up."

Winter tries to interject, but Bree presses on, almost uncontrollably, "Plus, now we *also* have proof that Brendon Pastures took the photo of Ali and Sky on the sofa together using Jeff's phone and texted the photo to He Who Must Not Be Named—"

"Hey." Winter holds up her hand, the banana peel dangling from her fingers. "I know. I know that it was Cliff."

The room goes quiet.

"Wh-what?" Bree stammers.

"How?" Marshall asks.

"He admitted it."

"To who?"

"Me."

"When?"

"This morning." Winter sighs. "I was planning to tell you before class starts in about"—she glances at the clock—"five minutes."

The three of us look at one another, dumbfounded.

"And?" Bree demands, gaping.

"And what?" Winter replies.

"What happened?"

"I walked him down to Principal Burger's office."

More silence.

"That's . . . *it?*" Marshall gawks.

"What was his punishment?" Bree asks, increasingly frustrated. "He was suspended, right?"

"I'm not sure yet," Winter says. "I'll talk to Principal Burger after school today and see. You should know, Cliff said a guilty conscience prompted him to confess—"

"That's supposed to mean something to us?" Bree interjects, heated. "We're supposed to feel sorry for him because he feels guilty that he's a terrible human being?"

"No," Winter says. "Not at all."

The three of us don't know what to say.

We've been building our case for days. We had all the puzzle pieces finally fitting. And he just . . . surrendered? He somehow found a way to suck all the joy out of Operation: Pin It on He Who Must Not Be Named.

Just like that.

Winter notices I haven't said a word. "You okay, Baker?"

The past twenty-four hours have been so amazing and sad and disorienting all at once, and now *this*—Cliff pounding the final nail into his own coffin? It's all the more dizzying.

I thought I'd be happier to see justice served to the worst human who's ever set foot in Rock Ledge. But whatever satisfaction I imagined washing over me in this moment isn't materializing. The highs and lows of the past month have all canceled each other out, I think, and now I'm left . . . numb.

I want off this roller coaster.

I don't want to tell Winter all that, though. Not right now. So I simply say, "Yeah, I'm fine."

She gives me a look. "Can we chat for a minute?"

I nod. Bree and Marshall give me deflated glances before stepping into the hallway.

Winter gestures for me to sit down. The only noise in the room is the buzzing of our overheating, ancient computers.

"You seem overwhelmed," she says, leaning against her desk.

"Well . . . yeah, I am."

"By what?"

I stare at her. "Have you *not* been at this school the past month?"

She nods and smiles gently before staring at the floor in thought. "You should know," she says, each word intentional and serious, "I'm incredibly proud of you, Sky."

I swallow hard.

Winter doesn't normally say things like that. You don't get these moments with her. She's the tough teacher you love because you have to work your ass off to get even the tiniest compliment. Winter vocalizing that she's *incredibly proud* of me? Is this real life?

I don't know what to say.

She walks around to the front of her desk, but leans back on it again, folding her hands in front of her. "Are you happy Cliff confessed to the hacking?"

I open my mouth—but close it again after nothing comes out. I'm not sure how to answer.

"I get it," she says after I stay silent. "Sometimes justice doesn't bring about the emotions we expect it to."

"That's what I'm learning now," I say. "It's like . . . I originally wanted to ask Ali to prom at the beach in front of everyone as a way to kind of stick it to Cliff and his asshole friends."

"Hey now."

"Sorry. *Idiot* friends. I wanted to show them that everything they say to me—the taunts, the way they imitate my walk, all that— wouldn't stop me."

"Stop you from what?"

"From being me."

She smiles. It's one of her really rare smiles, too. Because usually Winter only lets her lips curl up a tad to appease whoever she's speaking with. But now, her dimples are in full bloom. Soft wrinkles appear near her eyes.

"That makes a lot of sense," she says. "But really, you never have to prove yourself to anyone who doesn't accept you for who you are."

I roll my eyes and smile, because she sounds so cheesy saying it. "I know."

"I mean it. Screw 'em."

"Yeah."

"Can I ask, when were you the happiest this past month?"

"What?"

"Was there a moment—or a day, or a week—when you felt truly happy, even in the aftermath of the e-blast?"

I think.

The past few weeks have been such a whirlwind. I can barely remember how I felt five minutes ago, let alone a month.

"I don't know . . . our shirt-making party at Bree's? Or the first day I came back to school and everyone was so nice and support-ive?" I also think about swimming at the beach after Yearbook Prom planning this week and no one making a big deal out of Mars. But Teddy is mostly to thank for that good memory.

I don't want to go there with Winter right now.

"Do you feel like those moments were more important than sticking it to Cliff?"

"Of course," I say, as if it's obvious.

"I'm not surprised," she says, crouching down in front of me. Now we're at eye level, her dangling pink earrings sparkling in a ray of sunshine breaking through the windows. "Look, I've never been prouder of you for standing up for yourself, and making those shirts, and refusing to be silenced by your, ah . . . *outspoken* class president, and letting Principal Burger have it." She grins. "But for your own state of mind, for your own well-being, it's important to take a second and remember the people who love you and support you. The people who make you happy. The people who make you one of the lucky ones."

One of the *lucky* ones?

I've never considered myself to be one of those.

My mom basically disowned me and I'm borderline homeless. My one and only sibling hates me. I'm still not even sure how I'm going to pay for community college this fall. How am I one of the lucky ones?

I have nothing.

"I don't feel lucky."

"I get that," she says. "You've had it rough this year. You deserve better—from your classmates, from your school, from your mom, from this town. But you also have two best friends who'd go to the end of the Earth for you."

I laugh.

"I'm serious," she says, almost offended. "I see how much Bree and Marshall love you, Baker. They look up to you every single day. Friends like that are rarer than you think."

"Look up to me?" Winter must be stoned.

"Yes, look up to you—as evidenced by how proudly they've been wearing those shirts. They admire you because you're an admirable person." She stands back up tall, pulling her long, black ponytail in front of her shoulder. "I'd hold on tight to friends like them."

"I'll *try*," I say. "But they're ditching me."

"What do you mean?"

"In a few months, Marshall will have moved three hours away, and Bree will have moved three time zones away."

"Well . . . fight."

"Huh?"

"Fight to keep them in your life. For friends like Bree and Marshall, the fight is worth it." She pauses. "I wish someone had told me that when I was your age."

I know there's more to that story. I know she wants to divulge, but thinks twice.

Then the lunch bell puts an end to our conversation. Yearbookers begin pouring into the room. I think Winter blinks away a tear before transforming back into tough-teacher mode.

One of the lucky ones.

ONE DAY

Between being distracted as hell from my chat with Winter and still trying to process Cliff's confession, I have what has to be my least productive Yearbook class of all time. Seriously. I didn't get a single thing done on my movies spread, which is a problem because all our pages need to be 100 percent done next week if we want the books to print on time. (To say Bree would murder me if it were my fault we missed the publishing deadline is an understatement.)

Bree and Marshall are in foul moods because they, too, found the conclusion of Operation: Pin It on He Who Must Not Be Named to be depressingly anticlimactic. I don't know how we expected our mission to end—Cliff getting arrested in the parking lot with the whole school watching? Bree berating him with all our evidence in the middle of the hallway until he crumbled into tears?—but a quiet confession to Winter and discreet trip to Burger's office definitely was not it.

The bell rings, and everyone disperses their own ways. I turn left out of Winter's class—my mind still foggy from the insanity of the day—and look up to see the last person I expect walking down the hallway toward me. For a second, I think I'm hallucinating.

Charlie.

My whole body practically starts convulsing.

He looks confused, eyes darting between a piece of paper in his hands and the various classrooms surrounding us.

I run up to him, wrapping a sweater around my GAY FOR ALI shirt to avoid any questions. "Uh . . . hi?"

His eyes fall on mine. "Sky," he breathes, relieved to see my face. "How are you?"

"I'm fine, but—but what are you doing here?"

"I'm looking for room"—he looks down at the paper in his hands, a note from the main office—"forty-nine. The secretary didn't mention your teacher's name, so—"

"Room forty-nine is the Yearbook room."

"Yeah," he says, smile fading as he takes in how horrified I am to see him. "Listen, Sky, I'm not sure if you saw I called—"

"I did. I'm sorry for not calling you back."

"It's okay. You don't owe me an explanation. But I want to support the yearbook either way." He pulls his checkbook out of his coat pocket. Oh my God. After all this, he still wants to pay for the ad. "I was planning on dropping this off to your teacher—"

I grab Charlie by the elbow and rush him into the abandoned computer lab no one has used in years. Most schools may be dealing with overcrowding, but crumbling Rock Ledge High was built when the town was twice the size, so there's a dusty room stuffed with academic relics in every hallway. It's stuffy inside, the air reeks of mothballs, and the lights don't even come on when you flip the switch, but better trapping Charlie in here, even with the risk of inhaling asbestos, than Winter learning I broke our ad sales rules by promising a full-page to my dead dad's high school buddy.

"You can't go into the Yearbook room," I say sternly. "I'm sorry, but you just can't."

"Why not?"

I start pacing back and forth, overwhelmed by the absurdity of this week. Of this month. Of my entire senior year.

I can try to think of something on the spot to cover my tracks. Spew out a few more lies to save my ego from being eternally bruised. But I can't lie to Charlie any longer. I have to own up to it. I have to own up to how I got into this mess.

I sigh and shake my head, holding back unexpected tears. "I'm not Justin Jackson."

He smiles. "Well, yes, I know that," he says, walking toward a row of windows and pulling open the blinds to let some light in. "Haven't you noticed I've been calling you 'Sky'?"

"I didn't come over to your house to sell you a yearbook ad, either."

He pulls open the window. A slight breeze and a few chirping birds help break the suffocating stillness. "I kind of figured that."

"How did you know that it was me in your kitchen that day?" I don't know why I'm asking; I already know the answer. "It was Mars that gave it away, wasn't it?"

"Mars?"

"My burn scar?"

Charlie remembers—closing his eyes and tilting his head backward, like he's an idiot for forgetting. "Ah, right. Mars."

He loosens his gray tie and slides both hands into his pockets before gliding toward the front of the classroom. He stops once he's in front of the chalkboard, still dusted with the chalky remnants of the early aughts, and pivots on the heels of his feet to face me and the sea of empty desks. The front of a classroom suits him well, with his salt-and-pepper hair and black-rimmed glasses.

"This was definitely the room," he says.

"What room?"

He looks at me. "Mrs. Babcock's. US History. I sat over there." He points to his left. "I think your dad sat . . ." He thinks for a moment, scanning the space. "Oddly enough, right there." He nods at the desk nearest me.

I imagine my teenaged dad sitting just a few feet away. It feels like a weird, warm hug. Like two parallel universes from two eras colliding in the best possible way. "Seriously?"

"Seriously." He grins. "We sat next to each other for a few days, but your dad was a troublemaker. So we got separated. Fast."

"He was a bad kid?"

"No, no." He shakes his head fervently. "A kid who liked to press your buttons? Sure. A kid who sometimes didn't know how to keep his mouth shut during an exam? Absolutely. But a *bad* kid? No. Never." He almost lets out a laugh at the thought. "Your dad had a heart of gold."

I move toward the desk Charlie nodded at and slide my fingers across its spotty surface. This couldn't possibly be the same seat my dad sat in, of course. I bet a hundred kids and a dozen janitors have shuffled the desks around in here over the years—if they're even the same desks at all. And who knows, Charlie could be mixed up and this was never Mrs. Babcock's class to begin with.

But it doesn't matter. I still feel my dad in here. Like when I was in Charlie's den the first time, learning about what had prompted the *tough* quote. Or when I was lying on Bree's car after school in the parking lot, staring up at the eternal canvas of blue above.

"But yes, you're right," Charlie concludes, walking back up a row of desks toward me, his hands still planted firmly in his pockets. "You look quite a bit different than when you were a kid. But you felt familiar to me the moment I met you. And when I saw Mars again, it finally clicked. I knew you were Henry's son."

The warning bell rings, confirming I'm definitely going to be late for next hour.

"When did you see Mars before?" I press on.

"Your mom came to me with pictures of the scarring a few months after your dad died," he explains. "She knew I was studying dermatology."

"Did we ever meet in real life?" I ask. "Did I ever see you after the accident?"

He breathes in deeply, visibly uncomfortable for the first time since I met him. "It's complicated."

"How so?"

"Your mom sort of, ah . . . How can I put this?" He finally breathes out again. "She became closed off to many people after your dad was gone, Sky. I met you one time, before the accident, when you were about this tall"—he gestures to his thigh—"but that was it. I saw the photos of what became Mars, provided the best medical advice I could at the time, but never heard from her again."

That's tough to hear. But it's also not surprising.

I hardly remember anything that happened before my dad died, but between the cheerful, carefree family photos taken pre-funeral and the tales Gus told me about our cursing, weed-smoking *cool* mom that had vanished along with Dad, I assumed she left behind lots of people—just like she left behind her true self.

Charlie must have been one of them.

"I'm sorry," I say, hearing my voice tremble a bit. I try to keep it together. "I'm sorry she did that to you. And I'm sorry we didn't get to know each other better a long time ago"

"Me too." He smiles. "But I'm very happy I get to know you now."

"Do you know Mrs. Brandstone?" I ask.

Charlie thinks for a moment.

"Actually, you would have known her as Jennifer Graham."

He thinks some more. "Jennifer Graham . . . the name does sound familiar, but I can't place it."

I'm beyond embarrassed to divulge everything. But Charlie's been nothing but wonderful to me. I owe it to him to be up-front.

"She's my friend's mom," I continue. "She went to high school at the same time as you and my dad. I think she knew you were friends with him, and she wanted me to connect with you because . . ." I think about bringing up the promposal wall, and the e-blast hack, and my ensuing mental breakdown, but I can't right now. That's for another time. "She knew I was going through a rough time."

Charlie purses his lips, nodding.

"I think she thought if I met you," I explain, "it'd help me to just, like . . . sort some stuff out. I think she thought it'd make me tougher."

"I see."

"I chickened out, though. I was nervous. I made up the whole Justin Jackson thing and fake sold you a yearbook ad. It's all so stupid."

"No, it's not." Charlie leans against the desk that technically may—but probably, definitely not—have been my dad's, and folds his arms across his chest. He has a lot of important stuff to say, I can tell, but he's fighting the urge to spill it all at once. Instead, he mulls over every word before it escapes his mouth.

"You know when you were at my house and I was asking about Ram Ragers and nugget Fridays and all the things I cherished about my glory days here?"

"Yeah."

"Well, don't be fooled. For every Ram Rager and nugget Friday, I have twenty terrible memories of this place." He scans a wall of yellowed, torn posters describing how a bill becomes a law. "Growing up here was rough. It was really, *really* rough. But I wouldn't change it for the world." He clears his throat. "I grew some thick skin, which came in handy. I got a whole lot tougher"—he winks at me—"and I met some wonderful people, including my very best friend."

The tardy bell rings, echoing throughout the near-empty halls. I'm going to be way late for my next class on the other end of the building.

I look at Charlie. "I've got to go."

"Of course," he says, nodding. "I don't want to get you in trouble."

"Can I ask you a favor?"

"Anything."

"Please don't go to the Yearbook room. I kind of broke the rules by offering you an ad."

He laughs.

"I still want to sell you a full page!" I clarify. "I just—I need to work it out with our sales team first. And this time, I *promise* I'll give you a call and we can plan out the details."

He pats my shoulder, lips curling up into his dimples. "Sounds great, Sky."

Without thinking, I lean in for a hug. It may have surprised him, because he doesn't really react for a second. But his arms wrap around my back and pull me in too. The softness of his sweater vest feels so nice against my cheek.

"Thank you, Charlie," I say, before grabbing my stuff and rushing out of the room.

The rest of the day, I'm a ball of . . . something. A lot of things. Nerves? Dread? Excitement? Relief? All of the above, really.

I'm not exactly sure why, but Cliff's confession is still hanging over me like some dark storm cloud. And it's slowly sinking in that the Senior Beach-Bum Party is now a matter of *hours*—not days— away, which is utterly terrifying. But coming clean to Charlie took a million pounds off my shoulders—a million pounds I hadn't even realized had been weighing me down for days—and Winter's two cents from our chat earlier are still swirling around in my head like a song on repeat I just can't shake.

One of the lucky ones.

I get a kind of crazy idea in last hour. One that may just help me stop this Nerve-Dread-Excitement-Relief boulder from crashing

at the bottom of the mountain. I have no idea if Bree will be down for it, but I might as well give it a shot.

"Hey," I say to her as we cross the parking lot at the end of the day, her glittery DAYS LEFT: 1 shirt sparkling in the sunlight. "I know you were just making the e-blast for Monday in Yearbook today, but how weird would it be to have an e-blast go out on a Friday as well?"

She looks at me like I'm up to something. "What do you have in mind?"

ONE DAY

Hi there,

    I'm senior Sky Baker. I wanted to send out this special Friday night edition of the e-blast in order to talk about something important to me, Rock Ledge High, and, to be frank, our whole town. Here goes nothing.

As many of you saw, two very unfortunate photos were shared through this newsletter a few weeks ago. A student who isn't on staff was able to log on to our system and upload two personal pictures of me and another senior. They used slurs against us, too.

But this isn't about that student or that e-blast.

This is about what happened next.

I used to hate this school. Like, I've called it a heterosexual hellscape (in my head at least). And it's not like now I love it. It's still RLHS. The B-hall elevator is STILL broken. The science wing still smells like death (formaldehyde and burning incense). We still have homophobic, racist bullies here. And we still can't win a basketball game. No shade, basketballers.

I saw another side of Rock Ledge these past two weeks, though.

After the e-blast was sent, so many of you—SO. MANY. OF. YOU.—were there for me. Immediately. Not just my friends, Yearbookers, or other seniors, either; people I'd never even talked to before. You DM'd to check in, and you bombarded me with heart emojis, and you smiled at me in the hallway, and you proudly wore your gay shirts, and you gave me high fives, and you proved that you had my back.

No matter what.

Many of us feel like outsiders around here. I know I'm not the only one. I've felt like an outsider my whole entire life. But the past two weeks, and for the first time ever, I didn't feel like that was a bad thing.

I felt like one of the lucky ones.

Thank you for all the love, Rock Ledge.

Gay For You,
Sky

P.S. Just to be clear, I won't be promposing to Ali Rashid at the Senior Beach-Bum Party. Let's all just have some fun in the sun. Class of 2021. 🖤

P.P.S. Please don't unsubscribe if you're annoyed by this e-blast. Our editor-in-chief, who's worked very hard all year, wants me to note how much your readership means to us.

ZERO DAYS

I wake up the next morning finally feeling like myself again. Actually, feeling like myself for the first time ever.

I climb the stairs to the Brandstones' kitchen. *SportsCenter* is blasting away, although no one's watching it. Clare, wearing an apron covered in flour, is yelling at Petey for sticking his finger into some batter she's whipping up. Ray is nonstop scream-singing a line from a Beatles song on repeat. Bree is debating the nutritional facts of the hot cocoa in her hand with her dad. And Thelma and Louise are barking at a squirrel dangling outside the window like they're defending the house against burglars. Typical Saturday.

"Morning, Sky." Mrs. Brandstone spots me. "Oatmeal?"

"Sure, thanks." I climb onto the bar stool next to Bree, who doesn't even say hello before handing me an earbud so I can listen to whatever podcast she has on.

Before I get a chance, Mr. Brandstone, having driven home his final point on cocoa powder, commands everyone's attention. "Listen up. I know *you* have a swimming thing, and *you're* filming a YouTube at your friend's, and *you* two have your senior beach party, and *you* want to go to the animal sanctuary, *but*"—he gets serious—"today's the day. Spring cleaning. Everyone is pitching in with the yard before anyone leaves the house."

Petey groans in protest.

"No way anyone's getting out of it," Mr. Brandstone cuts him off, shaking his head. "Let's go."

I scarf down my oatmeal and am about to follow the twins outside, but Mr. Brandstone slides in front of the door, blocking me. We're the only ones left in the house.

"This came for you in the mail," he says.

He pulls out a thick manila envelope from behind his back and hands it to me. It's addressed from Rock Ledge Public Schools.

"Oh." My heart stops. The scholarship. "Is this . . . *it?*"

He shrugs.

"Do you think I got it?" I ask.

It looks like he's hiding a smile. "There's a lot of paperwork in there for a rejection letter. But what do I know?"

I breathe in and out slowly, sliding my fingertips across the seal.

"Do you want me to give you a moment?" he asks, sensing my hesitation.

I didn't think I'd be this nervous. I didn't expect to want privacy. But I nod.

He lets his smile show, says, "Okay," softly, and joins the rest of the family outside.

I sit down on the top stair to the basement, and Thelma and Louise appear on either side, nudging my shoulders with their wet snouts. I don't think they're looking for pats—they just want me to know they're there.

I take another deep breath and open the envelope.

Dear Mr. Sky Baker: Congratulations! is the first and only thing I read.

I jump up, throw my hands in the air, and scream. Thelma and Louise start going nuts.

I got the scholarship. I'm going to college.

I race out the front door waving the envelope above my head. "I got it!" Everyone turns toward me. "I got the scholarship!"

Mr. and Mrs. Brandstone rush in for hugs. Bree starts moonwalking across the front yard. Petey's jumping around like he just won a swim meet, and Ray follows his lead—even though I bet neither of them are quite sure what's going on. Even Clare sends me a smile.

"Amazing!" Mrs. Brandstone yells, beaming. She bends in closer to read the congratulatory letter in my hand. "Wow. This is fantastic, Sky."

"Proud of you." Mr. Brandstone ruffles my hair. "This doesn't get you out of spring cleaning, though."

It's sunny and in the sixties. Not necessarily ideal for a beach day, but basically magical for April in northern Michigan.

Mr. Brandstone puts Bree in charge of filling in freshly dug pits under the pine trees with dark red mulch, and I'm put on "weed patrol," as Mrs. Brandstone is calling it. Normally this would be torturous, but I'm on cloud nine right now; I could be shoveling Thelma's and Louise's poop all day and still be smiling from ear to ear.

College. *I'm going to college.*

I circle around their huge yard, which feels even bigger when it's your duty to pull up any and all disruptive growths, to find the little effers. When I'm about finished, I spot a tiny one busting through a crack in their driveway, but I decide to let that one stay. This is Rock Ledge, after all. We've got cracked concrete driveways around these parts, and sometimes a weed finds its perfect little home there.

I can relate.

Once the mulch is laid, the weeds are (nearly) vanquished, the porch is swept, and the yard is raked of all the dead leaves that have had their hiding places exposed now that the snow has melted, it's time to get ready. Because today's the day.

Zero effing days left.

I jump into the shower to rinse off all the late-winter gunk from my hands, knees, and face. I don't have a single shower-dream, either.

I'm standing in the bathroom, staring at my reflection, intentionally breaking my number one rule. There's Mars. Staring right back. Yeah, he's a million times more fire-engine red than usual. But I'm A-okay with that. He even looks a little bit badass.

Someone knocks on the door. "Sky?" It's Mrs. Brandstone.

"One sec!" I wrap a towel around my middle and slip on my tank top. "Yeah, what's up?"

The door opens, and the bright red rims of her glasses appear in the crack—way more hesitantly than they did thirty days ago. "Hey."

"Hey."

"There's a box of beach stuff in the closet next to your bedroom downstairs, in case you and Bree want to bring some stuff. Could be fun."

"Nice. Thank you."

"I told Bree, but I have a feeling she'll forget. A Frisbee, one of those Spikeball games—those sorts of things."

"Awesome. I'll definitely check it out."

She smiles at me and sighs, closing the door. "Okey dokey—"

"Hey." I turn away from the mirror to give her my full attention. "Just so you know, I appreciate everything you and Mr. Brandstone have done for me these past few months."

"Oh, don't worry about it, hon."

"No, seriously," I emphasize, because I don't think she really gets it. "Helping me with the scholarship, and giving me a place to stay, and allowing the Yearbookers to come over for the shirt-making party; it's all just . . . so nice. I don't know what I would do without you two and Bree. And Clare, Petey, and Ray. And Thelma and Louise. I'm lucky to have you all."

She laughs before pushing her glasses farther up the bridge of her nose. "We're the lucky ones, Sky."

A bit later, Marshall arrives right on time to carpool to the beach. "Hey, y'all," he says, as me and Bree drop into the back seats of his car with our towels, sunglasses, and beach bags.

Ainsley's wearing a massive, straw beach hat in the passenger seat that could basically cause an eclipse. "Who wants gum?" she asks, reaching back to hand us some.

"Thanks, but the gum can wait," I say. "Because I have some big news. . . ."

Marshall glances back at me, looking scared.

"I got the scholarship."

The car erupts in squeals. Bree and I crack up.

"That is *fantastic*," Marshall yells, reaching into the back seat to shake my knee.

"Let's see if we can get into some of the same courses first semester!" Ainsley says, before cupping her hands over her mouth excitedly. "Oh my God. I'll be so relieved to have someone I know in class. Study buddies!"

Marshall rolls down our windows and pulls off toward the state beach.

Once we're out of Bree's neighborhood, he cranks up the music too.

Loud.

"Whoa," Bree yells happily over the pulsating bass. "Seventy-year-old Marshall with the beat drop?!"

I catch Marshall's eyes in the rearview mirror.

We exchange smiles.

I don't want to jinx it, but everything feels okay for the first time in a really long time. I'm not riding some emotional high sparked by a GAY FOR SKY shirt—one that I know will inevitably crash—nor am I crying into a pillow with Louise at my side, wishing I'd never been born.

Being in this car, with these people, feels just right.

"Is Dan meeting up with us after the beach?" I yell at Bree, the wind whipping her hair throughout the car like a sprinkler gone wild. I have a flashback of the last time we stalked Ali together, because her hair was all over the place then, too.

"What?" she yells back.

"I said"—my voice gets louder—"is Dan meeting up with us later?"

She nods.

"You should prompose to him today."

"What?"

"I said, you should prompose to him today!"

She grins. "Oh yeah?"

"I'm serious!"

I *wasn't* really that serious when I said it the first time. But come to think of it, the two of them would make a great Yearbook Prom pair.

"Actually, I've been meaning to tell you something," she says, scooching over in the back seat so she doesn't have to yell. "I have a confession."

I tense up. "Okay . . . ?"

"You know how you thought I was mad at you the weekend of Ali's party?"

In the crazy aftermath of the e-blast hack, I almost forgot about Bree's horrible mood that weekend. "Yeah?"

"And I told you I wasn't, but, like . . . never gave you an explanation for why I was in such a terrible funk?"

"Yeah?"

"Well, I wasn't lying. I *wasn't* mad at you. But Dan . . . ah, Dan broke up with me that weekend. At Ali's party."

"What?"

"I said"—she raises her voice a bit louder—"Dan broke—"

"No, I heard you, it's just"—I pop my eyes, smiling from ear to ear—"why didn't you tell me you two were dating?"

She smiles back nervously with a shrug. "Surprise."

It makes perfect sense. I was just so caught up in all my own stuff,

I never put two and two together. Bree always melts into a pile of goo when Dan walks into a room. And watching Dan stare at Bree while she goes on one of her rants—like when she was catching him up to speed on all the drama when they were sitting on the hood of her car in the school parking lot, or going over Yearbook Prom ideas in the Brandstones' kitchen—he always has this sparkle in his eye.

I should have known.

"Well," I begin, unsure what to say next, trying to digest the news. "I'm sorry he broke up with you."

"I'm sorry I didn't tell you earlier," she cuts in. I can tell she's been dying to tell me. "He's been trying to navigate this whole coming out thing and we wanted to hold off telling people about us until he felt more comfortable in Rock Ledge."

"I get it, don't worry." I lay my arm across her thigh.

"Thanks." She lays her arm across mine. "But yeah. That's why I was in a mood that morning, and that's why He Who Must Not Be Named was able to successfully pull off the e-blast hack. I wanted to go to school early to meet up with Dan and try to talk things through—not make sure the e-blast got out okay." She drops her voice, ashamed. "I didn't give it a final read-through. I messed up. And I lied about it. I'm sorry."

"Brandstone." I bump her lovingly with my shoulder. "You don't need to apologize."

She wraps her arms around me tighter than ever before, squeezing the oxygen out of my lungs. "Thank you."

"Are you two having a moment?" Marshall asks, turning down the music and peeking up at us in the rearview mirror with a grin. "I'm having friend FOMO right now."

293

"Don't worry," Bree says. "I'll explain later."

"So it seems like you and Dan are still friends, though, right?" I whisper in her ear after Marshall's eyes go back to the road.

"Oh, we're back together. He only broke up with me because he didn't want to drag me through the messiness of his coming out as trans at school. He was trying to protect me. But I can protect myself."

"So wait." I look her in the eye. "You're telling me you have a *boyfriend*?"

She gives me a look. "Right?"

"You're telling me at least one of us *dateable*?"

"It appears that way, yes."

"Maybe there's hope for me, too."

Marshall pulls into the beach parking lot, and it's already crazy busy with seniors. All the jocks are running around shirtless for the world to see, and their hot girlfriends have picked out the prime sand real estate. There's a lot of skin, as expected, but a lot of hoodies and jeans, too. It's only sixty-something—what else can you expect?

But I'm not going to let the chilly breeze be an excuse for covering up. It's time for badass Mars to meet the world.

We step out of the car and start slipping on our sandals, stuffing our bags with snacks from the trunk, and searching the faces along the shoreline for familiar ones. Hopefully the Yearbookers have a good spot we can join.

Then Marshall takes off his shirt. And it's my turn to do the same.

I take a deep breath—remind myself to be tough—and slip it off too. The breeze hits my chest and the sunlight splashes across my face. The world hasn't ended. Not quite yet.

So I decide to roll with it.

Walking through the sand behind the others, I feel everyone's eyes are on me. It's like all Rock Ledge is watching—in my head, at least. My hips are swinging, but they're not swinging too much or too little. They're swinging just right. Because this is how I walk.

This is how I am.

We spot Ali, Christina, and Dustin along with a bunch of other Yearbookers, and gravitate their way. They laid out a bunch of towels to form this massive hangout spot with picnic baskets and umbrellas and speakers. I'm still nervous, but my Mars anxiety is slowly being replaced with excitement and the overwhelming smell of sunscreen.

Ali waves at me when we make eye contact. "Sky High!"

I wave back.

Hopefully enough people read my e-blast and know I'm not asking Ali—or *anyone*, for that matter—to prom. I want to have a fun time. That's all.

Just as we decide on a spot to claim as ours, I notice something's . . . happening.

Something strange.

"You should know," Bree whispers into my ear as all the Year-bookers stand up, "this was not my idea."

I look at her. "What wasn't your idea?"

They're all smiling at me. Then a bunch of other students around the group begin to rise too. And they're pulling white shirts over their bare torsos and bikini tops. It's not all the seniors at the beach—but it's lots of them. Dozens of them.

And all their shirts read GAY FOR SKY.

My heart is racing.

"Uh . . ." I gape as Marshall, Ainsley, and Bree all turn to me, beaming from ear to ear. The heat rises in my cheeks, and chills zoom up and down my spine.

"What's going on?" I keep repeating, but no one is answering me.

"Hi," Teddy says, appearing out of nowhere, green eyes sparkling in the sunlight. His face is peppered with grains of sand. His lips spread into a grin.

A Teddy Grin.

And my knees almost buckle, I swear to God. I think my vocal cords forget how to operate for a second too. But they finally get it together.

"Hi," is all I can muster in the moment.

He's not in a GAY FOR SKY shirt. He's wearing his orange Rock Ledge Rams track outfit. "I wanted to wear what everyone else has on," he says, voice trembling a little as he glances around at the sea of GAY FOR SKY shirts. "But Marshall said you'd prefer this one instead."

"Wait . . . what?"

I whip around to face Marshall, who's cracking up. "Sorry, man," he says, shaking his head. "I had to."

Teddy pulls yellow roses out from behind his back, along with the tiniest envelope I've ever seen. I take them both with shaky hands—all of this feeling far more surreal than even my craziest shower-dreams—and unseal the envelope. Inside are the old-school, vintage-looking ticket stubs from the first movie we saw together. The DuVernay one.

Then it all clicks.

This was Marshall's master plan. For *weeks*.

Those obnoxious questions he asked about promposing to Ainsley? About the yellow roses? About the movie tickets? About what he should wear when he asks her? They were really about *this*. The whole time.

My mind recaps all the little moments throughout the past month when Teddy tried to start conversations, tried to break the ice, tried to grease the wheels. When he complimented my shoes thirty days ago as we walked across the school's front lawn. When he attempted to ask me about my movies spread at Ali's party, but I was too distracted to care. When he showed me the No Context: To All the Boys I've Loved Before account after school, even though Bree's car was out of his way to track practice. When he was wandering up to the Brandstones' after jumping into Lake Michigan to check on me.

Maybe I've been Teddy's Ali Rashid this whole time.

I look around, hardly able to process what is happening. Dustin and Christina are standing there, taking photos. Carolyn, overcome with emotion, looks like she's straight up sobbing. I spot Ali, too, flashing the biggest Ali Grin ever. And Marshall's laughing even harder now, totally delighted that he helped pull this off.

"I've been gay for you for a while, Sky," Teddy says to me softly. "Will you go to Yearbook Prom with me?"

NEGATIVE TWENTY-SEVEN DAYS

Things settle down after the Beach-Bum Party. Thank God! Like I said: 70 percent introvert. Do you know the toll the past few months can take on a person like me?

I mean, sure, this semester was hands down the best of my life, all in all. But still.

I'm finally able to focus on school without all the extra gay attention and Ali's eyebrows distracting me. I convince Mrs. Diamond to let me resubmit a few assignments—proving that I *do* know what gonorrhea is—use my lunches to make up Anatomy tests I bombed, and retain just enough information in Trig to push myself up to a C-plus. Mr. Kam isn't impressed with me, but I sure as hell am.

I don't have to remind myself to be tough anymore either. I just sort of . . . am?

Sometimes walking around in your own skin and feeling good about it is enough to feel like a badass, is all. Tough feels good.

But today's a big day. And it has me on edge for three reasons.

For starters, it's my birthday (as Ray reminded me approximately one million times this morning in the kitchen). Eighteen. Officially a human adult.

Despite initially refusing to do so, Mrs. Brandstone eventually gave in last week and promised to keep it a low-key affair. Like, I made her swear on the dusty old Bible they keep in the living room cupboard that there would be zero birthday surprises.

Clare made a Boston cream pie (my favorite) for tonight, and Ray crafted a bunch of surprisingly elaborate 18! 18! 18! signs that he dispersed throughout the house. Teddy decorated my locker like the absolute sweetheart that he is, and Winter blew up some yellow balloons and tied them around my seat in class.

After a semester like the one I've had? That's about all the extravagance I can handle, honestly.

Secondly, the yearbooks arrived today. I'm freaking out to see how our year's worth of work looks in print. (Any anxiety I have is dwarfed by what Bree's been going through. She literally hasn't slept in days.)

And last but not least, Teddy's taking me to the appointment I booked with Charlie after school to deal with this whole Mars thing.

"You ready?" Teddy buckles up.

I breathe out with an anxious groan. "Sure."

He stifles a laugh, zipping up his maroon hoodie, looking especially cute today. "You nervous?"

"Yes!"

"It's going to be fine." He gives me a little peck on the cheek, and then nods past me, out the passenger side.

I roll my window down. "What's good, Christiansen?"

Dan bends down so he can see both of us in the car. "Just trying to survive this . . . what did you so appropriately call it in your e-blast letter? Heterosexual hellscape?"

"Bingo."

"Yeah, that. Trying to survive that. Also, happy birthday."

"Thanks."

"Whoa!" Dan's face lights up as he spots the brand-new year-book sitting on my lap. "That's right, they arrived! Congrats, dude. I've got to go pick mine up."

"Thanks," I say, staring down at its black cover. "Hot off the press. I'm surprised Bree hasn't made you look through hers four hundred times already."

"Don't worry." Dan sighs. "She will."

I haven't opened mine up yet. I know this may be weird, but I want to read it all alone at the Brandstones', where I can read every last word, appreciate each page, and let it all sink in. Now I have to use all my self-control not to give in and flip it open this second.

"I wanted to tell you," Dan says to me. "We're up to nineteen. I e-mailed you an updated member list about an hour ago."

"Damn," I say. "Two days ago it was eleven."

He shrugs, smiling. "What can I say? You helped a lot of people burst through their closet doors."

"We *both* did."

Dan and I are trying to get everything squared up with GLOW this year so that Dan can hit the ground running as the group's president next fall. Winter talked with Mrs. Choi—the brand-new Biology teacher who's a lesbian—about being GLOW's advisor too; she's stoked to help out.

Weirdly enough, as much as I can't wait to be done with high school, I'm kind of bummed I'll be missing out on GLOW stuff.

"Also, this might be a little strange, but"—Dan bends in a little closer to the car—"Cliff wants to talk to you."

I haven't given that asshole a second thought since I hit send on my e-blast letter weeks ago. "What do you mean?"

"Why?" Teddy asks over my shoulder. "Are you friends with him?"

"*No.*" Dan recoils. "He lives in my neighborhood, though, and yesterday he saw me shooting hoops in my driveway and pulled in to talk."

"You should have thrown the basketball at his windshield," Teddy says, joking—but not really.

"He heard about GLOW and how I'm friends with you and Ali. He apologized to me about the e-blast hack and asked me if I'd see if you and Ali would go to lunch with him sometime. Apparently, getting suspended can change a person." Dan holds his hands out to temper me, anticipating my reaction. "But I totally understand if you don't want to."

"Don't do it," Teddy urges. "He doesn't deserve it, Sky."

"I kind of agree, unless an apology would mean something to you." Dan straightens up and swings his backpack onto his back. "But your call. Just thought I'd let you know."

"Thanks." I don't know what to think. "I'll talk to Ali about it."

"What time should I come over to Bree's tomorrow to help set up for prom?"

"Probably four or five. I'll text you."

"Sounds good," Dan says, tapping the top of Teddy's car. "See you later, queens." He gives us a wink and walks off.

Teddy notices I'm quieter than usual on the ride to the

appointment. "You're really that nervous about Mars, huh?"

"It's not that," I say, staring into the trees. "I don't know what to do about Cliff."

"I hate that you're wasting a single second thinking about that idiot."

He's probably right.

It's nauseating just imagining being in the same room with Cliff again. Meeting up would almost feel like giving him an easy way out of his guilt, or something. Like, I don't owe him an opportunity to apologize. I don't owe him anything.

Just like I don't owe my mom anything either.

It's still impossible for me to think about one homophobe without immediately remembering that the other one exists too. Just like when Cliff mocked me in Health. They're still two peas in a pod.

At least Cliff reached out, though. At least he's trying to make amends. At least he won't condition anything on a cultlike summer camp.

"Hey," Teddy says, probably sensing my swirling thoughts. "Do whatever you feel is right. I've got your back."

I smile at him and push any thoughts of Cliff and my mom as far out of my brain as possible. That's for another day.

We arrive at my appointment, and the butterflies in my stomach are flapping around like crazy. Because today is the day I'm saying goodbye to Mars.

Well, sort of. Mars is getting a dramatic makeover.

"Sky! Happy birthday!" Brian yells, walking out from behind the counter of Traverse Tats wearing a party hat and beaming like a fireworks finale. I don't even have time to blink—he wraps me up in the biggest bear hug his body can muster. I made Charlie and Brian promise to be chill on the birthday stuff too, but that didn't stop them from hanging streamers from the ceiling.

"You must be Teddy." Brian tosses me aside to nearly rip off Teddy's arm in one of the most aggressive handshakes I've ever witnessed. But Teddy holds his own. Or at least he tries to.

Charlie, also rocking a party hat, comes striding out from the back. He's not quite as euphoric as his puppy-dog boyfriend, but he's definitely happy to see me. We hug too, and he shakes Teddy's hand. "Eighteen, wow." He sighs, crossing his arms over his chest. "How does it feel?"

I shrug. "Weird.

"Sounds about right." Brian grins.

"I'm glad we're doing this, Sky," Charlie says.

"Are you really, though?" I say, half kidding. "Because I'm kind of freaking out right now."

"Me too." He laughs. "Let's get this over with before I change my mind."

"Hold on!" Brian grabs my arm and pulls me behind the desk, where there's a tablet for booking appointments and taking payment. "I know it's your birthday, but it's technically also your first day on the clock, remember? We've got some training to knock out first."

Last week, Brian offered me a receptionist job, which I accepted in about point-five seconds flat. Yeah, it's a long drive from Rock Ledge, but Bree's not taking her car to California, so she's letting me borrow it indefinitely. Plus, Charlie and Brian said I can stay overnight at their house whenever I feel like it, which I'm thinking will be a *lot*. Summer on the lake splashing around with Bob and Teddy? Yes, please.

The best part is, the receptionist job pays eighteen dollars an hour, which means I'll not only be able to pay the Brandstones some rent money, but also have enough left over to hang out with Ainsley and Dan, and even visit Marshall a weekend in the fall.

After Brian walks me through the ins and outs of answering phones and booking appointments, it's finally time. We're doing this.

"You ready?" Charlie asks, sitting in the chair next to mine.

"As ready as I'll ever be."

Brian pulls out new tools and a freshly sterilized tattoo gun, along with a sheet of paper that has the design he created for me and Charlie: the initials HRB—for Henry Robert Baker—perfected in sleek black lettering. "Any last words?" Brian asks with a smirk.

"Um . . ." I exhale before slipping off my shirt. "Nope. Let's do this."

"I promised myself I'd never be sitting in this chair." Charlie sighs to himself, shaking his head in surrender. "Yet"—he turns to me with a smile—"here I am."

Brian carefully presses the design onto Mars; the outline of my dad's initials cover most of my pink, scarred skin. "You should feel proud of yourself, Sky," he says, gently peeling the paper off again, Mars now hardly visible. "Charlie's been tattoo-resistant since I met him. You've done what no one else has been able to do."

"I bet my dad would have been supportive of this idea, though," I say.

"I *know* he would have been," Charlie confirms.

"Can I get you anything?" Teddy asks, pulling up a chair on the other side of me and grabbing my hand. He looks just as nervous as I am. "Tissues? A glass of water?"

"I might ask you to start scrolling through those *To All the Boys I've Loved Before* memes at some point," I say. That would probably help ease my anxiety, come to think of it.

"Don't worry, it'll be quick and . . . almost painless," Brian adds, preparing the work space around him. "I'll be done before you know it."

Sure, you could say this was somewhat of a rash decision, seeing as I came up with the idea to honor my dad with a tattoo just four days ago, and then Brian sketched up the design less than twenty-four hours later. I should probably let the idea sink in another week before covering half my chest in eternal black ink. But this feels absolutely right. Every time I'm with Charlie and Brian, I've noticed, *everything* feels absolutely right.

Everyone's parents tell you not to get tattoos on a whim because it's something so permanent. Like, Mr. Brandstone probably would've locked me in my bedroom this morning if I'd told him about this appointment. I think the permanency is what I'll love most about it, though. Not only will I have a piece of my dad wherever I go, but I'll have this inerasable bond to Charlie and Brian, too.

It doesn't feel like a tattoo memorializing my dad as much as it feels like the first step in finally getting to know him—as the tough kid I know he'd want me to be, with a new family I know he'd want me to hold on to.

Brian's tattoo gun starts buzzing. Teddy squeezes my hand tighter.

"Hey," Charlie whispers quietly enough that I'm the only one who can hear. "I'm very happy you came over to sell me a fake yearbook ad, Sky."

I laugh a little before bracing for the impact of the needle. "Me too."

NEGATIVE TWENTY-EIGHT DAYS

So, guess what? Sleeping with a new tattoo on your chest is not fun. Shocking, I know.

I had to lie on my back the whole night, without a sheet or blanket covering me, just staring straight up at the ceiling and focusing all my energy on not itching Mars, cycling through mental checklists of every last thing that needs to get done before Yearbook Prom.

It sucked. But it was worth it.

The tattoo turned out even better than I expected. And Charlie loves his, too. He got all teary-eyed after Brian finished his work and we got to stand in front of the mirror together. For the record, I decided to officially discontinue my number one rule.

Saturday morning is pretty nuts. Bree and I run to the dollar store to get streamers, balloons, and paper plates, then drop in to Christina's dad's restaurant to finalize the food orders, then bolt to Lowe's two towns away to get the final supplies for the big canvas backdrop that Yearbook Prom attendees can take photos in front of. By the time we're standing in the checkout line there, we're both hangry but happy about how it's all coming together.

"Oh, what'd you think about the books!?" Bree asks, pushing our cart past a row of magazines near the register. "I can't believe we haven't talked about them yet!"

"What books?"

She gives me a look. "The *year*books."

Oh right. "I forgot to look at my copy last night."

"How did you forget? I read the whole thing, cover to cover, at least five times before I left school. Didn't see a single typo, by the way." She smirks proudly.

"I rushed off to my tattoo appointment, and I was so distracted by what Dan said, and I wanted to go through the book in a quiet place, all by myself, which sounds weird, but I—"

"Wait, wait." She holds up her hands. "What did Dan say?"

Damn it.

I wasn't going to tell Bree about the whole Cliff thing. Because out of everyone, she'll be the most irate over even the *possibility* that I'd give Cliff the time of day. And she's probably right in feeling that way.

I start placing our items on the conveyor belt rolling toward the cashier. "Dan told me that Cliff wants to meet up with me and Ali to apologize. . . ."

I pause, expecting an immediate explosion. A whole big scene. A fiery monologue on why He Who Must Not Be Named is basically Satan who deserves life in prison—not a chance to apologize to me.

But Bree just shrugs, pulling a roll of canvas onto the belt.

"That's it?" I say.

"I don't know," she says. "Do what you have to do."

"That is so not the reaction I expected from you."

"Well, I was talking to Clare, and she made a great point." She grabs a Snickers from the checkout row of candy bars and tosses it onto the belt. "Cliff isn't worth the anger I've spent fuming over him. He's a hugely insecure tool who sees the world in this sad, warped way. You know what I mean?"

"You said his name."

"Huh?"

"You said 'Cliff'—not 'He Who Must Not Be Named'."

"Right, that's another thing," she says, grinning. "I'm never letting another dude have that kind of power over me again. Screw it. I'm saying that asshole's name."

We pay at the register and start wheeling the cart outside.

"My point is," she continues, "do whatever you want to do. If you'd appreciate an apology, go forth. If you're over it, you should blow him off and never speak to him again."

"Yeah."

"Wait . . . are we forgetting something?" We come to a halt in the parking lot, both looking down at our cart. "Canvas, two-by-fours, glue gun . . ."

"Oh! My paint!"

I totally forgot. I promised Mrs. Brandstone I'd have my bedroom walls finally painted by Yearbook Prom. It was literally the only responsibility Bree's parents asked of me for living with them this entire time, rent-free. I can't *not* do it today.

"I'll be right back," I say, jogging inside.

"Hurry! We're behind schedule!"

I find the paint aisle, where I'm immediately berated by the plethora of swatches staring down at me. Apparently, there are ten million variations of gray—iron river, sparkling silver, cloudy day—and a hundred million variations of green—spring air, nature's bliss, wild forest—and an indecisive person like me could spend a year in this exact spot, tormented by the thought of choosing the wrong one.

"Can I help you with something?" asks a girl in a worker uniform, with bright-pink hair. She looks younger than me. "You seem overwhelmed."

"Yeah, I am. I'm looking for a color."

She laughs. "I could guess that much. Any color?"

"Any will do."

"We have a lot to choose from."

I start tapping my foot against the floor, knowing Bree's waiting impatiently outside in her car. I imagine her honking the horn, like the morning Mrs. Brandstone walked in on me shower-dreaming. "I need interior wall paint for a basement bedroom."

"You want to know a trick I came up with to help customers in your shoes? It's kind of random, but I think it works."

"Sure."

"Okay, so." She pivots to face the wall of colors. "Think of the best person in the world."

"Huh?"

"The best person."

"How do you define 'best,' though?"

"Don't overthink it."

"Um . . ."

Winter pops into my brain.

I should probably have thought about, like, Malala Yousafzai, or Teddy, or Greta Thunberg.

But it's Winter.

"Okay," I say. "Got it."

"What color does that person remind you of?"

"The blues are bluer up here," I mumble without even thinking. Winter's quote will always stick with me.

"Huh?" Pink-hair girl leans toward me.

"Nothing, sorry. The person reminds me of blue, I guess."

"Start there, my friend." She points to the blue section. "That's a great way to narrow it down."

I follow where her finger points. Just like with the grays and the greens, there are about a billion blue swatches to choose from.

"Thanks," I say, almost sarcastically. What a help she was . . .

Wait. She was onto something, though.

I don't know if it's God, or fate, or just some weird, cosmic coincidence, but—of all the colors laid out in front of me—my eyes immediately fall on the absolute most perfect swatch.

Sky Blue.

Back at the house, it's the calm before the storm.

Mr. and Mrs. Brandstone took Ray to go bowling, Clare went on a hike with Petey, and Bree is over at Dan's helping him with his suit and tie, because "All boys are hopeless at dressing themselves," as she put it—even though Dan has better style than any other guy I know. So me, Thelma, and Louise have the place to ourselves.

I won't be able to paint my entire room before Teddy, Dan,

Marshall, and Ainsley come over to set up Yearbook Prom—especially knowing the walls will need a second coat—but I should at least show the Brandstones I got the ball rolling. I put on some music and start painting away.

I stop right before I'm about to paint over the promposal wall, though. Because it's totally changed my senior year. My entire *life*, really.

It's kind of bittersweet, saying goodbye.

On one hand, the whole school discovering this wall was nothing short of traumatizing. On the other, the whole school discovering this wall definitely made me a tougher person.

I snap a picture before the words vanish into Sky Blue forever.

SKY IS GAY FOR ALI: PROMPOSAL IDEAS

DAYS LEFT: 0

My eyes well up. Because it feels like everything is coming to an end.

The end of giggling in the basement with Bree, multiple drywalls away from the nearest humans. The end of my trips to LMEP with Marshall, where we'd laugh and argue over movies and escape into a dark theater just long enough to forget the outside world exists. The end of Winter's class—the only place at RLHS where I felt like I belonged.

I wish someone had told me that when I was your age.

I remember Winter's advice that day. The Friday I sent out my e-blast letter. She told me to fight to keep Bree and Marshall as friends. To stay close with the people I love. My real family.

And I plan to.

My phone rings. It's Bree.

"I love you," I word vomit before she can get a hello in.

"Oh no. Are you binge-watching This Is Us *again?"*

"No. I just painted over the promposal wall, is all. I'm weirdly feeling sad about it, believe it or not."

There's a long pause on her end. Way longer than I'd expect.

"Yeah," she says. *"I know what you mean."*

Another long pause.

I swallow hard.

"I'll be home for Thanksgiving, Sky," she says.

"I know."

"Then my long holiday break is, like, a month after that."

"Yeah."

"And then I'll drag you back to LA with me."

I laugh. "All right. We'll see."

I get the feeling she wants to say something else, but she doesn't. I finally cut in.

"Anyway." I clear my throat. "What's up?"

"Can you do me a favor?"

"Shoot."

"Can you run up to my parents' room and see if my dad has a red tie?"

"Why?"

"Dan's tie is . . . not the right color."

"Yes it is, Sky!" I hear Dan yell out of desperation in the background. *"Don't listen to her! She's being a grouch!"*

"The red and the pink are clashing like crazy," she whispers into the phone.

"Give me a second," I say, climbing the stairs.

I step into the Brandstones' bedroom. I've never been in here before.

"This feels weird," I say, tiptoeing toward their closet.

"*How come?*"

"Your parents, like, *bang* in this room."

"*Oh my God, shut up.*"

"Okay." I flip on the light switch in their walk-in closet. "He's got a few yellow ones, a blue one, a pink—"

A box of storage catches my eye. There's a Rock Ledge High School yearbook from 1996 sitting on top of a bunch of junk. It has a scarlet-and-blue cover.

"*Sky? You there?*"

"Ah . . . yeah, it's just . . ."

"*Is everything okay?*"

I'm so confused. "I'll call you back in a minute."

I hang up right as she begins lecturing me about the importance of tie patterns, and I pick up the yearbook. The inside is covered in old signatures and messages from classmates.

"Holy eff," I mutter, reading through a handful. Because all the notes are addressed to Jennifer. As in, Jennifer Graham. *This* is Mrs. Brandstone's yearbook.

My heart begins pounding. Hard.

Because that means . . .

I run downstairs to my bedroom, grab my backpack, and pull out the 1996 book I've had this whole time—the one that actually *was* left on the Brandstones' front porch weeks ago with an anonymous note inside. Unlike Mrs. Brandstone's, this book seems to be completely devoid of classmates' signatures and well-wishes.

Whose yearbook could this possibly be?

The boulder starts rolling in my mind, gaining speed on a mountainside of critical questions I don't have the answers to. I close my eyes and focus on the *in* and *out* of my breath, like therapists in the movies say you should do. It surprisingly kind of helps. I flip to page one. Because there's got to be something *somewhere* in this book that gives away its owner's identity. I have to find it.

I get through the first twenty pages. Nothing. No stamp confirming it's the local library's. No class photos circled with a yellow highlighter. No hearts drawn in red pen surrounding a crush's school pic.

I get through the next twenty. Still nothing. I notice that, despite being the same age, the pages are crisper and spotless compared to Mrs. Brandstone's—no rings from coffee mugs, no torn corners. Whoever had this book, they didn't share it with the world. It was locked away somewhere safe.

It's not until I reach the end—on a blank, glossy white page that comes right before the back cover—that I see it. A note written in tiny letters crammed into the top left corner.

No wonder I never noticed it before.

Penelope,
Have fun exploring.
But come back quick.
The blues are bluer up here, after all.
Love you,
Henry B.

Henry B.? *What?* My dad signed this book?

The only Penelope I know is . . . Penelope Winter.

The blues are bluer up here after all.

Holy crap.

Holy, holy, *holy* crap.

I fall backward, and—seeing as my head doesn't split into a million pieces bashing into the concrete floor—I assume the futon catches me. The walls are spinning like I'm stuck in a rattling, sky-blue snow globe, though. Maybe it's the paint fumes, but it's probably more because I'm realizing that *it was Winter's yearbook all along.*

She left it on the front porch.

Winter must have been friends with my dad.

I sprint upstairs into the kitchen and look around for a set of car keys before remembering that everyone—along with their vehicles—is gone. Without even thinking, I fling on Clare's unicorn hoodie and dash out the front door wearing Mr. Brandstone's gargantuan flip-flops.

I don't care what the hell I look like. I need to talk to Ms. Winter.

I jog to the end of the Brandstones' 1 percent neighborhood, cars I'll never be able to afford beeping as I distractedly step too far off the curb. I turn right and pick up the pace, realizing I have two miles between me and my destination. There's the storefront of Wing Construction, which I've walked by a million times without ever really noticing before now; the ice-cream parlor where I served bratty tourists who wandered too far from the lake; the cross streets to Ashtyn Drive, where me and Bree would veer left for our stalking sessions. I stub my toe craning my neck to see if his car is in the driveway.

A part of me thinks I'll never *fully* be over Ali Rashid.

My feet thoroughly aching, I finally reach Winter's. I was here in the fall—Bree had to drop off yearbook proofs—but that feels like ages ago now. A lifetime, really. I'm a totally different person living under totally different circumstances.

It's a small but charming house tucked into the shade at the edge of a patch of woods, an expansive willow tree spreading its arms throughout the lawn. The shutters are a worn red, and two chipped chairs are rocking in the breeze on the front porch. It's weird. Just like her classroom, something about this place feels permanent and cozy—like it's been here as long as Lake Michigan's waves have been crashing on the shoreline a few miles away.

I knock on the front door and hear movement on the other side. A few moments go by, accompanied by the clicking of heels, before it swings open.

"Sky?" Winter's eyes widen.

She's wearing a moss-colored dress that covers her chest and arms in lace. Silver earrings pop in front of the blackness of her hair. It's the first time I've seen her wearing lipstick. I totally forgot Yearbook Prom setup is supposed to start soon at the Brandstones'.

"What's wrong?" she asks, glancing down at my feet, alarmed. "You're bleeding."

I'm suddenly aware of how ruffled I look in Clare's unicorn hoodie, my face covered with sweat and probably dirt, too, a stubbed toe leaking red onto her doormat.

"The blues are bluer up here," I say, holding up her 1996 yearbook. "You knew my dad."

NEGATIVE TWENTY-EIGHT DAYS

Winter places a pitcher of pink lemonade on the table between us before sitting down in the rocking chair next to me on the front porch.

"They're extra wild out here, I'm telling you." She sighs, nodding at a group of brown, bushy-tailed squirrels bickering with one another under the willow tree. "Every day they're out here fighting over something."

She tosses a Band-Aid onto my lap. I bend in half to wrap it around my toe right as my phone starts buzzing. I notice I have three texts from Bree that I missed on my journey across half of Rock Ledge:

Soooo did you find a tie?

SKY BAKER are you 🔪 ??

ok seriously call me back. Dan's suit is a national emergency lmaoooo we need to figure this out.

"Need to make a call?" Winter asks.

"No, I'm okay." I flip the phone over on the armrest so I can't see the screen.

A couple of cars drive by, a few nearby birds chirp soundly, and a slight breeze rattles the wind chime dangling by the front door. In theory, this is, like, the perfect combination to make me feel relaxed, but there's this anxious presence filling the space between us, begging me to ask all the questions swirling in my brain. I have no idea how to begin, though. I always feel comfortable around Winter, but we're usually surrounded by other Yearbookers—or, at the very least, Bree and Marshall.

Now it's just us.

"So—"

"Your—"

We cut each other off. And then laugh.

My phone starts ringing again.

"You should get it, Sky," Winter says. "Today's a big day. She may need you."

I don't want to sidetrack this conversation. I don't want to be anywhere but this porch, sitting next to Winter, the squirrels wrestling steps away, digging into a family history I never knew existed. But she's right.

So I answer. "Hey."

"*Where the hell are you?*" Bree bellows into the phone. I yank it away from ear, so as to not get hearing damage.

"Language, Brandstone," Winter says forcefully in my direction, grinning.

Bree pauses before lowering her voice. "*Was that Winter?*"

"Yes," I say. "I'm at her house."

There's a solid three seconds of confused silence. I can practically see Bree gaping on the other end of the line. "*Why are you at her house?*"

Winter and I exchange a look. "It's a long story," I say.

"I know you're not telling me something, Sky."

"Well, duh."

"What's going on?"

"I'll explain later."

"I'm coming over there."

"What? Bree, it's—"

But she hangs up.

"She's coming over here," I say sheepishly to Winter. "Sorry."

She smiles at me.

I start spinning my glass of lemonade in circles on the armrest, too overwhelmed to drink. "*You* wanted me to go meet Charlie?"

"I did."

"So . . . I take it you and Charlie were friends in high school too?"

"We were."

I knew Winter was around my dad's age and that she also went to Rock Ledge, but I never put it together. Winter and my dad have been orbiting in completely different solar systems in my head. The possibility that those universes ever collided never seemed feasible.

The idea that they were *friends*? Basically impossible.

"You didn't tell Charlie you sent me to see him, right?" I ask.

Because if she had, Charlie would have been expecting me. He would have known from the very beginning that I *wasn't* Justin Jackson—that I was Henry's teenaged son, who now happens to be in Penelope's Yearbook class. Unless he and Brian are excellent actors, there's no way that was the case.

"I didn't tell Charlie, no." She takes a swig of her lemonade and licks her lips. "I discovered his address through a friend of a friend, but Charlie and I . . ." She pauses to think. "We haven't talked in a while."

"How come?"

"It's complicated."

"Did you have a big falling out?"

"No, no, nothing like that." She shakes her head and crosses her legs, the bottom of her moss dress dancing in the breeze. "Do you remember the advice I gave you the day you figured out it was Cliff who hacked the e-blast?"

My mind jumps back to that weird, crazy Friday right before the Beach-Bum Party. She said a lot to me that day, but—like literally every word Winter says—I remember the whole conversation. I know exactly what she's talking about now.

"You told me I should fight to keep Bree and Marshall in my life," I say, recalling the firmness in her voice, the seriousness in her eyes. "You told me to fight to keep friends like that around."

She stares at me for a moment, eyes beginning to glisten with tears, before looking up into the willow's branches bending alongside the roof. "Yes," she says. "Exactly. I wish I had known that when I was your age—that people like Bree and Marshall are rare, and their friendships are worth fighting for." She pauses, neck still craned upward at the tree. "What I mean to say is: I didn't fight for Charlie, Sky, and I didn't fight for your dad."

Sadness grips my entire body. I can hear the regret in her voice—all the months she's wanted to confess this to me—and it feels like daggers.

Whatever happened—whatever she did or didn't do to stay close with Charlie and my dad—still haunts her. All those years Winter spent before finally *growing up*, as she put it, Winter left Charlie and my dad behind. And she doesn't want me to do the same with Bree and Marshall now.

She stands and leans forward against the porch railing to get a better view up at the insides of the willow. Or maybe she's looking at the sky—a completely cloudless canvas today. She thinks the blues are bluer up here. I'm beginning to think that too.

She starts brushing away the remnants of dead leaves and dust that have collected on the porch railing. The way her hands glide across the wood, the way her eyes pick out which imperfections to push aside—she moves the same way when she's organizing her desk at school. It's odd seeing her focus in this space, though, away from caffeinated Yearbookers and not balancing a million things at once. Winter's life is quiet and simple out here, I think.

A little lonely, too.

She stops and turns toward me. "I wasn't going to tell you that I knew your dad until after you graduated."

"How come?"

She hesitates. "Teachers need to be careful when it comes to these sorts of things and their students."

"But I'm not just *any* student, though, right?" I say. "I'm Henry Baker's son."

She tilts her head at me with a grin. "Maybe so. Maybe you're not just any student. But the last thing I wanted to do was make you uncomfortable."

"So why didn't you?"

"Why didn't I make you uncomfortable?"

"Why didn't you wait until I graduated? Why did you risk me seeing the note from my dad in your yearbook?"

She sits back down across from me. "The hacked e-blast," she explains, topping off her lemonade. "I thought meeting Charlie would help you realize that you aren't alone in this fight, Sky. You're never, *ever* alone in this fight."

There's a tingling in the back of my throat.

"I think you're pretty damn tough, and I know your dad would think so too," she continues. "But even the toughest people need to know they're loved, need to know they have people in their corner."

If Rock Ledge has taught me anything senior year, it's that I definitely do have people in my corner. Years from now—when everyone else has forgotten about how they wore a GAY FOR FRANCH FRIES shirt or planned that epic surprise promposal at the Senior Beach Bum Party for me—I'll still remember. I'll remember that people in this not-so-terrible town actually had my back.

The quiet on Winter's street is squashed with a sudden, raucous bass echoing down the pavement. It's the newish Ariana Grande song Bree is still obsessed with.

I don't want this conversation to end, though.

I don't want to leave this porch.

"Ah." Winter sighs, cranking her neck down the street. "A

blasting car stereo. The sweet sound of high schoolers with too much time on their hands."

A moment later, Bree's car comes to a screeching halt on the shoulder of the road next to Winter's mailbox. The passenger-side window rolls down, and Marshall hangs his upper body out of it.

"Hey, Winter!" he calls.

"Hi, Jones," she answers happily.

"What are y'all doing?" Bree yells from the driver's seat, clearly stressed. "We literally have an *entire prom* to construct."

The back seat window rolls down too, and Teddy's bubbly face appears. Dan's sitting next to him.

"Also, we have about an hour to plan said prom." Teddy's already in his light gray tux, a pale yellow tie draped around his neck. We lock eyes. The cuteness almost kills me.

"Do you want a ride over to my house, Winter?" Bree asks, turning down Ariana. "We have to pick up Ali and Ainsley, too, though, so it might be, ah . . . it might be a squeeze."

"As lovely as it sounds to be crammed into a back seat with three high school boys, I'll drive myself over shortly, Brandstone. But thank you." She turns to me. "We'll chat later."

I have so many other questions. We haven't even talked about my dad yet, and I'm dying to hear what Winter has to say about him.

Was he a nice guy? What did my dad, Charlie, and Winter do for fun? Did he get into trouble a lot, like Charlie mentioned? Would the three of them partake in nugget Fridays? What about Ram Ragers? How often would they skip? What was it like being his friend?

Did he ever have a crush on Winter?

Did Winter ever have a crush on him?

I know there's so much more to their story. But I also know this is the first of many conversations with Winter on this porch. I have the whole summer to get to know my dad.

"I'll see you at Bree's in a bit," I say, handing over the 1996 year book to its rightful owner. "Thank you for everything."

She takes it from me. "Anytime, Baker."

"Have you ever thought about reaching out to Charlie?" I say, walking backward toward the car beneath the creaking willow tree. "He's a great guy. I think he'd like to see you again."

Her mouth spreads into a larger smile, eyes and earrings glistening in the sun. "I might have to give him a call."

I hop into the back seat, give Teddy a kiss, and share a smile with Dan.

I expect to get berated with questions from the front about why I'm over at Winter's in the first place, but I don't. Bree and Marshall just glance backward at me with grins before Marshall nudges the volume up, Bree shifts into drive, and the car pulls away.

ACKNOWLEDGMENTS

A million thank-yous to:

My agent, Moe Ferrara of BookEnds Literary—the first person to believe in Sky's story. I'm forever grateful for your vision, commitment to inclusivity, and patience in fielding an unending barrage of stupid questions from a debut author. (Please thank corgi intern Winston with a belly rub as well.)

My editor, Amanda Ramirez, and the extraordinary folks at S&S BFYR. Amanda, your Twizzlers insight is invaluable and your skill communicating edits via memes in the margins is superb. I don't know how you so expertly sifted through my messy manuscript to find the shiniest storytelling gems (witchcraft?), but I'm eternally appreciative that you pulled it off. From the start, Sky Baker was in the best of hands.

The amazing readers at Salt & Sage Books, Cameron Van Sant and Helen Gould. You both helped me create authentic residents of Rock Ledge, adding depth and heart to *The Sky Blues* in ways I couldn't have created myself.

My mom, my dad, Melanie, Doug, Carson, Parker, Max, Sean, Vy, and Carlee. "Home is people. Not a place." Author Robin Hobb wrote that, and I agree with her. All of you are my home. And I never would have been able to create Sky's story without the impact you've had on my life.

All my boos in the group chat (you know who you are). Your jokes, inappropriate GIFs, and boundless encouragement helped power me through this book in ways you'll never know. I love y'all. When's the next reunion?

And to every Ms. Winter, Mr. and Mrs. Brandstone, and Charlie Washington who has made the skies a bit bluer for the LGBTQ kids in their corner of the world.